S0-AYC-497

The BOOK OF THORNS

Also by Hester Fox

The Witch of Willow Hall
The Widow of Pale Harbor
The Orphan of Cemetery Hill
A Lullaby for Witches
The Last Heir to Blackwood Library

The BOOK OF THORNS

HESTER FOX

GRAYDON
HOUSE

GRAYDON
HOUSE®

Recycling programs
for this product may
not exist in your area.

ISBN-13: 978-1-525-83156-0

The Book of Thorns

Copyright © 2024 by Hester Fox

All rights reserved. No part of this book may be used or reproduced in any manner whatsoever without written permission.

Without limiting the author's and publisher's exclusive rights, any unauthorized use of this publication to train generative artificial intelligence (AI) technologies is expressly prohibited.

This is a work of fiction. Names, characters, places and incidents are either the product of the author's imagination or are used fictitiously. Any resemblance to actual persons, living or dead, businesses, companies, events or locales is entirely coincidental.

® is a trademark of Harlequin Enterprises ULC.

Graydon House
22 Adelaide St. West, 41st Floor
Toronto, Ontario M5H 4E3, Canada
www.GraydonHouseBooks.com
www.BookClubbish.com

Printed in U.S.A.

To my darling boys.

And to all children,
who deserve a soft and gentle childhood, free of thorns.

Content warnings:
sexual assault, miscarriage, graphic descriptions of warfare.

The lily has a smooth stalk,
Will never hurt your hand;
But the rose upon her brier
Is lady of the land.

There's sweetness in an apple tree,
And profit in the corn;
But lady of all beauty
Is a rose upon a thorn.

When with moss and honey
She tips her bending brier,
And half unfolds her glowing heart,
She sets the world on fire.

Christina Rossetti

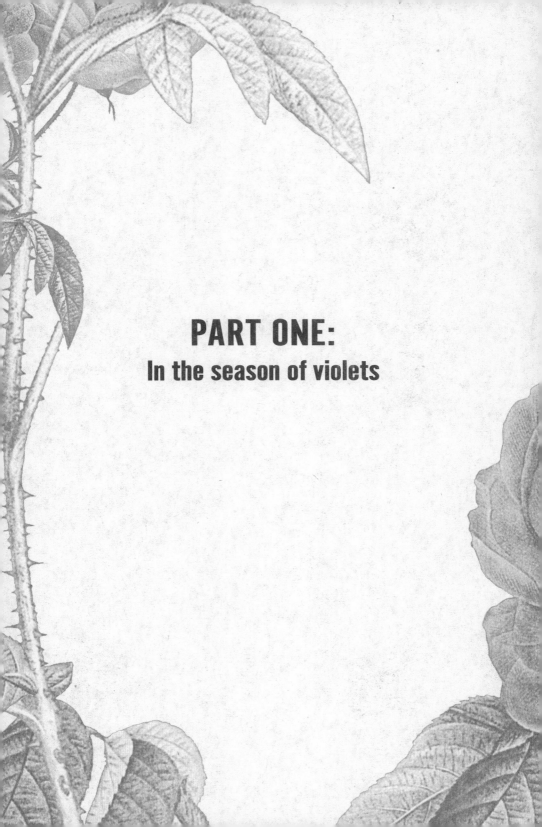

PART ONE:
In the season of violets

Le Moniteur Universel
January 10, 1815

Dearest reader,

There are few things more detestable than an unwanted suitor who will not take *no* for an answer. Whether it is due to an unadvantageous match or simply a disagreeable temperament, what can one do when one is unable to deter the attentions of such a determined beau?

I have designed a bouquet for young ladies who find themselves in the unfortunate position of not only having to decline an offer of matrimony but of having to do so *repeatedly*. As ladies, we understand that we are at a disadvantage when it comes to pressing our cases, especially when we suffer under the care of an unsympathetic guardian. However, we are not without recourse.

Take up your shears, take up your knives. Cultivate the life of which you dream. Drive away those unwanted suitors, and save yourself for the match of which you are worthy.

Pennyroyal: flee away
Rue: disdain
Pasqueflower: you have no claim over me
Wild tansy: I declare war against you

A bouquet comprised of these flowers and placed on the windowsill will not only dispel the attention of unwanted suitors but grant you a greater power over your own destiny. And remember, be not afraid to prune away that which does not serve you in life.

Madame Dujardin

One

CORNELIA

BEGONIA: a favor repaid, a warning foretold,
a promise delivered in darkness.

Sussex, England, February 1815

I can feel Betsy watching me from the doorway.

She hovers like a bee, rehearsing some small speech in whispers. I pretend not to notice her fidgeting and instead focus on the vase of narcissi before me, the weight of my pencil in my hand. Betsy clears her throat, twice, but I am already arcing out the path of the dainty stems and unfurling petals. There is something calming about reducing the flowers to splashes of grays and blacks, finding beauty in the absence of light.

Betsy lets out a throaty cough. "You might as well come in and be done with it," I tell her without looking up.

"Yes, miss." She drops a curtsy, her gray ringlets bouncing under her cap. "It's just that there's a man in the drawing room with your uncle, miss, and your uncle asks that you join them."

I continue sketching, watching the frilly petals take shape on my paper. "Please make my excuses," I tell her. Uncle likes to bring me out when he has business meetings, the same way he sets out the good claret and crystal goblets with the old family crest. With no wife and no children of his own, I make a pretty addition and bring a touch of softness to his otherwise hard demeanor. "There's a cake in the kitchen and cold ham as well that you might bring them," I add as an afterthought.

But Betsy doesn't leave. She wrings her hands and tuts about like a fussing hen. "No, miss. He's for you."

I carefully set aside my pencil. This is what I was afraid of. Closing my eyes, I rub my temples, wishing that it was anything else besides this. My time is not even my own, and I hate being pulled out of my work just to oblige Uncle.

"Very well." I dismiss Betsy and take a moment in front of the mirror in the hall. Uncle's friends and associates are mostly stodgy old men, but there is always the possibility that it could be someone young, someone exciting. I pinch roses into my cheeks and tease out a few of my yellow curls. If have control of nothing else in this house, I at least can take pride in my appearance.

I take a deep breath and let myself into the drawing room. "Betsy said you wanted me, sir?"

Uncle stands and tugs at his waistcoat. "Cornelia, come in."

Though not more than fifty years in age, his poor temper and taste for rich food and drink has left my uncle with a ruddy complexion and portly figure. He is not a healthy man, and his jowls are loose, his complexion jaundiced. What he lacks in polished comportment, though, he makes up in his wardrobe, opting for elaborate cravats and showy brocaded waistcoats that never quite fit him but speak of money and an account in good standing at the tailor. Uncle waves me over, impatient. "Come meet Mr. Reeves."

Obedient, I come and position myself near the window where I know the soft gray light is especially flattering to my fair complexion. The man unfolds himself from his chair. He is tall and spare, his black frockcoat well-cut and his boots shined. He looks familiar, perhaps from church or one of Uncle's interminable business dinners. I suppose some might consider him handsome, but there is an intensity in his dark eyes that is more predatory than charming. "Miss Cornelia," he says, taking my hand and bowing over it, "a pleasure."

"Mr. Reeves." I withdraw my hand. "I hope my uncle is not boring you with land yields and livestock accounts."

He shares a confidential look with my uncle. "On the contrary. Our conversation has been on the most enjoyable of topics."

"He's here to see you," Uncle says, plowing straight into the heart of the matter as he always does. "Mr. Reeves comes as a suitor."

Uncle makes the outcome of this meeting perfectly clear in the sharp downturn of his lips. His patience with the matter of my marital status is wearing thin.

Well, that makes two of us.

I don't fancy marriage, but I certainly don't fancy spending one more day than I have to under my uncle's roof, either. My dreams of publishing a book remain foggy and out of reach, and the money from my illustrations published in a French newspaper under a nom de plume pays only a pittance. It is not enough to live on, and certainly not enough for a young woman who enjoys fine things and an easy life. A husband would solve at least two of my problems, but it would create a host more.

"I'll leave you two alone to talk," Uncle says, cutting me with a look that says there will be hell to pay if I emerge from this room without securing an engagement.

The air usually lightens, the room sighing a breath of relief, when Uncle leaves, but Mr. Reeves's presence prickles me under my stays, makes me fidgety.

Betsy is posted outside the door, her needles softly clacking as she knits some horrid bonnet or muffler. Outside, a fine mist has rolled over the gentle Sussex hills. A smile spreads over Mr.

Reeves's sharp features. "Your uncle says you're a spirited filly. That you need a strong hand to break you."

Ah, so it is to go like that, then. I pour a cup of tea, ignoring my guest's outstretched hand, instead lifting the cup to my lips. "That does sound like the sort of nonsense my uncle would say."

Mr. Reeves regards me, his dark eyes calculating. "Your uncle was right, but I think he also underestimated you. I can see you possess some wits, so I'll not mince words." He crosses his long legs. "I am looking for a wife, and your uncle is looking to expand his landholdings to the south of the county."

If the man who has sat down across from me was meek, pliable, then perhaps I would have more patience in hearing his suit; I don't need someone who will get underfoot or try to handle me. Even some doddering old lord who might die quickly and leave me a widow would be acceptable. But Mr. Reeves is irritatingly young and looks to be in good health.

"My uncle was mistaken. I am not in need of a husband." I offer him a cold smile, my mind already back on my flowers, my fingers itching to hold my pencil. The light has shifted with the gathering clouds, and I will have to rework my shading.

He pours himself a cup of tea. "Come, wouldn't you like to have a fine house? Be mistress of a whole host of servants? I can see that you enjoy some degree of freedom, and I can give you that. You will have a mare and a generous allowance."

"I should think it would be terribly lowering to have to lure a wife into one's home with promises of horses and gowns. Shouldn't you rather wish her to come of her own volition because she holds you in some esteem?"

"You are naive if you think that marriage is anything other than a business transaction. You are a young woman of beauty and some small means but a drain on your guardian. I am an enterprising man, with successful business dealings and a good bloodline looking for a wife who will elevate his status and ornament his home. I hold a commission in the army and anticipate traveling to the Continent shortly. It is a good deal for you, and you would be hard-pressed to find a better one, especially with your lack of polish and manners."

"It's a little late to be going over to the Continent, isn't it? I believe we quite vanquished Napoleon."

Irritation animates his dark eyes before he glances away, taking what I suspect is an intentionally long sip of his tea.

I study him over the rim of my cup, imagining the way I would draw the sharp angle of his chin, the aquiline nose, before finally placing where I've seen him. "You were married before, were you not?"

There is an almost imperceptible stiffening of his body. "Yes, I make no secret of the fact that I am a widower," he says shortly.

"And how, exactly, did your first wife die?" The roses in the vase on the table beside me are vibrating, warning me. I pretend not to notice, pretend that I am a normal young woman who does not receive messages from flowers.

His lips thin. "An unfortunate fall."

"Mm. She did not bear you any children, did she?"

"Barren." He tugs at his cravat, irritated. "You would do well not to let your ear wander to every housemaid that has a piece of gossip to peddle," he says coldly.

"In any case, I am not interested." I move to put my cup down, but a hand closes around my wrist, hard. I look up to find that he has leaned in close, his breath hot on my neck.

"Perhaps you've also heard that I have certain...proclivities."

The roses in the vase strain toward me, singing, setting my teeth on edge. My fingers begin to tremble, but I do not let him see it. "Why would you tell me that?"

"Because I think, dear girl, that you are under the impression that I would use you poorly." He leans back, but only slightly, the air around him still charged and menacing. "I can be a very hard man when I'm tested, but I can take my pleasures elsewhere, so long as my wife is obedient."

His gaze is sharp, his grip painful, and I realize that here is a dangerous man, one who is not just a brute but also clever. He cannot be fobbed off with witty barbs or batting eyelashes.

"This conversation bores me," I tell him, standing. "I will not be your wife. I'm sorry that you wasted your time in coming here."

But he makes no move to stand, his cool gaze sliding over me in a way that leaves me feeling horribly exposed. "I've seen you often, Cornelia. In church, sitting so demurely with your hands folded in your lap. You may think to have everyone else fooled, but I see the spirit in your eyes. A woman like you can never be satisfied with the life of a spinster, put on a shelf here in Sussex. I can offer you fine things, take you to exciting places abroad with me."

And I've seen you, I think. *I've seen how cruelly you used your first wife, the bruises on her pretty face. The way she faded little by little every week in church, until she was just a ghost in a dress, her final service that of her funeral. That will not be me.*

"Surely there are other young ladies that would be flattered by your attentions," I tell him.

"None so beautiful, none that I would take so much pleasure in breaking. The more you deny me, the more determined I am. Ask your uncle. I am a man who gets what he wants, one way or another."

All the promise of gold or Continental trips would not be enough to tempt any marriage-minded mama to let her daughter enter into an arrangement with a man like Mr. Reeves. But of course, I have no mama to arrange such matters for me, to keep me safe.

"Then, perhaps it was time you lose for a change. Do you not find it dull to always get what you expect?"

He stands, drawing close and jabbing a finger into my bodice. It takes some great force of will to stand my ground and not let him see my fear. "You may think yourself clever, but this visit was just a courtesy. Your uncle and I have all but drawn up the contract already."

He storms out, and the room grows quiet in the wake of the front door slamming. Betsy startles from her seat where she had fallen to dozing. I close my eyes, take a breath, wait until my heartbeat grows even again. Then I return to my waiting drawing in the parlor.

If I work quickly, I can still finish it and have it ready for tomorrow's post. But for now, there is no waiting publisher, no silly French pseudonym; it is just the light and the shadows and me, a silent dance as I commit them to paper. Mr. Reeves and his odious proposal quickly fade away from my mind.

But then a raised voice shatters the silence, breaking my concentration, and there is the thundering velocity of Uncle coming down the hall.

"I caught Mr. Reeves in the front drive," he tells me, his shadow falling over the paper. I do not pause in my sketching, and I can feel him puffing with exertion above me. "I don't suppose you know what he told me?"

"I can't even begin to imagine."

The shadow shifts, and then his hand is covering the paper, forcing my pencil to land crooked. "You will look at me when I address you."

I know better than to provoke him, though some days I will gladly take his fist for the pleasure of ruffling his feathers first. But today I am tired, and so I stay my tongue and obediently lift my gaze.

His lips thin in triumph, though his anger quickly returns. "He says that you rejected his proposal out of hand. Not only that, but you insinuated that the man killed his own wife."

Uncle is looking for me to deny it or perhaps gild the story with some more palatable details. "Well?"

I lift a shoulder. "He speaks the truth."

Uncle's arm comes down, slamming my little desk and spilling the vase's water all over my sketches. Hours of work stream down in front of me, my chance to make tomorrow's post in time gone. "And you find that acceptable? I've fed you, educated you, kept you in the finest clothes, and catered to your whims. Now, tell me, do you think I am being unreasonable in expecting you to do the one thing you were bred for? You are not going to get a better offer than Josiah Reeves, and I am certainly not going to play at matchmaking until by some miracle you deign to accept a curate's son or clerk in the city, or... or..." He devolves into a coughing fit that robs him of breath.

Crossing my arms, I watch as his face grows red. I could counter that he might have kept me in fine clothes and fed me the best meat and drink but that he also has used me ill, taken liberties when he's in his cups.

The paper has absorbed all the water now, the faded lines of the narcissus warping and twisted. I know the next part of his little speech well enough by now, but still my blood heats as he launches into it.

He has finally regained himself and wipes the spittle from his mouth. "You take after your spoiled mama, and is it any wonder? To say she was a fool would be putting it lightly—forming an attachment with a French soldier and following him to Paris! She was a whore and—"

"Don't speak of my mother like that."

His lip peels back. Few things delight him so much as besmirching my mother's character. But then the predictable speech veers off course into new and unspeakable waters. "You either accept Reeves or I take matters into my own hands."

There is a cruel glint in his eye, and I know that he is about to land a decisive blow. But what could he take away from me now? What could he do that would be worse than that which he has already done? "And pray, what does that mean? You already sent my maid away. There is nothing else you can take away from me."

Color creeps up Uncle's neck. "Your *maid*," he says, nearly choking on the word. "Is that what you call her? For all of your perversions, you might at least speak plainly. She was your—your *lover*," he splutters, "and I should have sent you away to a convent in Scotland the moment I discovered your devious activities. So now I will do exactly that and be glad to rid my house of your polluting presence."

Neither of us has uttered Anna's name since that awful night, and it feels like a broken truce. But this threat of his, it's a bluff. It must be. As much as he wants to be rid of me, and I him, a convent would be a costly endeavor and would do nothing to improve his standing in the eyes of the local gentry. We stare at each other, this man who has raised me and I. Like a cat and a mouse, this is the game that Uncle and I play—sport for the cat, deadly for the mouse. "Am I understood?"

I manage a stiff nod. There was a time when I could conjure choking ivy, poisonous nightshade, when I could bend flowers to my whim. But any power that I had left with Anna and my broken heart. Satisfied, Uncle leaves me to try to salvage my sketch and revive the wilting narcissus. Both are beyond saving, so I take up my spencer and slip outside.

My mother left me a garden watered with tears, a name, and not a single memory of her. The bells of the village church ring in the distance. I close my eyes and let my fingers brush across the papery petals of a long-dead rose, then give myself over to the pricking of a thistle. These are the flowers that taught me patience, guided my hand to the gentle pursuit of sketching and watercolor. Throughout every long season of my life, they have grown and died and grown back again, constant and comforting sentries in their continuous cycles of life.

But they do not whisper of patience or art today. How the flowers speak to me is not something I would ever tell anyone, least of all my uncle or the men he brings home. What well-schooled girl would admit to something so outlandish? Anna was the only one who ever knew, who accepted me despite it. And now she is gone.

Through the window, I can see Uncle hunched at his desk furiously scribbling in his ledgers. When he is working in his study he might as well be dead to the world. A cloud rolls over the sun, and the garden grows cool. Uncle stills, his coat taut over his wide shoulders as he turns in his seat, as if he can feel my hateful gaze on him. He meets my eye, and something passes between us, something that I couldn't name if I wanted to, but that sends a chill down my neck all the same. A bleak wind blows through the garden, and I suddenly know that I am on a great precipice.

Run, the flowers tell me. And so I run.

Two

LIJSBETH

PEONY: a bashful bloom. Looking inward, protecting delicate secrets.

Brussels, the United Kingdom of the Netherlands, Winter 1815

There is a ladybird tangled in a spiderweb above the gaping maw of the kitchen sink, a ruby jewel thrashing and quivering in the dusty light. The poor thing will soon be too tired to fight any longer and then will be slowly wrapped and eaten alive by the spider that is waiting just out of sight. I put aside my mending and stand on my tiptoes, carefully pulling her from the web and releasing her. She takes wing and lands on the kitchen window.

When I'm satisfied that she's no longer in danger, I take up my mending again, but my mind is far from the stitches. I track her progress across the windowpane, a cheery spot of red against the cobblestones and mud of the street beyond.

But my wandering mind does me no favors, and there is a flash of pain as my clumsy needle plunges into my thumb. I know I should not relish the pain, should not wait with detached glee for the inevitable crimson blood to bubble out, but in a dreary world of mending and scrubbing and serving, it is a novelty, a different sort of sensation to take my mind away from the usual aches and pains that plague my body of twenty years like that of an old woman.

"Are you mad?" Annette stalks over and yanks the lace out of my bleeding hand. "You've ruined Madame's favorite fichu. Touched in the head is what you are," she says, forcefully bandaging up my hand while I look on like a scolded child. "Stutter my foot," she grumbles, "I've never heard you say more than three words since I've been in this house." Annette has been in this house for as long as I can remember. She is old enough to be my mother twice over, and though she might look matronly with her graying hair and gently creased face, she has never been affectionate.

"Here," she says, thrusting an apron at me when the bandage is tightened to the point of constriction. "The pie crust needs rolling. Leave off that lace for now, and I'll look at it later to see if it can't be salvaged." There is a touch of pity in her voice but not warmth or kindness—there is never any warmth or kindness in this house.

She bustles out to fetch a hen, leaving me alone in the suffocating stillness. Outside the distant sound of a city in which I have no place rumbles on. Through the window I can just see the edge of the little garden if I crane my neck, and it is upon the thirsty flowers I meditate while waiting for the feeling to come back into my fingers. Idle moments are dangerous, not just because of the risk of reprimand but because that stillness is a fertile ground for impossible fantasies and dreams to take root.

"Master Isidore has returned," mutters Annette as she passes through the kitchen with tonight's supper still feathered and twitching. "And he looks like he's in a right fiery mood. He's already upset Maggie and her pups and threatened to drown them if they spook his horse."

Hastily wiping my hands on my apron, I set aside the pie crust and go to the other window to peek at the caravan of coaches that has come to bear the young master and his belongings home from university. It has been six months since he left, but I had only just started to relax my shoulders, breathe a little freer in the house. Now my skin prickles at the memories of his wandering hands and hungry eyes.

I hear Isidore's footfalls before I see him, the polished boots clipping purposefully down the hall. I turn to hurry from the kitchen, but in my haste I stumble, and in the time it takes me to right myself, he's found me.

He's gotten bigger since I saw him last, taller and broader in the shoulders so that his bottle green coat pulls taut across his back. His face has filled out a little too, and aside from the smirk that still pulls at his lips, I would almost call him handsome. Almost, because I know what lies beneath that polished veneer.

"Well, Lijsbeth? And are you glad to see me?" He extends his hand to help me up, but I struggle with my heavy wool skirt and scramble up myself. He purses his lips. "Still stubborn as ever, I see."

Isidore sucks the air out of the room, makes it feel hot and small. His smile is too bright, his dark eyes too sharp. He has never been told no, never been denied anything he desires. He has never had to fend for himself or imagine a world in which he is anything other than the center.

He takes another step closer, forcing me to back into the table. "Annette," he says, without taking his hungry gaze from me, "I believe you are needed in the parlor."

When she has scurried from the room, Isidore nips at my ear. "Now, then, sweeting," he whispers, "is that how you greet your employer?"

He's not my employer, his father is. But that has never stopped him from taking liberties. Even in the days when I was still his playmate, his companion, before the little orphan girl was usurped by a real sister of blood and relegated to the kitchen. Even then, he took liberties.

The space between us shrinks, and suddenly his silk waistcoat is brushing against the wool of my bodice. His hands come behind me, quick, squeezing me to him.

I hate how my heart thumps when he's near me, how my body trembles as if I have no control over it. He makes me feel small and powerless. Even if I could scream, could tell him *no*, I would not. In the currency of society, I am the bad bargain, a girl without a family or protector to speak for me. I am simply a possession, and no one would fault the golden son for making use of his plaything.

His hands roam over me, until he takes the locket about my neck in his fingers, idly playing with it. The silver locket is the closest thing to proof that I once had a mother, one who had planned to come back for me at the orphanage. Feeling the chain tug around my neck is more of a violation than his hands on my body. The locket is not just mine, it is a promise, a link to the mother I never knew. Seeing it in his hands makes me feel sick.

"You still insist on wearing this," he says with mild interest. "Perhaps I should bring you back a gold necklace with a ruby next time I am in the city. Something that would remind you of me when I am away." He leans in close, his lips brushing my ear. "Would you like that, Lijsbeth?" he asks in a drowsy murmur.

I close my eyes, waiting for the demands his lips make on me, my body tense, but they never come. Instead, I hear the sound of my mistress's voice floating from somewhere down the hall.

"Isidore? Is that you?"

He pulls back abruptly, and he's smoothing back his dark hair when Madame van den Berg breezes in. Her gaze narrows when it lands on me, and I lower my eyes, wishing that I could disappear into the creaking floorboards. There has been no love lost between Madame van den Berg and me. I was never the daughter she wanted, never a proper substitute even before Isidore's younger sister Thérèse came along.

Isidore shifts from rake to doting son as easily as a snake sheds its skin. He takes his mother by the shoulders and kisses her forehead. "I was famished from my journey, and Lijsbeth was just putting together a plate for me. Isn't that right, Lijsbeth?"

I give a nod, and Madame sniffs. "Come," she says, looping her arm through her son's elbow and leading him away. "I want to hear all about Paris. Is it true that the czar drives about in an armored carriage?"

"We will finish this later," he whispers in my ear as he passes, then laughs at something his mother is saying. "The Russians may think themselves victors in the whole affair, but mark my words, Bonaparte will be back."

Their footsteps disappear down the hall, and I fall to the ground, hugging my knees to my chest. Instinctively, I search out the tips of the lavender in the garden out the window, but a tiny splash of red catches my eye instead.

The ladybird has flown back into the web, and this time she is too hopelessly tangled to escape again.

Three

CORNELIA

WATER WILLOW: freedom, a newfound independence.

"You'll have to get off here, mademoiselle."

I blink up at the coachman through the gathering dusk, certain that I've misunderstood him. We have been rattling about on pitted roads since Calais, and the landscape is still mostly empty fields, with only the occasional town or village in the distance. One of my traveling companions breaks wind as he shifts in his seat, then falls back asleep. "This isn't Paris," I tell the driver.

"I should say not. You've not got enough money for Paris." The coachman hawks up something vile from his throat and spits it into the road. "I let you stay on past the last stop because Jean here was enjoying your pretty face. But I've paying passengers who need the seat now."

I'm unceremoniously deposited by a reeking canal. It's dark, and there is not another living soul about. "Where am I?" I call back to the coachman who is already flicking the reins and trundling away.

"Amiens," he calls over his shoulder.

The coach's lantern grows smaller and smaller until it disappears around the bend, and I am left with only what I can carry in an unfamiliar city.

The folly of my plan and what I left behind becomes terribly clear as soon as I begin walking. I thought by now I would be in Paris, my cream-colored cotton dress with delicate embroidery fashionable, not a hindrance as I try to navigate about the narrow streets without bringing undue attention to myself. My boots blister my ankles, the leather stiff from never being used for more than a turn about the garden. My breath quickens as I attempt to maneuver around twisting canals in the shadow of a great cathedral. A group of men loitering outside a tavern whistle and call out something lewd which I will not repeat. In Sussex, I was a young lady of some standing, and never wanted for anything—anything material, in any case. Here I am prey, a fresh piece of meat for a carnivorous city.

Footsteps clip behind me as I dart into a cramped alley. Is it the result of my overwrought nerves, or are they following me? I hasten my step, and the footsteps match my pace. I am running now, my hem clutched in one hand, my bag awkwardly slung over my shoulder. Another desperate turn, and I find myself in a well-lit square full of carts selling trinkets and mouthwatering pastries to strolling couples.

The footsteps gone, I can finally catch my breath. With my back against a stone building, I close my eyes and slowly my heartbeat begins to steady again. Lord, but I am hungry. I would sell every stitch of clothing on me for hot tea with a tray of cakes. Instead, I dine on some of the cold meat and bread I took with me when I left Hill Cottage. All the money I saved over the past year barely has lasted me a week, and I use my last coin to pay for a shared bed in a boardinghouse where I can hear the mice and rats scurrying through the straw on the floor all night.

The last few days of travel have not been kind to me. As I do my best to make my toilette at the boardinghouse's grimy mirror, I hardly recognize the tired eyes that stare back at me. I left behind a house heavy with secrets, its walls buckling under the weight of them. But for all that it felt like a prison, it was the only home that I had ever known, the cold halls the only connection to my mother.

The morning is little better, and my body aches from the night spent on a straw-tick mattress. A pigeon lingers on the front step of my lodgings, regarding me with cocked head, and I fancy I see a trace of pity in its vacant eyes. But then it takes wing, and I am once again alone with my growling stomach.

I take my luncheon of the last of my bread and cheese to a fountain in a little-trafficked square. What am I to do in this small city in the middle of nowhere? What opportunities could there possibly be here? All these years I spent suffering under my uncle, I thought that I only had to get away and everything would fall into place. I would make money publishing my book of flowers, live an elegant life of a literary woman, and visit the best salons. It is only when I look about me at the sleepy square that is so clearly *not* Paris that I cringe at the realization that I have been harboring some secret hope, expectation even, that my mother would be there. My fingers go to the locket at my neck, the pressed rose petal that rests there quietly humming.

I cannot believe that the woman who planted such beautiful roses could have been as low of character as Uncle insists. The miniature of her that I keep in the other side of the locket shows a graceful young woman, beautiful, with frank, gray eyes. I would like to think that I would have been enough for her, would have been a balm for her broken heart, but the departure of my father robbed me of the opportunity of ever knowing.

In the absence of a true history of my father, sometimes I like to build my own, imagine the kind of man he might have been. I like to think that he was an adventurer at heart with lofty ideals and no place in which to realize them. The unrest in France and subsequent revolution was too alluring for him. Kissing my pregnant mother goodbye, he pledged that he would return to her once reason and justice ruled the land. Whether he intended to fulfill this pledge or not, I shall never know. Likely he perished in some cobbled square, rivers of blood running through the gutters, with the cry of *Égalité! Liberté!* on his English lips. Or perhaps he was swept up in the lasting romance of it all and is somewhere even at this moment living the life of a libertine.

My poor meal finished, I brush away my useless melancholy. *Come now, Cornelia,* I tell myself, *will you really admit defeat so quickly?* I cannot return to Sussex, but there may be a way to get to Paris yet. I find an empty chapel and change into the only spare gown I have brought with me, carefully stepping into the violet silk. My reflection in a shop window shows me that despite being a little rumpled, I look presentable. With my portfolio tucked under my arm, I tilt my chin up and start walking.

A little boy kicking rocks into the canal points me across the bridge when I ask him if there is a publisher in town. The steps to the stone town house are well-swept, and I have a good feeling as I notice the window boxes full of thriving geraniums. Knocking, I step back and put on my blandly polite smile that always sways things in my favor.

A spare man, balding and neatly dressed, opens the door and gives me a suspicious look from behind his wire spectacles.

"Bonjour, monsieur," I say brightly. My French is quite good, and I have always prided myself on sounding like a native. "I am a published artist and author of the popular floral column in *Le Moniteur Universel.* I am seeking a space in your publica-

tion to reach a greater audience and showcase my work. May I come in?"

He glances at the portfolio and then back to me where I stretch my smile a little wider.

"*You* are Madame Dujardin?" he asks finally.

"I am."

Gray eyebrows rise from behind the spectacles. "How do I know that is your true identity? Aren't you rather young?"

I was prepared for such a question, and I go to show him one of my correspondences with my publisher as proof of my identity. But my hand closes around nothing, and too late I remember the packet on the floor of the coach, where I declined to bend over to pick it up lest I give the man across from me a free glimpse of my chest.

The man at the door shakes his head. "Just as I thought. We are not looking for a lady's column at present, in any case. Good day."

"Please! I have my drawings right here, I can show you—"

He closes the door before I have a chance to protest or show him my work. I am likewise summarily dismissed from half a dozen other publications. My only comfort is the small slip of paper that I always keep in the pocket sewn into my skirt, my last letter from Anna. That, at least, I did not lose in the coach. My hand closes around it now as I struggle to come up with a new plan.

There is nothing so humbling as to be caught completely unprepared after what you had thought was the more careful of research, the most particular of planning. Not only that, but I had thought myself made of stronger stuff, thought myself nearly invincible after surviving all that I had at Hill Cottage. I am the young woman who could charm Uncle's business friends at dinner and then put them in their place when they came up the stairs to continue the conversation. I am the young woman who once stole the translation book right out from under her governess's nose and used it to answer my exercises in perfect Latin so that I might never have to sit through a boring lesson again. But here, I am just another face in a crowd, and as the city darkens around me, I feel for the first time in many years as a small child, alone and frightened.

Four
LIJSBETH

COLTSFOOT: justice shall be done to you.

Brussels, March 1815

The air is alive and buzzing as I hurry to market with my basket on my arm. Church bells toll, and partisans wearing the colors of the French Republic hang out of windows, waving flags and scattering violet petals on the cobbles below. *"Vive l'Empereur! Vive le Roi de Rome!"* A man in a threadbare cap catches me up in a jig, spinning me around before releasing me dizzy and confused. "Emperor Bonaparte has escaped his unjust bonds," he explains, when he sees my bafflement, "and it is only a matter of time before he sets his sights on Brussels."

Perhaps I should return his grin, kick up my heels and leave off my errands, but the name of the man on the throne makes little difference to the maid who is forever under the heel of her master and mistress. Napoleon could ride into Brussels tomorrow on a lion and a crown of laurels and I would still be responsible for scrubbing the hearth and seeing to the coal scuttles.

It is late in the day, but the flower market is still thronged with customers, the sweet blooms struggling to overpower the rotten petals trampled on the cobblestones. There are many reasons to fall into despair now Isidore has returned, but there is at least one bright spot, and that is there will be parties and balls now. And balls and entertaining means that Madame will want the house filled with flowers.

I can't remember how it first came to be that Madame asked me to arrange flowers, but it has fallen to me to keep the house full of fresh blooms and eye-catching arrangements. The flowers speak for me, say what my stubborn tongue cannot. Thorny roses for encounters with Isidore, sweet-smelling lilies when I am alone in the kitchen, working quietly in the soft shafts of sunlight.

Today it is peonies, fresh and bursting with the heady scent of spring. Perhaps it is the air of celebration, or the soothing pink of the flowers, for my steps are light, my chilblains nearly forgotten. Even the cloud of Isidore's return hanging over my head is no match for the triumph of spring.

I return with my basket full of blooms and go straight to the kitchen to begin my work. My little knife slices through the stems, flashing in the mellow light spilling in from the window. It is second nature to me, and I fall into an easy rhythm of cutting and sorting, bringing new life to the thirsty flowers. Petals unfurl, sigh great breaths of relief as they slide into place in the urn. Pinks and pale blues deepen, like the sky at sunset.

Sometimes, when I am deep in work, I fancy that I can hear the flowers speak to me. Of course, it is only the fancy of my wandering mind, but still, it feels as real as any conversation. Realer, even, because I am included. They whisper comfort to me, promises of better things to come. Today, there are no whispers, but when my fingers close around a rose stem, the strangest vision flashes through my mind. I see a young woman in a violet silk dress, standing on a bridge over a canal, staring down at the water. The residue of some leftover dream, no doubt. I shake the image from my head and finish my work.

But no sooner than I carry the arrangement to the alcove in the hallway than the smell sours and the blooms recoil as a dark figure steps out of the shadows.

"We were interrupted before," Isidore says, pressing me up against the wall.

His breath smells of expensive port or maybe brandy. He is strong but graceless. I go stiff as his mouth finds my neck, and he clumsily kisses a trail down to my collarbone. He has been at his club: I can tell because of the smell of cigars on his coat, the unhappy pinch of his brows that tells of a day spent losing money. I hate that I know him so well, this man who torments and fawns over me in equal measure. I hate that I must calculate my every movement, my every breath to draw as little attention as I can from him. Most of all I hate how some small part of me craves his attention, knows that it is the only proof I have that I am more than just a ghost. That I exist, even if it is just as an object to be used.

"You taste sweet, Lijsbeth. Not like the girls who paint and powder themselves in Paris. Do you know how many nights you filled my dreams? How many nights I was robbed of sleep because your lips were all that I could think of?"

Above the stairs there hangs a gilded picture of some saint. A placid smile touches her lips as she gazes down at us, and I wonder what she would think if she knew the extent of the sin which she is witnessing.

Isidore pulls back and then slams his hand down hard on the wall next to my head, snapping my attention back to him. "Damn it, Lijs. You have this power over me, and you won't even look me in the eye. Sometimes I think you know exactly what you do to me, that you relish the torture that you impart." He wrenches my chin in his hand, forcing me to meet his flashing gaze. "You are a spiteful little bitch, aren't you?"

Isidore's voice fades as I retreat into myself, and I hardly notice his arousal pressed against my thigh. The sickly-sweet scent of roses fills the room, fills my head. They are thorny and beautiful and cannot be tamed. No man can pick a rose without drawing a drop of blood. Isidore is fumbling with my skirts, his cold hand making an intrusion between my legs, followed by his member. The saint's smile stretches thin, her eyes unseeing. I am at once terribly stuck in my body and yet outside of myself, high above with the saint. I watch my own hand close around the knife in my skirt. Though soft and made of bruised petals, I have thorns all the same.

Isidore's scream is punctuated by a dramatic spurt of blood on the tiled floor. He pulls away from me, and my legs go weak with his withdrawal. "You stabbed me, you bitch!" He staggers backward, bloody hand gripping his shoulder.

The house comes alive with commotion. Thérèse is the first to arrive, Madame on her heels tying her dressing gown belt. And then Monsieur van den Berg, looking as if he was just roused from a deep slumber.

Madame rushes to her son, face drained of color. "Isidore, what has happened?"

My head spins as the hall crowds with voices. There is a persistent ache between my legs. The knife, which I am still clutching, is pried out of my trembling hands by someone.

I feel my entire world tip on its axis as I wait for Isidore to accuse me of assaulting him. It doesn't matter that he was the one to force himself upon me. It doesn't matter that no one would look between us and think me a seducer or anything other than an insignificant maid. I will be found guilty simply because *he* cannot possibly be anything other than innocent, and I will be turned out of the only home I've ever known.

He holds up his hand, inspecting the blood. Frowns. His cravat is crooked and his color is high, his dark hair falling out of its carefully swept-back coiffure. Isidore holds my fate in his hands. It would not behoove him tell the truth about what we were doing—what *he* was doing, even if he faces no formal consequences. So long as I am under this roof, I am at his mercy.

"Lijsbeth was pruning the flowers and was careless with her knife." His words come out unevenly as he gasps through the pain. "It slipped when I tried to assist her."

His face is pinched, his hand pressed tight to stanch the blood on his shoulder. The bloom of pink on his cheeks is quickly fading, leaving him gray and drawn.

Thérèse looks incredulous. "But in your shoulder? Oh, Izzy, how will you manage to fence now? Come, we must get you stitched up." Her hatred radiates off her as she brushes past me, arm around her brother's waist.

The commotion dies down as everyone hurries out to prepare a comfortable bed and hot drink for Isidore, fussing over him as if he was a sick child.

The ache between my legs is throbbing, and I want nothing more than to soak in a hot bath, but I will have to settle for scrubbing with some cold water later tonight in my basin.

My heart is pounding, my hands shaking as I return to work. Because that is what girls like me do: we are used and sullied, and then we get on with the never-ending grind of life.

I begin to gather up my things, and that is when I see it: the flowers quivering in the vase, rearing like snakes ready to strike, thorns dripping thick with blood.

Five

CORNELIA

MONKSHOOD: knight-errantry. A wanderer is found.

The little church and its nunnery sit behind high stone walls on the edge of Amiens, tightly buttoned against the sins of the outside world. It is quiet here, the sounds of a celebration in the city muffled and distant, forcing me to sit alone with my thoughts. What irony that I ran from Sussex to avoid being sent to a convent, only to find myself penniless in France and contemplating that very existence as a means of circumventing my poverty.

The garden is peaceful, full of early spring blooms. They do not speak to me like the flowers in my uncle's garden, but I know what secrets they hold all the same. I cannot remember a time when I did not hear the whispering of flowers, could not close my eyes and see a network of roots spreading below the ground. Perhaps it is simply a degree of observation that most people do not possess or, rather, do not have the inclination to perceive in a world that values action. For I quickly learned that I was singular in my ability to hear flowers and learned faster still that it would behoove me to keep my mouth shut and not tell the lady callers that came round hoping to win my uncle's fortune that the rosebush had imparted all its secrets to me.

I settle myself on a sun-warmed rock, pulling the boots off my blistered feet and massaging away the aches. It's so still here, so quiet save for the light song of a lark. Though I am used to being alone, I am not used to having to depend upon myself for everything from my meals to having a place to lay my head at night. I think briefly of Anna and how good it would be to have a companion with whom to share all my worries and burdens.

But it seems I am not the only one who has sought refuge in this field on the edge of the known world. A slash of deep blue and silver interrupts the bobbing narcissus, moving toward me. It grows closer, and I can make out a soldier's plumed shako hat and gleaming saber. He sees me and changes his course.

Instinctively, I hug my sketchbook to my chest. I have none of the protection afforded to me by my uncle's house or name here in the abbey garden. I have nothing but my wits, and I am not so sheltered that I do not know what a soldier with pleasure on his mind can do.

When he is close enough that I can make out the gold braid on his hat, he looks at me, then squints back toward the city, as if trying to deduce how he came to be here, of all places. He is young, my age or a little less perhaps. Handsome in a classical way. Black hair, dark, soulful eyes, and a well-cut jaw, very pale skin. His blue coat is crisp, his boots free of mud.

A cannon shot across the field shatters the birdsong and is shortly followed by distant cheering. The soldier seems unbothered, though I have taken refuge behind the rock. "Are we at war?" I ask.

"Better!" he says, extending his hand to help me up. Too rattled to be frightened by him, I allow him to help me to my feet. "The emperor has escaped his imprisonment and is even now riding to Paris."

I put my distance between us again, my sketchbook a shield across my chest. So, as I was escaping the bonds of my uncle's house, Napoleon was escaping from Elba. The cannon fire has died down, and a breeze sweeps across the garden. I can only assume that if this young man had some dark design on me, he would have acted on it by now. I have received no warnings from the flowers that surround us, so I decide to stand my ground.

"Are you a lover of violets?" he asks. His French is musical and has a provincial charm to it. He is looking at me as if awaiting the answer to the most important question ever asked. The little blue flowers stretch in a luscious blanket around us.

"Well, yes, I suppose I am," I say. "They are one of my favorite flowers."

This answer seems to please him, his dark eyes shining. "I, too, have longed for the violets to return all this winter."

"You'll excuse me if I don't believe that a soldier has come here simply to admire the violets."

Palms up, he gives me a disarming smile, lopsided and genuine. "You've nothing to fear from me, mademoiselle." His gaze quickly rakes over my stockinged feet and muddy hem before landing on the abbey at my back. He looks surprised, as if he had not realized where he was. "*Mon dieu*, you are much too pretty to become a penitent. Please assure me that you are simply lost and not truly considering giving yourself over to God?"

Oh, I have longed for good conversation, a bit of light flirtation. The weeks since I left Sussex have been a trial, but the years before them were bleak, too. So I allow myself one of the few truly diverting pleasures of life.

"One must first know one's destination in order to then realize one is lost," I tell him. It is a small truth, stretched thin for the sake of flirtation as well as my safety. "And as for becoming a penitent..." I look up at the windows and the cloistered lives that are unfolding behind them. I will not exchange one cage for another. "I am not disposed to silence, and I am much too fond of my hair."

His grin relaxes further, and an understanding passes between us. We are alike, I think. Both good-humored and fond of a little harmless flirtation. "As you should be," he says. "Such a color, like the golden hour before dusk. What are you drawing, then?"

I seat myself on the stone in a wordless invitation, and he settles beside me, close enough that I can smell his pomade. Opening my sketchbook, I tilt it toward him.

"You drew all these? Truly?"

A blush steals over my face. My work has always been my secret refuge. Once it leaves my hands and goes to print under my pseudonym, I have little to do with it. I did not realize quite how hungry I was for validation until he shone some on me. "Of course," I say, leaning over to see which picture he is studying.

"Where do you find them? The flowers, I mean. Some of these look quite exotic."

I could tell him that Uncle had an orangery, full of such flowers and fruits that are only found in the hot climates of the Indies. That although Uncle was a hard man, he liked to be seen as a gentleman and made certain he engaged in all the requisite pastimes of one. But it would not do to tell the soldier where I came from, who I am. After all, he is French, and I am English. "Ah, here and there. A florist's stall, the gardens of Versailles."

His gloved fingers trail down each drawing as he reverently turns the pages. I try to imagine my work through his eyes, through any eyes other than my own. I know that I am proficient at drawing, but Uncle was never one to offer me encouragement, and my governess declined to have anything to do with it when she discovered my particular talents. "Well?" I ask. "How do you find them?"

He looks as if he wants to say something, his dark eyes appraising as he drums his fingers against his calfskin breeches. "I think you ought to come with me," he finally says.

When I meet his eye, there is no flirtatious glimmer there, just an earnest interest. In the distance a rocket explodes, and there is another round of cheering. Soon it will grow dark, and without the safety of a bed, I will be at the mercy of the streets. "And why would I do that?"

Standing, he extends his hand down. I stare at the white glove. "Because there is someone you should meet."

I snap my sketchbook shut. The flowers around me issue me no warnings. In fact, they are almost nodding as if in agreement. But what an odd request from a soldier in the garden of a convent on a sunny day. "I'm not in the habit of accompanying strange men," I tell him. "And to unknown locations, no less."

He grins. He is boyish and young, cocky. "Not even with men in dashing blue coats and epaulets?"

"On the contrary, your colors are the very reason for my hesitation. Don't tell me girls are usually so easily swayed?"

That bright grin again, cutting through the solemn air of the nunnery. "Oh yes," he says, and his confidence is almost enough to persuade me to accept to his invitation. Almost.

"I would be a fool to accept the invitation of a man whose name I do not know, blue coat and epaulets or not."

"Forgive me," he says, sketching a neat bow from the waist. "Armand Boucher, Fusilier Sergeant in the Emperor's Grande Armée. And who is the enchanting young artist who has taken refuge in the field of an abbey?"

"Colette," I say, giving him my pseudonym.

The quick, downward tug of his brow tells me that I have not fooled him by omitting a last name, but he smiles graciously all the same.

Behind me the sisters of St. Clare are prayerful and obedient but with full bellies and warm rooms. Beyond the cloistered walls is a city awaiting the return of a despot. I belong in neither, yet I must choose.

My stomach rumbles, and on impulse I accept the hand he

extends to me. He pulls me to standing, with just enough force that I find myself perilously close to his chest. He murmurs an apology and takes a step back, but not before I catch the heady, masculine scent of his pomade again. I feel restored a hundred times over, as if I have slipped easily back into the pretty games of drawing rooms and balls, but this time with no uncle breathing down my neck or the threat of a badly made marriage. I only wish that I was dressed to the best of my advantage and had the benefit of a good, hot bath.

"Who are you taking me to meet?" I ask him.

His smile is cryptic. "Someone who appreciates the importance of the natural world."

He says no more, and I ask no more. I find that I am glad to have a blank page spread open before me, with no hint of what is to come. Adventure is so much more tolerable when there is no longer the question of where one will sleep or from where one's next meal will come.

With ease, Armand slings my bag over his shoulder, and I am only too grateful to not have to burden my aching arms any further. We begin walking back toward the city, our pace leisurely. "Do you know, there are not actually any nuns in there," he tells me with a sidelong grin. "The convent was turned over to the gendarmerie after the Terror."

I give him a playful slap on the arm. "Wicked man! If I had not agreed to go with you, would you have let me go in there and embarrass myself?"

"Perhaps I knew that you would say *yes*," he says. "And so there was no danger of you discovering the truth."

"You are dreadfully arrogant, aren't you?" But I'm laughing, delighted at my new friend's humor.

As we leave the abbey behind us, there is something in the breeze, a promise that tells me that my life has just taken a bold new direction, that nothing will ever be the same again.

Six

LIJSBETH

WHITE VIOLETS: to take a chance, whether on love or on one's self. To step out into the unknown.

March 1815

Isidore stalks the house like a hungry cat, drawing pleasure from watching me look over my shoulder, seeing me jump whenever I come upon him in a room. At any moment he could say the word and see me turned out of the house, but he seems content to let me dangle like a fish on a hook instead. My body shrinks into itself further, my mind scattered and distant as I work throughout the day. But tonight there is an air of excitement, a current that runs all the way through the old house and into the kitchen where I am sorting flowers in big buckets of water.

Madame is hosting a party to celebrate Isidore's return from university as well as the escape of Napoleon from Elba. Annette says that he has landed in Golfe-Juan and is already now marching to Paris where he will reclaim the throne. Madame seems to think this will mean good things for the family, so she is in high spirits. There will be sweets and a harp concert, and best of all, Isidore will be preoccupied with the young ladies that Madame is no doubt inviting to try to tempt her rakish son.

I spread the fragrant blooms before me, running my fingers over them as a pianist might the keys before he begins to play. As I carefully find a home for each of them in the vase, I try to not to dwell on the strange way the flowers soured and recoiled, the blood that I imagined dripping off their thorns the day that I stabbed Isidore. My mind is always wont to wander when I am arranging, my hands working of their own accord. But tonight, it is as if I were in a trance, watching my body from far away. It is easier to see my life through the petals of flowers, to imagine myself simply an extension of their brief yet beautiful lives. This body is a burden, a painful reminder of just how low I am, how little I am worth.

When I come back to my body, I stand back and study the arrangement as if seeing it for the first time. It is unlike anything I have ever arranged before. The tulips brush the table with their frilly heads in a great sweep, and the roses stand thorny and defiant. Colors that looked soft and dainty in the market now appear brash, almost sinister. I imagine Madame's brows drawing down in dismay when she sees the arrangement that's meant to celebrate her son's return. But the sound of carriages outside tells me it is too late to begin again, so it will have to do.

Once I've delivered the flowers to the front hall, I melt back into the belly of the house before the first guest arrives.

I'm scrubbing the kitchen floor when Annette plows in, her wide skirt swishing about her. "Madame wants you," she says. "She's in the drawing room with the rest of them. Wants you in there now."

The panic must be writ large on my face because she scowls. "Well, are you just going to stand there a-dripping water everywhere?"

I have never been called into the drawing room before and

certainly not when there are guests. I feel the eyes of a dozen well-dressed young ladies and smart gentlemen on me as I slip inside, sweating hands clasped at my waist. Gazes quickly slide away in disinterest, like water running off the back of a drab waterfowl.

Conversations flow in both Dutch and French, switching easily and sometimes in the middle of a sentence. "If Napoleon comes to Brussels, you can be sure that the city will welcome him with open arms," a man in a gold waistcoat is telling his companion.

"Not if the Dutch have a say."

"I heard he escaped in the middle of a masquerade and landed in the clothes of a masked jester," a woman says behind her fan.

I make my way to the settee where Madame is holding court, fanning herself like an empress beset with ennui, a glass of sherry in her other hand. She doesn't see me, and I stand awkwardly, as young ladies in gowns as soft and pale as summer clouds with quivering ostrich plumes in their hair regard me from suspicious eyes. Isidore's oily stare lingers on me, and I feel my cheeks flush hot as I drop a hasty curtsy and finally catch the attention of Madame.

"Lijsbeth, there you are," she says crisply. "Madame Dubois was most complimentary of this arrangement," she says, the curl of her lip making it clear that she is not in agreement.

The flowers are taller than I remember, the unruly stems reaching out of the vase and toward the window like the desperate claws of a bird of prey.

"Lijsbeth cannot speak," Madame van den Berg tells her friend, and Madame Dubois makes a little noise in the back of her throat, which might be pity but is more likely disinterest. "But she is a hard worker and has a way with flowers."

Madame Dubois rises from the sofa in a bustle of silk and feathers, inspecting me through a little opera glass.

"I am looking for a girl who can do light housework, as well as arrange flowers," she says, not quite to me but at no one else in particular. "I entertain often, and my maid now is a butcher with the flowers. I would have my five girls learn the art of arranging. If you accept my offer, you will start tomorrow morning. But be warned," she says, wagging a finger full of heavy rings, "I do not tolerate laziness or insolence."

The offer—or, rather, order—is made so quickly and so casually that it takes me a moment to understand her meaning. Isidore may be content to let me dangle, but Madame wants me out of her house. She knows that Isidore's injury was no accident, and she is probably regretting not casting me out when Thérèse came all those years ago.

Madame Dubois is watching me expectantly. Isidore is lingering at his mother's shoulder, his lips pressed tight as he pretends to be absorbed in spinning the signet ring round his little finger. I don't know what sort of mistress Madame Dubois is. Does she raise her hand to her servants? Does she scream and rail if the silver has streaks? Does she have a scoundrel for a son? I have only ever known this home, but really, it is just a house, not a home. Madame and Monsieur van den Berg, Isidore, and Thérèse, they are a family. But I have been shut out, relegated to the kitchen and back stairs when my role as pet and plaything became obsolete. Who needs an orphan girl from the gutter when they can have their own shining golden child?

Isidore finally meets my eye, something hot and angry simmering behind the cool facade, and I know that the next time I may not escape with my life.

Seven

CORNELIA

CROCUS: mirth, a joyous beginning.

"Goodness, is this all the work of one day?"

Armand is leading me through the camp which has sprung up on the other side of the city like an eager spring daisy. My curiosity—excitement, even—is enough to keep the hunger at bay as we walk, and I can put the unpleasantness of the last few days behind me.

"We knew that the emperor would return," Armand explains, "and so preparations were already underway when we received word that he had made his great escape. Now we must work on conscripting more forces until we join with him in his march across France."

Everywhere the smell of smoke and churned earth hangs in the air. There is a jovial atmosphere with fluttering banners and flags, boys playing tin penny pipes. For being in the business of killing, the men seem remarkably lighthearted, taking part in games of piquet and whist.

Armand guides me around a line of soldiers doing a drill, and I jog to keep up with him, hem in hand in a vain attempt to keep it out of the mud. I come to a sudden stop. "Is that a cannon?" The metal contraption rumbles past us, hauled by a mule and a team of sweating men.

Armand hardly spares it a glance. "One of them, yes. This way!"

When we arrive at a large brick barracks, I am breathless and my only good dress damp with perspiration. My escort finally stands still, his dark eyes bright as he turns to me. "Are you ready?"

"It's not..." I look at the rather plain brick building. "That is, the emperor is not—"

Armand throws his head back and laughs. "No, he is a hard traveler, but he is not so quick as to have appeared from Golfe-Juan since this morning. But come, he is important all the same."

I wish that I looked a little more presentable, that I did not have limp curls and a wrinkled dress. There is nothing worse than meeting the unknown looking anything other than one's best.

I have never given much thought before, if any, to what goes on in a military barracks. I suppose if I were pressed, I would say that they are cold and dreary places, with somber men in tricornes pushing pegs about on a map. Instead, I am greeted by a spacious office, with etchings and prints of flora and fauna hanging on the walls. Someone has gone to great lengths to turn the old room into a sanctuary with thick rugs and animal hides on the straw-strewn floor. I turn to Armand, my smile spreading. "These are all flora of France and Italy!"

A throat clears, and Armand guides me with a light hand to the back, where two men in blue and gold regalia are conferring over some papers with a third man seated at a large desk. Here are the military men I envisioned, buttoned up in dark blue coats and gold tassels, rigid with self-importance.

The seated man looks up, dazed, as if he had forgotten about his surroundings while he was absorbed in the papers. He is unremarkable in appearance, other than a scattering of healed pockmarks and a formidable square face. The other two are a little older, portly and pale, as if they have not seen action on a battlefield in some decades. They break off in their conversation and turn to stare at me.

"Sergeant," the seated man with the scars says, the single word holding both a question and a condemnation. "You are not expected."

Unbothered, Armand sketches a hasty bow and presents me as if I were a debutante at a ball. "General Guérin, forgive me, but I came across something most unusual this morning and am eager to share my finding with you. This is Mademoiselle Colette—she is an artist and naturalist."

The question in the general's sharp blue eyes deepens, and an unreadable look passes between him and the other men, who he then dismisses with a wave, leaving me the center of his attention.

He makes an impatient motion at my sketchbook which I have been clutching. Reluctantly, I watch his big hand swallow it up as I pass it to him.

I dare not breathe as I watch him examine my sketches. I do not know why Armand has brought me here, but the expectant air of the office feels like a test, like the course of my life very well may depend on what this harried man thinks of my work.

He quickly scans the illustrations, thumbing through pages that took me years to fill. He looks surprised when he comes to a lady's slipper. "You are familiar with orchids?"

"Of course." I do not think it wise to tell him that I'm more surprised that he, a general, is familiar with a hothouse flower.

"Mm." He makes a distracted sound and goes back to the portfolio. "Your accent... Where are you from?"

I try not to bristle as he implies my French is recognizable as anything over than that of a native. "Brussels," I tell him, though I don't know why that, of all places, passes through my mind.

There is a long, brittle moment until he tosses my sketchbook onto his desk and crosses his arms. "You understand, we cannot simply grant any girl that walks into our camp access. We must be certain that she is not a spy. Or English," he says, a distasteful emphasis on the last word.

"Come, General," Armand says. "You can see mademoiselle is harmless. Only think how pleased the emperor will be when he arrives and finds a naturalist who can continue the work he started. If we are to build an empire on reason and science, we must employ the best, most talented minds. Just think of all the other places in the empire that must be taken in hand. We need another Egypt, a grand expedition that—"

"Do not speak to me of Egypt, boy," the general snaps. "You were still in short pants when I was sweating with fever and putting down the natives."

There is some sparring between the general and Armand, and I am left with the impression that this is not the first time my young friend has crossed his superior. All the same, the man finally removes his hat, rakes his hand through his graying hair and mutters an oath under his breath. "She will be in my custody," he says after a weighty pause and continues before Armand has a chance to argue. "When the emperor returns, he will make the final decision as to her fate. In the meantime, she will be under constant supervision." Turning his attention to me, the general pins me with his steely gaze. "Do you understand, mademoiselle? There is to be no fraternizing with the men or unsupervised activities beyond partaking in meals and attending to your necessary needs. You have set foot in this camp as a civilian of unknown origins, and I cannot allow you unchecked freedom."

The fact that I walked into the barracks a guest and am now apparently a prisoner rankles me. I am used to being examined, however subtly, by the men that Uncle would bring to dinner, but it does not mean that I appreciate feeling like a horse at market. I did not ask to be taken here or put forward for inspection. "Perhaps you would be so kind as to tell me what it is I have just interviewed for," I ask him coolly.

The general stands, gestures to some of the frames on the walls. "The emperor is a science-minded man. Naturalists, botanists, astronomers, and all other manner of scientists are important for the expansion and legitimacy of the empire. I cannot say that the emperor thinks highly of women who set their sights outside of their domestic duties," he says with a tightness suggesting he is of one mind with the ruler, "but talent is talent. There are to be no grand expeditions into the Orient or Africa for the time being. You will follow the camp, document whatever flora you can find along the way, and then we shall see if the emperor is pleased with his new acquisition."

The space of a breath is the only time I need to think about my answer. "I accept," I tell him, tilting my chin up as if I had a choice in the matter. I suppose I could walk out of the barracks and keep going, forgetting this strange chapter in my brief foray into the world. But he is offering me security—at least, for now—and besides, what else is a woman in my position to do?

He holds my gaze a moment longer, then gives a curt nod, putting to rest whatever lingering doubt he was still nursing. "Do you have boarding in the city? No? You will have a tent in the camp, then. Lieutenant!" he calls, and a soldier materializes out of the corner. He must have been there the entirety of the interview, yet I did not even notice him. Surprising, given that he is tall and remarkably well-built. "Lieutenant Peusol will be your guard here in the camp. You understand that you are not to get underfoot." The general switches his attention to Armand. "Consider my debt to your father repaid, and then some," he says. "And if I hear so much as a whisper of impropriety or anything untoward, it is your person which will bear the fault."

Armand gives a tight nod, and I wonder why he was so eager to call in a favor with this hard man, all for a woman he has known but two hours.

I emerge from the barracks a new woman. Only two weeks ago, I was the ward of a country esquire of some small importance and no prospects. This morning I was nothing more than another hungry face haunting the cobbled streets of Amiens. And now? I will travel with the army of Napoleon himself. If only Uncle could see me now, attached to the army of the little Corsican whom he hated so fiercely.

Lieutenant Peusol shows me to my new lodgings. The tent is only just tall enough to accommodate me, and my silent guard looks on as I examine the thin bedroll on the cot, the tin basin in the corner. Perhaps this was the life my mother chose. Perhaps my father is one of the men in this very regiment, a hard-faced soldier who still fights for the ideals he so fervently believes in. Perhaps my mother is waiting for him in some cottage. Perhaps fate has brought me to exactly where I am meant to be.

Eight

CORNELIA

EVERGREEN CLEMATIS: ambition, climbing to great heights. The threat of a fall, poverty.

I awaken stiff-backed and hungry, my body unused to stooping in the low tent, sleeping on the hard cot. Well, let it be a reminder of my freedom. I might have slept in a feather bed and eaten from a silver plate at Uncle's house, but I was not free.

Except I am not free here, either, I remember as I emerge into the brisk, smoky morning and my guard greets me with a wordless nod.

"Well?" I ask him. "Where may I make my toilette?" My stomach is rumbling, but I think it's rather more important to attend to the horrifying state of my hair and dress before finding something to eat.

If my guard finds his new assignment tedious or beneath him, it does not show on his expressionless face as he leads me to the water pump. He is a rather beautiful man, his broad shoulders and impressive height softened by the fullness of his lips, the almost sorrowful wash of his light gray eyes. When he does speak, it is low, rough, and with a provincial patois, thicker than that of Armand. I wonder how he was chosen to act as my guard.

Lieutenant Peusol shows me how to pump cold water for my basin (which I am instantly hopeless at) and introduces me to the victualler who provides the camp with hot cooked meals. I jog to keep up with him, my head constantly swiveling to take in the sights of my new surroundings. The camp is like a city unto itself. Women barter for goods, while shrieking children run underfoot. It could be London with all the different languages that I hear being spoken, people of all skin colors and origins. The men's uniforms are often ill-fitting, and boot soles are worn thin. Still, an air of camaraderie permeates everything. There is one thing conspicuously absent from the camp, though, and that is flowers. How I am supposed to document the botanical wonders of Napoleon's empire if I am consigned to a field of mud in France?

Though I was told that I was not to fraternize with the soldiers, I cannot stop the curious looks and eventual introductions of some of the men at the large trestle tables where a breakfast of some kind of porridge and ham is being served.

"We are all equal under these colors," a young soldier tells me when I voice my observation about the camaraderie. He cannot be more than seventeen years of age, and his eager eyes shine as he speaks.

"If you rise here, it is through your merit on the battlefield alone and not because of the name you bear or the connections of your father," says another young man with dark brown skin and a gold hoop on each ear.

I glance at Lieutenant Peusol, who is waiting for me across the table, his arms crossed, his expression a carefully studied look of indifference. His coat is barren of some of the heavier and flashier medals and ribbons that the other men wear, yet there is an air of importance about him, a deference that the other men afford to him. It is hard to imagine him engaged in combat, charging on a battlefield. It is hard to imagine any of these men using their hands for killing.

Lieutenant Peusol returns me to outside my tent. It cannot be ten o'clock in the morning, yet it appears as if I am meant to bide here for the rest of the day. "I need to see something posted in the mail," I tell him as he turns to leave me.

He reaches out his hand. "I can take anything you need."

"That's kind of you, but I must see it posted myself."

Lowering his hand, he regards me with renewed interest. "Are you a spy, then?"

"What? No! It's just…it is a private matter. A *feminine* matter," I say, hoping to strike an enigmatic air.

But he doesn't look in the least bit perturbed. "A feminine matter?"

I flush, stamp my foot. It's very unbecoming of me, I know, but it is beyond the pale that I am being treated as a prisoner. "It is no business of yours."

"That is where you're wrong, mademoiselle. It is my only business. Is this it?" He plucks the packet from my hands, and before I can snatch it back, he is holding it well above my head to inspect it. I fruitlessly try to snatch it back, but he easily holds it aloft.

I give up and cross my arms, watching helplessly as he tears open the packet and empties the contents. I was happy enough to share my work with Armand, but in the hands of this brute, it feels like a violation.

He's gone very quiet above me. "What is this meant to be?" he finally says, lowering them.

I snatch them back. The seal is mangled, and I try in vain to press it back on. "Are you satisfied now? They are merely some silly drawings bound for publication in a paper."

"I can't let you send them."

The papers fall from my hands. "Why not?"

"Could be a code of some sort."

"A code," I repeat. He cannot be serious, yet there is no hint of humor in his hard gray eyes. I have come so far, but my position is far from secure. What if the men in camp are licentious and I am blamed for it? What if the emperor is killed en route and the whole camp disbands? My pencil and paintbrush are all I have.

"Are you crying?" Lieutenant Peusol looks horrified. He takes a step toward me, hand out. "Don't…don't do that."

No young lady worth her salt has not, at least on one occasion, resorted to summoning tears at will. But no sooner than the first tears fall than I find that they are flowing in earnest. Mortified, I try to sniff them back, but it is too late. The dam has broken. I am alone, far from home, and what little security my drawings provided is about to be taken away from me.

The lieutenant pulls me into the tent, away from the curious gazes and laughter of soldiers passing by. In the cramped space, I am nearly flush with his chest. "Stop that," he says gruffly, thrusting a cloth at me. I dab away the last of the tears, only to see something like a flicker of pity in his eyes.

"I'll post the bloody pictures," he says. "But if I find that they are anything other than harmless drawings, I'll quarter you myself."

There is no heat in his words, and I'm inclined to believe that it is all bluster on his part. "Oh, thank you!" I throw myself at him, and he goes stiff in my arms, but he is warm and does not try to pull away.

That night as I lay in my cot, my worries come bubbling back up. There is no guarantee that I will be able to post my column again, not when Lieutenant Peusol was so reluctant. And besides, where am I to get flowers to study? I am stuck in a tent on a muddy field in the north of France, with a guard who is never more than a few paces from me. I can conjure flowers in my mind, commit them to paper, but it is no substitute for becoming intimately acquainted with the idiosyncrasies of an individual bloom. I rather doubt that I am even capable of conjuring up flowers anymore, and I am not inclined to try lest I find that I have truly lost my touch since Anna.

I turn over, clutch the thin pillow to my chest. It is a rare night that I allow myself to wallow or indulge in memories of Anna, but tonight, here in this strange place, I do just that.

Armand is leaning against the water pump the next day when I go to fill my pitcher. My heart instantly lightens as my gaze falls upon the closest thing to a familiar face.

Lieutenant Peusol takes my basin and begins to pump water for me, but Armand stops him. "No need, Lieutenant," Armand tells him with a bright smile. "I can assist mademoiselle."

My guard does not look happy about the gesture, but then, I think that he probably never looks anything other than painfully serious. He stands back, and Armand takes the basin and begins to pump.

"You are the belle of the camp," Armand says, when the basin is full. "I think military life suits you. Though, I daresay you would shine even in the darkest catacomb."

His compliments are restorative, more so than any cold water or breakfast could be. "You are a dreadful liar," I tell him. "For I know for a fact that I look a fright."

"Mademoiselle, it is impossible for you to look anything other than utterly enchanting," he says, a bolt of heat in his words.

The lieutenant coughs, and out of the corner of my vision, I see him roll his eyes.

"Very well, I won't argue with you. I can see that you are quite decided on the matter."

A dimple shows as he smiles. The man is as charming as a fox, and he knows it. "Quite right. So how do you find camp life thus far?"

"I can't say that it is sparkling and gay, but I like it well enough, I suppose."

Leaning against the pump, he crosses his arms and gives me an appraising look. "Yet something is bothering you."

"My work is my life," I tell him. "But I cannot work if there are no flowers."

"And there are no flowers in a military camp. I see." He tents his fingers in thought, gives a long pause. "Well, we shall just have to go find some."

"But what of Lieutenant Peusol?" The lieutenant is standing only a few paces away, doing a miserable job pretending not to watch me from the corner of his eye.

Armand gives a little snort. "Do you mean to tell me that the girl who boldly questioned General Guérin is afraid of her guard?"

"Of course not!"

He grins, offering me his arm. "Then, come with me."

I glance back to where Lieutenant Peusol is distracted by a conversation with another soldier, then take Armand's hand and allow him to lead me to where the flowers grow.

"I have a confession to make."

Armand has brought me to the river's edge beyond the camp, where a maze of floating gardens winds through the countryside. The day has grown mild and pleasant. Little boats skim by, rowed by men in straw hats selling bundles of vegetables and flowers. Armand lies on the grass, hands laced behind his head, as he squints at the overcast sky. I am sketching the most exquisite lily and hardly glance up as he speaks.

"Oh?"

"Yes, and I hope you don't think me a villain when I tell you."

"I could never."

He sits up, rests his chin on his knee as he watches me work. "I did not just come upon you in that field."

This causes my pencil to stop. "No?"

"No. I saw you at the pont du Cange and I confess, I followed you. You looked so forlorn, staring down at the water from the bridge."

I lay my work aside and look at him. Yes, he truly is a fox. Clever and watchful and always planning his next move.

"Do you think me very wicked?" he asks, his dark brown eyes watching me intently.

"That depends. Are you contrite?"

He pushes himself up the rest of the way so that he is kneeling before me. "Never," he says, the vehemence of his words taking me aback. "How could I be, when my actions brought me to such a perfect moment as this, with such an extraordinary woman?"

I give him a playful rap with my pencil on his arm, his gaze tracing the movement. "You are very naughty, but I forgive you," I tell him, going back to my work. I like having admirers. I like being the object of adoration and cannot fault him for playing a game in which I myself so often take pleasure.

"Ah, Colette. You do not even blush. I think that you must have many admirers."

"Do you wish to see me blush? Or perhaps fan myself and apply some sort of smelling salt? Because I find all that to be rather silly."

He laughs and returns to his supine posture, idly swatting away a bee. "You are right, of course. I shouldn't like you half so well if you were a silly creature like that. Come, show me some of these flowers that so occupy your time."

I show him the drawings, explain to him how each one is imbued with its own special meaning. How together they can tell a story, convey a deeper message. I do not tell him I know because the flowers tell me themselves.

He listens, rapt with attention. "You say they all have secret meanings? How is one to know which bloom means what?"

"One would need to read Madame Dujardin's column in the newspaper to decipher them," I tell him, watching to see if he has figured out that the very same sits before him right now.

He seems to consider this. "And what sort of messages might one send? Are they solely the tokens and promises of lovers?"

"Not necessarily, though they lend themselves to lovers' assignations and secret rendezvous. They speak very well to friendships as well and sentiments where the spoken word often fails to convey the appropriate intention." I consider him for a moment. "You are very interested in flowers."

"I am very interested in anything concerning you, Colette."

His gaze is a little too sharp, his eyes a little too bright as he says this. But it is a beautiful day, and for the first time since coming to France, I feel the freedom that I have so longed for.

It is well past dusk when Armand and I return to camp.

"I must say farewell to you here," Armand tells me when we see the flicker of the torches through the dark. "But I hope that you will do me the honor of allowing me to abduct you again and sever your manacles."

I laugh and reward my friend with a light kiss to the cheek.

Lieutenant Peusol is pacing outside of my tent, his face drawn in the torchlight. As soon as he catches sight of me he strides over, so close that he nearly bowls me over.

"Where were you?" he demands, his nostrils flaring. He looks like a bull—a very strong, very angry bull.

"Goodness. No need for all that. I only went out for some company and a change of scenery."

"With who?" he demands.

"It was only Sergeant Boucher, and—"

"Who?"

I swallow despite myself. The muscle in his jaw is straining, and I can practically feel the heat radiating off him. "Sergeant

Boucher. I'm sure you know that we are friends. He is, after all, who brought me here."

My pulse quickens in my throat, but I hold the lieutenant's violent gaze. He could take me before General Guérin, have me turned out of the camp. Or the way he's looking at me he could very well strike me. I tilt my chin up, daring him.

"Damn it," he mutters, breaking our standoff and removing his hat to scrub at his short hair. I let out a slow breath. "You know that you are not to fraternize with the men and certainly not to leave the grounds with one. Never mind *him*, of all people."

There is something in his tone that gives me pause. "Why? What is it about the sergeant that you find so objectionable?"

Lieutenant Peusol seems to be searching for a satisfactory answer, before finally saying, "I don't like him." The fire in his eyes has dimmed a bit, and he strikes a less formidable posture, leaning back against the tent post. But his gaze is still sharp, his attention honed on me.

"No?" I ask, amused. "You mean to say you don't find him all things charming and amiable? I think quite a few ladies would disagree with you." I was hoping for a smile at the very least, but my guard remains stone-faced.

"You should mind yourself around him."

The lieutenant would no doubt be apoplectic if he knew the circumstances of how Armand and I met, how quickly I placed my trust in him. But I suppose that's the nature of men, quick to jealousy, quick to form judgments. "He's harmless," I tell him. "And in any case, I can take care of myself."

He grunts, perhaps the closest thing I've seen of a smile so far hovering at his lips. "I've no doubt. Still."

A breeze sends the flags fluttering and a chill racing across my neck. Lieutenant Peusol's color is still high, and I cannot help but be touched that he is so concerned for me. I nod. "Yes, I'll mind myself. And of course, I have you."

"You have me," he repeats softly.

Another chill runs through me, one that makes me wish for a warm body to lean into, or at the very least, the hand of a friend to take. Somewhere in the distance, a horse whickers. Light flirting and harmless banter are one thing, but there is an air of prickling expectation as I stand with my guard. Suddenly, I find that I am quite tired, eager for my bed. "Good night, Lieutenant," I tell him through my tight throat.

He gives a curt nod, and I return to my cot, dizzy with racing thoughts. Long after our conversation, I can still just make out the strong lines of the lieutenant's silhouette through the canvas walls.

Nine
LIJSBETH

CLEMATIS: safety after a journey. Joy.

Everything in the Dubois house is from somewhere else, somewhere far away. The flocked wallpaper in the parlor has been brought in from Paris. From the Orient, porcelain so thin that sunlight shows through it when held to the window. The plush carpets on the floor were woven in the Far East, and imported by way of Constantinople. Oil paintings from Italy sit heavy and important in their gilded frames. It is a house meant to showcase the collecting acumen of its owner, and I am simply the newest addition.

But I don't mind. Mellow sun spills into the parlor where I am dusting, my sleeves pushed to my elbows, skin warm. With the light chatter of Madame Dubois's five daughters around me, I work comfortably, breathe freely. I may still be nothing more than a shadow, but at least I am one that need not fear harm. The family is kind enough—some of the daughters more than others—and Madame Dubois comments often that she is pleased with my work. I think that this is the closest to happiness I have ever felt.

But the peaceful scene is shattered as a carriage rumbles to a stop across the street amid much jubilant shouting and fanfare. Rosalie, Hippolyte, and Virginie spring up from where they were embroidering and race to the window, squealing. "It's the Duke and Duchess of Richmond!" Hippolyte exclaims. "Look! You can see the arms on their carriage." Though only a few years younger than me, her voice is high, girlish still. She is the second youngest of the five and something of a pet to her sisters.

Eugenie sets aside her embroidery and takes a sip of her tea. "We are quite under siege from the allied forces, it seems," she says dryly. She is the eldest of the girls, and looks like a Greek statue come to life, serene and very beautiful. She catches my eye and winks, and I immediately return her smile, unable to hide the pleasure it gives me to be recognized by one so lovely and kind.

All week, forces from England have descended upon Brussels, preparing to put an end to Napoleon's romp across the Continent after his escape. The constant stream of arrivals has provided no end of entertainment and fodder for the family's gossip, and the Duke and Duchess of Richmond's taking of apartments across the street is the latest cause for excitement. Their graces have fourteen children, at least a few of which are the correct sex and age, and Madame Dubois has made no secret of the fact she thinks she might foist one of her surplus daughters on a Richmond heir.

Madame's mother is peeking through the curtains next to her granddaughters, tutting at the entourage of carriages and scurrying servants. "You would think it was a Continental tour and not a war! Look at all those trunks, probably full of shapeless English gowns and poorly stitched stockings. I—"

"Grandmama, come away from the window, you are like a gawping playgoer, and they will surely see you," Octavie says, her voice chiding as if she was speaking to a small child. Octavie is my least favorite of all the girls.

The old woman waves her off. "As if that wasn't their design in coming in here! Tell me they don't wish to be gawked at when the duchess is traveling with *three* ostrich feathers in her hat!"

I pretend to be absorbed in dusting a candelabra, though it has been clean for some time now.

"Their design in coming here is quite of the military persuasion," Madame says firmly, drawing her ancient mother away and throwing her daughters a warning look. "And a good thing, too, as it will take all the might of the allies to banish Bonaparte once and for all. Isn't that right, Jacques?"

"Hm?" Monsieur briefly comes up from behind his newspaper. "Quite right, quite right," he murmurs before returning to his reading.

When the excitement has been contained to a simmer, Madame informs me that it is time to give the eldest girls a lesson in arranging. She thinks it will be a feather in their cap in the marriage mart. All the girls already speak French, Dutch, English, and some Latin, are proficient with watercolors and an embroidery needle, and can play the spinet or pianoforte. But with five on her hands, Madame is leaving nothing to chance.

Eugenie and Rosalie join me in the back hall where I have laid out flowers, their stems already trimmed and lower leaves stripped. We have found a comfortable routine, one where they chat and laugh quietly between themselves as they copy my example in their own vases.

"Lijsbeth, you're so clever with flowers. Do you think we could make this instead?" Eugenie produces a newspaper clipping and places it on the table. "It's Madame Dujardin's latest column," she explains.

I study the illustration. I've never seen anything like it before. The jonquil comes alive, frilly white petals, and stamens so real that it could be plucked right from the page and transplanted into the royal gardens. "Every week she features a different flower and expounds upon its secret meaning. Then she shows it in a bouquet with other flowers that tell a story. Isn't it divine?"

"Ooh!" Rosalie leans over and snatches the paper from my hands. "What does she say it means? Lijsbeth, we really must try to incorporate some of her designs. All the girls are making bouquets for their sweethearts with messages from Madame Dujardin's columns. With the soldiers coming 'round, we will need to be ready."

I've never heard of Madame Dujardin, and even if I wanted to, I can't read what the words say. But there is an intimacy about the delicate sketch, and I fancy that I can gather what the artist is trying to convey, even without the benefit of the accompanying text.

When the girls have finished their arrangements and are admiring each other's work, I quietly palm the forgotten newspaper clipping. As I slip it into my pocket, I can almost see the hand of the woman who painted the picture, a glimpse of a face that is at once familiar and dreamlike. But then Eugenie is asking me something, and the image disperses, like a flock of startled doves.

Soldiers and officers are all that the Dubois girls talk about for the next week, and the city is soon crawling with redcoats. The Duke and Duchess of Richmond's lodgings abut the house in the back and share a carriage yard, so we are privy to their every coming and going. When Isidore was very young, Madame van den Berg bought him an automaton clock where a little soldier would march out of the face on every hour. It might have appeared to be chaos with gears and springs snapping and grinding every which way, but every piece had a job, and even one tiny screw out of place would render the entire thing useless.

And that is how it feels to work at Madam Dubois's house now that Brussels is preparing for Napoleon's arrival. Soldiers come and go at all hours, and there are always lively games of whist and loo and spontaneous salons to which Madame invites all the new Brussels society. Monsieur Dubois teases his wife that she is the only Anglophile in all of Belgium, if not the Continent. She tuts and raps him on the arm, but it is true. She follows all of the society pages from London and would love nothing more than to be attached to a great English family.

But with the arrival of the soldiers comes an end to the reprieve that I had enjoyed my first few weeks here. Though I no longer have to be attuned to Isidore's drunken slur or clipped boot steps, now I find myself forever ducking into alcoves, disappearing behind curtains, as red-coated soldiers lounge about, laughing and speaking loudly in English.

"Marie!" Madame's mother's shrill call rings out down the hallway to the kitchen, where the other maid, Marie, and I are scrubbing potatoes.

My job is to leave the house more beautiful, to arrange the flowers, and then to help with any other light household work. Marie is the all-about maid, and though she is responsible for everything from filling the scuttles to scrubbing the floors, she has no qualms about relegating some of her more unpleasant tasks to me. "It's the old woman's gut," she says with a grimace. "Can't handle all that rich gravy she insists on eating with her fish. Go on," Marie urges me, "you go and see what the old dragon wants."

There is little point in refusing, so I hurry to the old woman's chamber where I find her squatting over the pot, her skirts hiked up over her knees. The smell is thick and sour, but I force myself to give her a pleasant smile.

She grunts, hardly sparing me a glance. "My gut is giving me trouble again."

I stand there for a moment before I realize she expects me to help her. She catches my hesitation and scowls. "Well? Don't tell me you're too good to help an old lady?"

Taking her elbow, I help her position herself in a deeper squat, and she lets out a relieved sigh as her bowels rumble. I turn my head away, choking back my gag.

"What, turning up your nose like you're some high lady? I wouldn't have thought a girl who can't even speak such a prude." She lets out a rattling laugh that devolves into a coughing fit, and she sends me on my way with the pot to empty.

I am carefully making my way back down the hall, a linen placed discreetly over the pot when I collide with a soldier walking briskly the other way. It is all I can do to tighten my grip and make sure that the pot doesn't go flying.

My eyes slowly travel up the neatly pressed red coat and find a man a few years my senior, his expression caught somewhere between surprise and amusement. There have been so many soldiers about lately that I can't say for certain if I've ever seen this man before, but something tells me I would remember those clear blue eyes, the soft sweep of golden hair if I had. By some small mercy, the contents of the pot have stayed inside, but the smell is pungent, and there is no mistaking what I am transporting. We both stare at each other, at an impasse on the stairs. Perhaps I should be grateful that I am holding this stinking pot, that it makes me all but undesirable, or else I could find myself at the mercy of a soldier who has no compunction about taking advantage of a maid.

But the soldier only crinkles his nose, and he takes a hasty step back. "Good God!" he exclaims in a heavy English accent. "Well, don't go through that way! You'll pass right through the drawing room, and Madame Dubois will never recover." Moving so quickly I don't have a chance to back away, he takes me by the elbow and leads me back up the stairs and then down the hall to the other end of the house. "Our gracious hostess is assembling her evening salon, and I daresay she would not appreciate having her guests routed en masse by whatever *that* is," he confides, as he continues to propel me down the back stairs.

His grip is firm and warm, but not so hard that I would not be able to pull away if I should wish it.

Before I can so much as blink, we emerge into the carriage yard in the back where the Richmonds' horses are stabled. "Here we are." He nods toward the water pump. "Acquaint that with some water before you bring it back in," he advises.

I've not even had a chance to start the pump, when a group of soldiers amble out of the house, lighting cheroots and laughing among themselves. The bowl is growing heavy in my hands, my cheeks hot as they cast their gazes around the yard. "There you are, Norton! What the devil are you doing out here? Hazards are about to start, and you're needed."

"I was just escorting the young lady out of the path of Madame Dubois's delicate constitution," he says with good humor and not a drop of condescension or malice.

The young lady. Not *servant* or *girl* or any other perfectly reasonable label he might have assigned me.

My soldier joins his friends, but not before giving me a jaunty salute and holding my gaze for what feels like a moment eternally suspended in time. His accompanying smile is like a sunbeam, reaching right into my chest and flooding me with warmth, and I almost forget that I am standing in a noisy carriage yard, holding a soiled pot. Then he is gone, in a dazzling cloud of laughter and brightly colored uniforms.

Ten

CORNELIA

PURPLE LILAC: the first stirrings of love.
An awakening after a long period of dormancy.

Growing up in Sussex, there was precious little in Uncle's house to read, or rather, precious little that was worth reading. Certainly, there were books, though they were mostly treatises and dusty old sermons. But Uncle did keep a stack of journals, the *Courier de l'égypte* among them (though why, I cannot fathom, as I am certain he never studied them). I read them under the guise of improving my French, but really I was being transported to a land of windswept deserts and crumbling pyramids. It seemed impossible that the same sun which nourished the flowers in our garden could also bake clay into hard bricks and warm the backs of scaly crocodiles.

So when Armand plucked me from the verge of sisterhood, I had expected verdant jungles, campaigns in the Orient or even Africa. I imagined myself an explorer, traveling the far reaches of the known world, documenting hitherto undiscovered flora. Instead, I am stuck on a muddy field on the outskirts of Amiens.

I am largely left to my own devices as the men run drills and prepare for the emperor's return. On occasion I catch sight of Armand, but after our clandestine excursion, I dare not repeat our caper, lest my guard decide to stop helping me post my columns. And so, I am completely without friends.

The morning after my excursion with Armand, Lieutenant Peusol is obliged to join his regiment in a drill, and he leaves me with strict instructions not to wander from my tent. He needn't worry, for I have a headache and am not inclined to subject myself to the din of rifle fire. Instead, I toe at the mud outside my tent, watching the once-fine kid leather of my boots wick up the dirt. The garden in Sussex might have been my refuge, but it was never quiet. The earth sang in flowers, birds adding their own trilling verses. If I were to slip out of the house in the dark of night and stand barefoot on the ground—and I'm not saying that I did, mind you—I would have been able to feel their song through the soles of my feet, reassuring in its constancy.

That same thrumming runs through the ground here as well, deep and old. I fancy that somewhere far beneath the surface I can hear the groaning of roots as they twist through the darkness in search of nutrients. The sound of men shouting and loading rifles fades as I let the sound twine through my bones.

No, not *hear. Feel.*

I step back. A tiny bud, white as a bleached bone pokes through the mud, straining up to the weak sun. It greens before my eyes, growing and growing. In the space of one breath to the next, it has grown what should take days, if not weeks.

Too transfixed to be frightened, I crouch down closer. It is the first time since Anna's departure that I have caused anything to grow. Flowers used to blossom around us as we spent lazy afternoons hidden in the apple trees behind the stables. Anna never questioned it, never condemned me, and perhaps it was that sense of safety, of acceptance, that allowed me the space to commune with those deepest, purest parts of me. So why now? Why here?

I can feel the little bud's struggle, feel it as if it were pulling the blood through my veins along with it. The fresh air on my own tender flesh, exposed after months spent dormant below the ground. The relief, the promise, the sheer joy of—

"What are you doing?"

The spell breaks, and I spring to my feet to find a young woman with a basket on her hip watching me. She cranes her head, trying to see past me to where the green shoot still quivers. "Bit muddy to be planting flowers, isn't it?"

I hastily brush the dirt off my skirt. Her light brown skin is freckled, and her sable hair streaked through with gold, as if she has spent many days working in the sun. She adjusts the basket on her hip as she regards me from eyes as green and brilliant as emeralds.

"Is it against the rules to garden in the camp?"

She laughs, a musical sound that soothes away the jangle of the drills and shouts. "Do I look like a marshal? It's none of my business what anyone gets up to."

I think that is going to be the end of it, but she lingers. "You're the new healer woman, aren't you?"

Her question surprises me. "Who told you that?"

"Word travels. My aunt was a healer in our village, so I know what it means when someone says they're a naturalist or what have you."

"I *am* a naturalist." I hesitate, gauging the interest in her pretty face and direct gaze. "Though, my interest in flora does extend to the healing properties of plants as well. Perhaps you've need of a tisane or compound?" Really, I have no business making such claims, but I find that I want to give her anything she needs or wants, just for a chance to be in her company a little longer.

The laugh again, surprisingly rich coming from someone so small and elfin-looking. "No, I've no need for your services."

There is something warm and appealing about her, and I find myself looking to prolong our conversation. "Are you a wife of a soldier here?"

She levels a withering look at me that draws blood to my face. "I'm no man's wife. I do the laundry. It's a good life for me, for anyone who would rather not sit about or toil at home raising a brood."

I feel eyes on me and realize that Lieutenant Peusol has returned and is watching me from the little avenue of tents. I'm not supposed to speak to anyone, but he doesn't seem compelled to interrupt us. The young woman catches sight of the lieutenant, and a swift, unreadable look passes between them.

"Do you know Lieutenant Peusol?" I ask her.

There is a touch of pink at her pointed little ears, and I'm not sure if it's jealousy that makes my chest tighten just a little. And if it is jealousy, I am not sure on whose behalf I feel it.

"We've crossed paths before" is all she says, hefting the basket from where it has slid down her narrow hip.

Though I never gave much weight—well, I never gave *any* weight—to Uncle's opinion, I cannot help but see myself through his eyes right now. His cruel words to me before sending my Anna away. *Unnatural is what you are. A perverse creature that has no place in polite society.*

I shut Uncle's voice away. "My name is Colette," I tell her, unprompted.

"Sophie," she responds. "I should be going."

"Will I see you again?" I sound like one of the village boys I always scorned, hopeful and pathetic, but I cannot help myself. She has unnerved me, thrown me into that delicious, heart-pounding state that comes from meeting someone whose good opinion suddenly means everything.

"I should think so," she says with a charming smirk. "I can be summoned by leaving your used linens out."

I watch her walk away, her pale blue dress gently swaying

as she hums a pretty tune. I am likewise turning to go back to my tent and my guard, when a splash of color against the dirt catches my eye.

The little plant, which before our conversation had been nothing more than a seedling, has sprouted rich green leaves and a head bursting with pale blue petals.

Eleven

LIJSBETH

DOG ROSE: the exquisite pain of love,
the sharp pleasure of yearning.

I never thought myself a thief, but the newspaper is just lying forgotten on the sideboard, the petite roses in Madame Dujardin's latest column calling to me. I quickly glance behind me to make certain there is no one about and then stuff it into the folds of my pocket. Later tonight, after Marie is asleep and snoring, I will add it to my growing collection. I hoard the columns under my pillow, letting the flower illustrations dance into my dreams each night, the papers growing soft and faded with my constant folding and unfolding. Only once does Hippolyte express confusion when she goes to look for that morning's newspaper, and she ends up deciding that it must have accidentally gotten tossed in with the tinder.

I run my finger across the gracefully confident lines of the rose stems, marveling at the way the artist has used shadows to give life to the flower so that it looks as if it could be plucked right off the page. Last week, one of the soldiers gave Octavie a bouquet, and the girls spent hours poring over Madame Dujardin's columns, trying to decipher the soldier's intentions. I could have told them that the soldier was a shameless flirt and only bought the first flowers he saw at market, but then, I suppose that's not the fun of it.

"Pardon, I did not realize anyone was in here."

I spin around at the sound of the foreign voice, the papers scattering at my feet. I fall to my knees, trying to sweep them up as they seemingly multiply. It is bad enough that I should be caught idling by anyone, but it is not just anyone, it is the soldier with the topaz blue eyes and disarming smile.

"Allow me," he says, quickly springing into action and joining me on the floor. With his body only a few inches from mine, I can smell the rich scent of his soap. Before I can protest, he has swept the papers up in a neat pile, helped me to my feet, and pressed them into my hand. "There we are," he says, his fingers lingering on mine for the briefest moment before releasing me. It's a little gesture, and he will surely forget both it and me the moment he walks back out the door. But oh, I think I will remember the warmth of his gaze focused solely on me for the rest of my days.

His kindness is enough to shatter the flimsy armor that I've built up around myself, and before I can stop myself, hot tears well up and are falling onto the papers. I have been so emotional lately, every little thing bringing me to the brink of tears.

"Oh no. No, don't cry." The panicked look that flashes across his face would be amusing if not for the fact I am the cause of it. But ever the gentleman, he quickly regains his composure and offers me his handkerchief. It smells of his soap. "There now, no need for tears," he says gently.

He could leave, he *should* leave, but he stands patiently, if not a little awkwardly, while I sniffle and wipe away the tears. Any moment Madame or one of the girls will come in and find me alone with a soldier, and it will not be him that pays the price of the indiscretion. Madame would surely send me back to the van den Berg house, back into Isidore's hungry claws.

I finally come to my senses and give him back his handkerchief, our fingers brushing. Yet he still does not move away. "I've seen you about the house, and..." There is a catch of hesitation in his throat. "And there is something I would have of you."

A cold weight settles in my chest, dispelling any romantic delusion under which I had been laboring. He has me alone in a room, and I, a fool, thought he only meant to help me. I am less affected by the actual prospect of what is surely to come than by the utter disappointment of learning that he is no different from Isidore, from any other man.

He must sense my dismay because he pulls back slightly, and a frown creases his fair brow. "No! God, no. What a devil you must think me." There is a feather-soft pause, then a vulnerable quiver of a bird settling on a brittle branch. "Your name," he says, gently. "I only wish to ask you your name."

"There you are!"

The glassy moment shatters as Eugenie breezes into the room. I jump back, but the soldier does nothing, except give Eugenie a short bow, as if conversing with a maid alone in the dining room is the most normal thing in the world.

"I had the house upside-down looking for you," she tells me. "I need your help with my arrangement, for I am afraid I am still utterly hopeless when it comes to getting the tulips to stand up straight. And Captain," she adds with a warm smile, "my mother will wish to invite you to dinner if you would be so obliging."

"I would be honored," he says, though there is a tightness in his otherwise-gracious smile.

Eugenie leads me away, looping her arm in my elbow as if we are old friends. "You must show me how you managed that clever trick with the lilies." she exclaims. "How elegant it looked!"

I am swept along with her, the papers in my pocket no longer simply precious because of their contents but because of whose fingers have touched them.

★ ★ ★

"I saw you with that soldier," Marie says that night as we are undressing for bed.

My back is to her, but I can hear the curiosity coupled with hostility in her voice. I shrug, concentrating on tying off my braid. I had not expected to make friends among the other servants here, but neither I had expected to be treated with such animosity, either. Perhaps Marie is annoyed that she must now share her room, or perhaps she is just a bitter person and would not be friendly to me regardless.

"Wouldn't have thought a girl in your position to be so stupid, but then I suppose you *are* simple," she continues. "Between you and me, you should have a care. Madame isn't hosting all these parties and salons just because she enjoys the society. She's looking for matches for the girls. You wouldn't want to be what comes between a good match, would you?"

I could have told Marie that much, but what I don't understand is why she is giving me any advice when she so clearly dislikes me. I turn, and she must see that very question in my face, because she gives a little snort. "I'm not telling you because I care what happens to you. I'm warning you that it will be bad for all of us if you forget your place."

Twelve

CORNELIA

JONQUIL: I live in hope of a return of your affection.

I would be lying if I said I did not walk through the camp hoping to catch a glimpse of a diminutive figure with a basket on her hip. I would also be lying if I said that I have not had more than one dream about said diminutive figure.

So the last place I expect to find Sophie is standing outside of my tent, waiting for me when I return from the water pump the next morning.

"I need your help," she tells me, hands on her hips, her little pointed chin jutted up. Her tone leaves me to understand that this is not a favor: she speaks with all the authority of Napoleon himself, and I am expected to comply. But she doesn't know that she need not resort to such commands. I would gladly do anything she asked of me.

"Oh?"

"Marion usually helps with the laundry, but she's caught cold and is abed resting. I need you to come help me rinse and hang the linens. There's a good stream just down the way."

Whatever I expected her to ask of me, it was not this. "I don't know how—"

She throws me an impatient look. "It's the easiest thing in the world. Come," she says, taking my hand.

Lieutenant Peusol, who has been watching silently throughout this confusing exchange, steps in front of us. "You can't take her," he tells Sophie.

"I'm not taking her anywhere. She's *coming* with me."

"All the same," he says, crossing his arms across his broad chest.

Sophie gives a little pout, and I am completely enraptured by her feminine charm. "It is only to the far field," she tells him, her tone sweeter and higher. "Well within the sight of camp. Where is the harm in that?"

I watch them negotiate, aware that Sophie does not need my help; she has the lieutenant completely in hand.

He looks as if he wants to argue, the muscle in his jaw tensing, but he must decide it's not worth the argument. His gaze lingers on me as he sternly says, "I come with you."

The negotiation complete, we set off, Sophie tugging me along by the hand, the lieutenant never more than a few paces behind us.

As we leave behind the tents in camp, Sophie flashes me an impish grin, then takes her skirt in her hand and starts running. "Let's see if you're too much of a lady to run the rest of the way."

"Is that a challenge?" I've never run before, but I find myself taking my own hem and letting my legs stretch long to catch up to Sophie. Behind us, Lieutenant Peusol grumbles to himself as he's left to haul the baskets of laundry.

We arrive breathless and laughing at the stream and collapse on the ground while we catch our breath. I have spent probably no more than half an hour in Sophie's company between the first time I met her and today, yet it feels as if I have always known her. She is easy to be with, her joie de vivre infectious. Lieutenant Peusol arrives shortly after us, plunking down the baskets and watching us with wary interest from the corner of his eye.

Crouching by the edge of the stream, we plunge the linens into the clear water. Sophie shows me how to rinse them, explaining that they have already been boiled with lye. It doesn't take long for my arms to begin to ache, but I would rather die than admit as much to my new friend. She is eyeing me as she works, her movements brisk and efficient. "I could wash your gown for you, you know," she says.

My once-lovely violet gown is now more of a muddy purple, and the hem has been dragged through more than I care to think about. I wish, once more, that I had been more judicious when packing and had not brought only what I considered my loveliest gowns. My clothes are ill-suited to life in a military camp. "Yes, perhaps that would be a good idea," I tell her. Sophie sits back on her heels, staring at me expectantly. "What?"

"Well?" she asks.

"You mean to wash it here, now?" I glance about at the clearing beyond the stream. "I haven't anything else to wear," I say, lowering my voice.

Rolling her eyes, she scrambles back from the edge and stands with hands on hips. "And? We're both women. Lieutenant Peusol will turn around, won't you?" she calls out.

Although we are some distance away, I fancy I can see the lieutenant's ears turn pink. He mumbles something and then obliges.

I have never suffered from being overly modest, and with Sophie impatiently tapping her little foot, I disrobe down to my smallclothes, giving her even my petticoat to wash. She produces a sliver of soap. "It won't be as clean as it would get with a boiling, but it will be a sight better all the same."

Her brow is furrowed as she scrubs at a particularly stubborn stain. "This is a very fine frock," she comments. "I've never seen such fine silk. I don't think it would even do to boil it, anyway."

There is a question in her voice, but I can offer her no answers about why her friend dresses like a fine lady but finds herself in a military camp in the north of France. The furrow at her brow deepens. "What is this?"

I look to see a small piece of paper fluttering out from the pocket that I usually wear under my skirt. "It's nothing," I say, reaching to snatch it away.

But Sophie is too fast. She yanks the frock back and holds the scrap of paper aloft. *"Anna?"* she says, reading the smudged writing. "Who is Anna?"

That little piece of paper is the only thing I have left from Anna, and my heart pounds from hearing that name spoken aloud, and by my new friend no less.

"It's no one." I finally am able to grab it back, only to overreach and send both myself and the letter tumbling into the stream.

It is really more of a river, I discover as I surface, my feet barely able to touch the bottom. The water is cold but not terrible. It actually feels rather nice, like the bath which I have been craving since I left home.

I blink the water out of my eyes to find Sophie doubled over, her shoulders shaking, my letter nowhere to be found.

"Are you *laughing* at me?" I sputter.

"I'm sorry..." she says and gasps between breaths "...but your face..."

She is not sorry at all, but I don't mind. I even find that I am not inclined to search for the letter, ruined as it must be. She looks very appealing, her cheeks rosy and her green eyes wet with tears. I swim up to the bank and, while she still has her head tilted back in laughter, give her a good pull so that she is forced to join me in the water.

She splutters and gasps as she topples in. Too late, I realize that she may not be able to swim. I try to grab her arm and pull her to me, but she goes under the water and, fast as a minnow, swims over and yanks my legs out from under me.

We surface in a tangled mess, gasping with laughter. I try not to notice the way her dress hugs her breasts, or the provocative swell of her hips, the water droplets clinging to her lips like dewdrops on a rosebud.

It doesn't occur to me until I tear my gaze away from her that we are not alone. I look back at the bank to see Lieutenant Peusol watching us. He catches my eye and swiftly looks away.

"Join us, won't you, Lieutenant?" I call, laughing. But he does not seem to find the humor in the joke.

He stands, his deportment stiff. "Come, it's time to go."

"We still have to hang the linens to dry," Sophie tells him.

With an impatient gesture, Lieutenant Peusol lets us know that we are to finish the task at hand without any more capers. Sophie gives me one last splash, the wicked little temptress.

Wading back to the bank, I haul myself up, then offer my hand to Sophie. It's just as well we still have to hang the linens, as we both need time to dry out from our spontaneous dip. The breeze makes me shiver in my wet smallclothes, and I wonder if Sophie is as curious about my body as I am about hers. For his part, the lieutenant has turned away from us and is doggedly studying the passing clouds.

Sophie runs a thin rope between two tree branches, and I help her tie it at both ends. Then she shows me how to toss the linen sheets up over the rope so that they hang down with space for the breeze to circulate around them.

"Careful, I have need of someone tall to help me with this," she tells me. "I might have to recruit you again in the future." I assure her that nothing would give me greater pleasure, and indeed, I am nearly glowing from having her undivided attention lavished on me.

I am reaching for a linen, when my hand brushes hers. Though

I thrill at the touch, there is something startling about the texture of her skin. "Sophie!" I exclaim. "What has happened to your hand?"

She glances down to see what I'm looking at. "It's from the lye," she says with a shrug.

"Doesn't it hurt?"

"I'm used to it."

"But you shouldn't have to be." The burns look painful, even though some of them must have scarred over long ago. I wish that I could reach out and bring her hand to my lips, kiss away the pain and marks. But of course, I cannot do that, so I settle instead for saying, "Let me make a poultice for you."

She shrugs again, and I hope that I have not embarrassed or offended her. The laughter and camaraderie we shared in the river seem to have evaporated, and Sophie works in brisk silence.

Since there are hours yet before the linens will be dry, the lieutenant grudgingly agrees that I might gather the herbs and flowers I need. For every stem that I pick for Sophie's burns, I also pick one for my reference later. By the time the linens are dry, my basket is full of plants, and I can't help but be glad that I will have an excuse to be near Sophie again.

Back at camp, Sophie sits still for my ministrations. When I'm done applying the salve, I reluctantly let her hands go. "You really should keep them bandaged for at least a day with the salve. It needs time to work."

"I haven't got days to sit about, doing nothing," she says. Perhaps I am studying her too closely, but I can't help but feel there is a slightly accusatory edge to her words.

"Here." I hand her a bottle of the extra salve that I prepared. "Apply this to your hands before you do the wash next time, it will protect them from the worst effects of the lye."

Sophie nods, pocketing the bottle. She is so young, and I wonder that, even though she finds freedom in being a laundress, she hasn't also consigned herself to a life of backbreaking labor that will one day leave her blind and stooped.

When she stands to leave, I feel my heart give a jump of protest. "Stay a moment." Sophie stops, looking at me expectantly. "This afternoon… Thank you for inviting me to do the washing with you. I enjoyed myself."

I can see her try to hold in her smile, but it escapes at the edge of her lips, and she lets out a little snort. "I don't think anyone has ever uttered those words describing the washing," she says.

"It wasn't the washing that was so enjoyable," I tell her. "It was the company."

My heart is beating fast, and I can't remember the last time that I was so content to not be in strict control of myself.

The smallest flush of pink touches Sophie's cheeks. "Good night, Colette," she says, slipping out of my tent. I stand there for a long time, wondering what has happened to the young Englishwoman who once would have rather died than risk showing anyone even a glimmer of her soul again.

Thirteen
CORNELIA

YARROW: courage in adversity, a healing balm. Love.

On a damp Sunday morning with a sharp wind and heavy clouds, the mud is deemed passable, and like a lumbering pack mule, the whole camp is packed up and heaved onward. Napoleon is predicted to arrive shortly in Paris, where he will need all the support he can get if reports about the allied forces and Prussia are to be believed.

I leave behind my little garden, a small piece of me rooted to this liminal space that no longer exists. Though I was only here for a fortnight, it had begun to feel, if not like home, then at least familiar. How and why the plants appeared and bloomed is not something that I am interested in examining too closely. Perhaps it was a coincidence, perhaps the soil in Amiens is particularly favorable. Whatever the reason, I am only glad that no one aside from Sophie seems to have noticed, that no undue attention was drawn to me. For I am still very much an outsider here. Only the thinnest of threads keeps me respectable so long as I am in this camp under guard. And until I receive payment for my latest column, I have nothing to my name.

Our first night is spent in a rocky field not far from the road. Lieutenant Peusol wordlessly pitches my tent and sees that I'm comfortably situated before disappearing to attend to his own accommodations. Through the canvas walls I can hear the sounds of equipment being unloaded, and the excited chatter of soldiers who are glad to finally be on the march. I am just brushing out my hair when a tremendous explosion rattles the night.

There is a great deal of shouting as several smaller explosions rock the air, sending debris raining down and pelting the tent.

"Are we at war already?" I ask Lieutenant Peusol as I throw on my wrap and rush outside.

He is already shedding his coat. "A powder cask," he tells me by way of explanation. "Go back inside."

But my feet are rooted to the ground. There is a flurry of activity as torches are lit and men rush through the night, assessing the damage. Soon stretchers begin going by, bearing the injured.

I've never seen burns before or so much blood. It makes my stomach clench, my head go light. Is this what war will be like? Burnt flesh and gaping wounds? Men vomiting and screaming in pain? Bile rises in my throat, and I suddenly feel rather small.

"Colette."

I tear my gaze away from the carnage to find the lieutenant at my elbow. His closeness brings me back into my body, his clean smell blocking the acrid smoke. I allow him to guide me back to my tent with a firm hand to my lower back.

He's no sooner seen me safely deposited back inside than he turns to leave again. "Where are you going?" I cannot help the panic that pitches my voice high.

"To help," he says shortly. "Stay here."

Feeling rather useless, I am still only too glad to follow his orders. I lie in my small cot, but my head is too full of the screams of injured men to find sleep. Outside, the commotion gradually dies away, replaced by an eerie silence.

I am teetering on the edge of sleep when there is a sharp whistle, unmistakably close to the entrance of my tent. Throwing on my wrap again, I slip outside to find a small figure shivering in a cloak. They push back their hood, revealing a familiar face.

"I haven't any linens," I tell Sophie, wishing very much that I did so that she might linger a little longer at my door.

"It's not to do with linens," she says, a bit testy. "Why would I be collecting linens in the middle of the night?" My heart begins to beat a little faster. Sophie is stomping impatiently against the cold. "Can we come in?"

She could tell me to parade through camp in nothing but my chemise, and I think I would, the way the moonlight is spilling over her pixie features and illuminating her sharp green eyes. I imagine her curled up in my bed, warm and soft and sweet-smelling.

I don't have time to ask her who *we* is before she's glancing over her shoulder and leading a soldier into my tent.

"This is Jean. He was hurt in the explosion," she tells me as she settles the young man on my chair and begins fussing about like a mother hen.

He is thin, almost willowy beneath the too-big coat, his dark hair matted under his cap. He is looking away, making a point of not meeting my eye, but I can see the labored rise and fall of his chest, the dark blood at his collar.

"Well?" Sophie is tapping her foot, watching me.

I pull my gaze back to her. "Well, what?"

"You'll treat him?"

"Treat him? Surely he should be brought to the medic. How long has he been bleeding? He should have been there already, receiving care."

"He can't go to the medic," Sophie says, suddenly cagey.

I don't want to disappoint Sophie. I want her to come to me

when she needs something. I want her to come to me when she doesn't need anything, when she just wants my company. "What makes you think that I can help him?"

Though we have only recently met, Sophie levels a look at me as if we had been over this a hundred times. "I saw you with those flowers," she says. "You have a touch. You can heal him. Look," she says, putting her hands out, palms down to show me the smooth brown skin where once there were scars. "Your salve, it worked."

As I said, Sophie could instruct me to do any number of impossible tasks, and I would indulge her. "Very well. I will look."

I expect that she might effusively praise me, thank me. For I assume that this young man is her beau, despite what she said about having no wish to be a wife. I find myself desperate to win whatever little approval I can from this woman, to see her break into a wide smile, perhaps to even throw her arms about me. But instead, she only gives me a tight nod and stands back to allow me space to examine my patient.

I bring him to the bed and pull the only lamp close. He is younger than I first supposed, his pale face with no mustache or whiskers to speak of. "I don't know that I will be able to provide much in the way of relief," I say, giving voice once more to my reservations. Inwardly, I pray that there is not too much blood, that all of his organs are inside where they belong. I touch his collar and start to unbutton the ragged linen shirt, but the soldier grabs my hand with surprising force, stilling it. His eyes are bright, not quite wild, but close.

"I'll be gentle," I assure him.

He goes very still as I carefully finish with the buttoned placket and then tear it the rest of the way. I frown. "Why, you're already bandaged!"

The soldier looks to Sophie who steps forward and places a protective hand on his shoulder. "Jean dresses this way for his protection."

Jean finally clears his throat; his voice comes out low and soft. "Mademoiselle, I beg you, treat me as you would any other man who found himself under your care."

With only those few instructions and a dawning understanding, I promise him that I will. When I have unwrapped the bloody bandages, I see the wound, a jagged slash just under the breastbone.

"Yarrow," I tell Sophie. "That will help stanch the bleeding. But I don't have any, and it is too early in the year for—"

"I will find it," she says, disappearing and leaving me alone with my patient.

"This is a dangerous profession for a woman," I say as I dab at the edges of the wound. I am relieved to see that it is not too deep.

Jean winces but remains admirably still, and I realize the wince is more for my words than for his wound, that he does not wish to be referred to as a woman. "I'm not the only one," he tells me. "There are others."

"Do all of them disguise themselves as you have?"

There is a downward tug to his lips at my question, though it may be from the pain of my ministrations. "Most of them fight as vivandières, true to their sex."

I want to press him, ask him why he has anatomy familiar to my own but finds himself dressed and fighting as a man. The lamplight flickers as I clean and dress the wound as best as I can.

"What shall I call you? Surely you have another name, one that—"

He stops me with a firm shake of his head. "My name is as I gave it to you. I am Jean. My old life is not one that I wish to live."

"Sophie… That is, how did you know to go to her with your complaint?" I endeavor to sound nonchalant in my question, but I am burning with curiosity.

"She's a fine girl," he says. "She is the only one here who knows who I am. You won't say anything, will you?"

"Upon my honor, I shall not."

Sophie returns with the yarrow, though she does not say where she found it. I instruct her to crush it up with a stone and add water until it forms a fine paste, which I apply to Jean's wound before dressing it with clean linen. He stoically sits through the entire process and seems to take the whole thing a great deal better than I do, for more than once I fear I might retch from the scent of the blood.

When he is dressed, I help him to his feet, and Sophie is quick to loop her arm around his waist to help him walk.

I try to convey with my eyes my gratitude for the trust Sophie has placed in me, but in the dark it's hard to tell if she returns the sentiment. I bid them good-night and watch Sophie bear my patient back out into the darkness.

My fingers still sticky with blood, I lower myself to my cot, taking shaky breaths. It is hours yet before I am able to find sleep, to rid myself of the scent of burnt flesh in my nose. Only the thought of Sophie's small hands holding the yarrow brings me any peace. I am learning that Sophie is a collector of broken and forgotten things, that her heart is pure and noble, and that I would do anything to be worthy of a place within it.

Fourteen

CORNELIA

LANTANA: a rigorous trial. Exhaustion.

I can hardly keep my eyes open at breakfast the next morning.

The victualler, an impossibly ancient woman with no teeth and a hunched back, has made a great pot of rice and onions, which the men descend upon like hungry wolves. From somewhere deeper in the camp wafts the smell of roasting chicken, and my stomach grumbles. I would give anything to be dining on squab with capers in a cream sauce or even just a hot muffin slathered in butter. I never thought myself terribly fastidious when it came to food, but then, I never had to subsist on hard bread or rice and onions before.

Lieutenant Peusol brings me a bowl of the questionable substance, then seats himself on the ground outside my tent and begins shoveling his serving unceremoniously into his mouth. "You should eat that," he tells me between bites when I still have not touched mine.

Now that we are on the march, everyone eats wherever they

can find a seat, some perched on carts, others on blankets on the ground. I poke at the bowl of colorless mush, trying my best not to get my skirt wet from sitting on the damp grass.

I push the bowl to him. "I haven't the stomach for it," I tell him. "You may have it."

He's a big man, tall and broad, muscled, and I can't imagine that the rations even begin to fill him properly. But he doesn't move to accept my offer. "You'll need to eat to keep your strength up."

"Perhaps we will pass through some town or village with an inn or tavern," I tell him. "I shall wait for something more palatable."

Lieutenant Peusol doesn't say anything, just regards me for a moment over his spoon before returning to eating.

I haven't time to think about how hungry I am, for soon a bugle sounds, and it is time to begin the day's march.

The first part of the day I spend on horseback, borne like a queen, with Lieutenant Peusol leading at the bridle. When the horse needs to rest, I dismount and walk beside the lieutenant. General Guérin rides up and down the length of the line, inspecting the troops. He briefly catches my eye but gives me no sign of recognition. The march is monotonous as we snake through the French countryside, sometimes met by cheers, other times by villagers hurling rotten vegetables at us. Most of the women and families are toward the back of the caravan, and I do not see Sophie, though I look out for her all morning.

I quickly fall to ruminating about the events of the previous night. "I suppose I should be worried about Jean, and if he is doing better this morning—and I am: I truly hope he is—but I cannot help but going back to the memory of Sophie watching me as I bandaged Jean up. Was her serious expression one of admiration? Or did she see the way I was doing everything in my power to stop myself from fainting from the smell of the blood? I wonder if she thinks I am too weak to be worthy of her respect. And why do I find that I care so much what she thinks of me?

"What's the matter with you?" I come out of my thoughts to find Lieutenant Peusol regarding me with an interest that is perilously close to amusement. He has been silent as we march, a bag slung across his broad shoulders, his long legs showing no signs of tiring.

"Who said anything was the matter with me?"

"Your face, and the fact that you haven't complained once about the march. Lover's quarrel with Sergeant Boucher?"

My cheeks heat, not with shame but anger at his impertinence. "The sergeant is *not* my lover," I tell him. I assume my face is starting to show how uncomfortable I am, with my boots chaffing my heels and blisters starting to form. But I will not complain, will not give him the satisfaction of being the snobbish young woman he so clearly thinks me.

The lieutenant only shrugs. "He's not? My mistake."

I stew in my annoyance a little longer. Lieutenant Peusol seems content to walk in silence, as we pass by a small town, church bells tolling the hour. My blisters are becoming almost unbearable. "If you *must* know, I am bored," I tell him, desperate to distract myself from the raw skin chaffing on my heels, the gnawing hunger in my stomach.

He raises a brow, but otherwise looks unimpressed by my admission. "Bored? I didn't think ladies were prone to boredom."

"What on earth would give you such an impression?"

Shrugging, he squints up at the sky as if more absorbed in the weather than our conversation. "I thought ladies were used to sitting about and striving to be ornamental. Besides, don't you all have piano lessons and dancing masters and that sort of thing?"

I can hardly countenance the insult. "If we are used to sitting about and looking ornamental, as you say, it is only in the way a canary bird must be content in his cage. You *men* are not content until you lock us all up and clip our wings."

Lieutenant Peusol has, at least, the decency to look somewhat ashamed at this.

"In any case, I have my work," I tell him, not content to let the matter lie. "Or I did."

He slants me a questioning look before returning his gaze to the road ahead. "You haven't asked me to post anything for days."

"There seems little point in relying on the vagaries of the French post," I say, bitterness creeping into my voice. "Besides, I am never given leave to conduct my work, especially now that we are on the march. When, pray tell, shall I find time to draw when we spend all day trudging through cornfields?"

"That is not the Colette I know," he says, still looking at anything and everything besides me. This time it is the arc of a bird taking wing from a nearby tree.

"I wasn't aware that you knew me," I say, a little taken aback to hear my name from his lips.

He gives a Gallic half-shouldered shrug.

"No, no. Do tell me. What have you learned about your captive?"

Heaving a sigh, the lieutenant shrugs the bag a little higher on his shoulder and gives the question due consideration before answering. "I've learned that she has a taste for good food, and—"

"You cannot fault her for that," I put in.

"No, you cannot," he concedes. "Do I have your leave to continue?"

"By all means."

"I've learned that she would much rather be engaged in conversation and have an audience than be by herself. She favors her left hand for drawing and her right for writing. She pretends that she does not care for the children of the camp but will teach them how to make flower crowns or assist in nursing a wounded doll when she thinks no one is looking. Furthermore, she is a terrible liar, though she prides herself on being sophisticated and unreadable. She is quite beautiful, but not in the way she supposes. Her true beauty lies in her unguarded moments, when she thinks no one is watching her."

I nearly stumble, momentarily rendered speechless at hearing myself reduced to such intimate details. Smoothing out my skirt, I force a bright smile. I refuse to let him see how he has rattled me, left me uncomfortably exposed. "Why, Lieutenant! You are a regular flirt. I think there might be hope for you yet."

But he doesn't seem pleased by this observation. His throat bobs, and the heat from his words fades. "I am your guard, nothing more."

"Oh yes, how could I forget!"

We continue to walk in silence as I nurse my pride, and the lieutenant is preoccupied with whatever it is he's thinking about. The steady clop of horse hooves and the rumble of carts and men's chatter fill the space between us.

"May I ask you something?" I venture after the silence has become unbearable.

He doesn't say anything, so I continue. "You told me that you do not trust Sergeant Boucher, and you clearly dislike him. Why is that?"

I thought that Lieutenant Peusol would have to think over the question, but he answers immediately, without hesitation. "He is false. There is nothing but self-serving interest under his charming surface."

"Did he do something to offend you?" I ask, for I can think of no other reason a man should care very much what another man has beneath the surface.

"Offend me? No. We fought together, on the peninsula, and I saw for myself what sort of man he is."

"And what sort of man is that?" I prod the lieutenant to give me some particular details, but he refuses to elaborate.

"A soldier should not speak badly of his fellow soldier, no matter his personal opinion of him" is all he will say on the matter.

"Now it is my turn to ask you something," he says, surprising me by the sudden change of subject.

I incline my head to let him know he might proceed, curious as to what turn this strange conversation could possibly take now.

"Have you ever considered writing a book?" He has finally met my gaze, though it is a long and slow path his eyes take, shy at first, then intently interested and genuine. I forget for a moment that this is a soldier—my guard, no less—and not some young man come to call on me.

"A book?" I echo, unable to follow his flow of thoughts.

"Yes, have you heard of them?"

I draw on some deep reserve of patience. "Yes, I believe I am acquainted with the concept," I say drily. "But what makes you ask?" I don't tell him that it is my dearest dream to one day publish a book, and one with my own name on it, no less.

"Might be easier to collect up whatever it is you're working on into one volume. No point in sending it piecemeal when you aren't even certain they'll reach the newspaper or your payment will reach you."

I miss a step, then quickly right myself. I am suddenly seeing Lieutenant Peusol in a new light. "Lieutenant, that is a very sensible idea."

The only sign that he is at all pleased with my pronouncement is the faintest duck of his head, the smallest tug of his full lips. It is the first indication that perhaps my guard is not so disagreeable after all.

Shadows begin to lengthen around us. We have been walking for hours, and my feet are aching, my blisters rubbed raw. Whatever stoic demeanor I had been trying to preserve is crumbling fast. Looking about me, it seems that no one else is struggling. The soldiers are quieter now but still march doggedly. Though every muscle in my body is crying out for rest, I will not be the one who brings us to a halt.

My stomach rumbles again. The rice and onions are long

gone, and I, a fool, was too proud to eat what was placed in front of me. One foot in front of the other. I trip, stumble, and would fall on my face into the rough road if it weren't for Lieutenant Peusol catching me.

"I'm fine. I'm fine!" I swat away his arm, but his hold is strong as he lifts me easily to my feet. When I move to put weight on my leg, my ankle turns, and I sway.

He catches me under the arm again and maneuvers me to the side of the road, leading his horse with his other hand. "You should have said that you needed rest," he says, not unkindly.

I have no choice but to lean into him and give him some of my weight. My pride is wounded, but my body is only too glad to feel his steadiness beside me, his warmth. "And have you think me weak?"

"There's no shame in needing to rest. We have been walking for miles, and at a hard pace."

I set my jaw. "If the other women are able to march, then I am too."

He looks down at me, his gray eyes unexpectedly warm. "The other women take shifts in the carts."

"You might have told me and saved me a great deal of trouble, as well as embarrassment," I grumble.

The lieutenant doesn't say anything, just lets out a shrill whistle. A moment later a young sergeant comes cantering up on a bay horse. "Yes, sir?"

"When does the general think we'll make camp?"

The man points over the bend in the road, where the sun is sinking fast. "Not even a mile now," he says.

Lieutenant Peusol thanks him, and the man touches his heels to his mount, cantering off. Now that I know we are so close, I muster a bit of energy and steel myself for the last stretch. All I can think about is sinking into my cot, eating a bowl of something hot and filling, even if it is flavorless.

I can feel the lieutenant watching me from the corner of his eye as I begin to limp back onto the road, merging with the soldiers bringing up the rear. "Yes, Lieutenant?"

"You're white," he tells me. "You aren't going to faint again, are you?"

"I did *not* faint. I tripped and—" But before I can protest any further, he is taking me by the waist and lifting me back up onto the horse. What had made me feel like a princess earlier in the day now strikes me as a great indignity, especially when so many of the men are on foot.

"Get me down this instant," I hiss at him.

In response, he reaches up but not to help me dismount. Instead, he swings himself up behind me, bracketing me between his arms as he takes the reins and clicks to the horse.

"We don't give out medals for false acts of heroics," he tells me, his voice close to my ear as we canter ahead of the line of soldiers. "Lean back."

I want to fight him, but I am tired, and my body is aching in a thousand different places. So despite my exasperation, I allow myself to lean into him, the rocking motion of the horse's gait and Lieutenant Peusol's strong arms around me lulling me to sleep.

Fifteen

LIJSBETH

CINQUEFOIL: maternal affection.
The enduring power of a mother's love.

Working below stairs has taught me to eat whatever is placed in front of me, and to eat it quickly. There is no telling when a bell will ring and I will be called away from my meal to attend to some matter or help one of the girls. But today the cold luncheon of boiled turnips, sausage, and hard bread and cheese turns my stomach even more than usual.

"What, too good for blood sausage, are you?" Marie says, eyeing my plate. "You had a high look about you as soon as you came here. Didn't I say as much, Cook?"

"That you did," the old woman replies blandly. She doesn't look up from her food which she is cutting into meticulous pieces, each scrape of her knife sending a blinding pain radiating through my skull.

When I cannot stand the stench of sausage and cheese any longer, I push the plate away and bolt to the slop bucket in the corner just in time. Another wave crashes around me before the first has receded, and I heave until it feels as if my body will turn itself inside-out.

"That's good meat," Cook calls from the table, accusation in her voice. "It can't be what's making you sick." She mutters something else, then rises and limps out to the yard.

Marie watches me from the corner of her eye as she chews. "You really cannot be as simple as all that," she says in exasperation.

I raise my head from the bucket long enough to catch her rolling her eyes at me.

"When was the last time you had your courses?"

Another wave of sickness washes over me, and I retch again. My courses were never regular, made worse by hunger, but now that she mentions it, I can't remember the last time that I bled.

She clucks her tongue as realization dawns on me. The implications are too big, send too many ripples spreading through my mind. But I know without the shadow of a doubt that it's true, can feel everything shift slightly within me and fit into place.

"I wonder who the father is," she says as she idly fidgets with her knife. "Can't be Monsieur, he's much too old." Her eyes go wide with unfettered delight. "It's one of the redcoats, isn't it? Is it the one I saw you mooning over in the dining room?"

I hardly hear her as she ticks off the possibilities, her voice gleeful. I know I should be frightened—and I am, of course I am—but all I can think of is the seed planted within me, growing. My hand goes to my abdomen. I am no longer alone. I serve something greater now than any family or even God. My body has become a home, and my purpose is to care for this little seed of love, to nurture it and see it bloom.

When I realize it has been some time since Marie has said anything, I wipe my mouth and rock back on my heels from where I was crouched in front of the bucket. There is an appraising glint in her eyes that I don't like. "Madame wants the carriage yard cleaned, and I'm tired," she says. "I think it ought to be you that does it."

If there is one chore I hate, it's cleaning up after the horses. Even if my stomach weren't still churning, I wouldn't be able to bring myself to sweep up the manure. It ought to be the job of a groom or driver, but for some reason it always falls to us. I shake my head.

"Do you know what happened to the last girl who found herself in your condition? Turned out without a recommendation, and selling her body on the streets. So I think you will do whatever I ask, unless you want me to tell Madame about it." Marie's lips curl into a cruel smile. "Though, I suppose it's only a matter of time before your dress tells the whole story."

It should be the thought of losing my position, of being turned out or, worse, being sent back to the van den Berg house that spurs me to acquiesce, but no, what occupies my mind is the thought of providing for someone else, someone who depends upon me entirely.

Even with the usual bustle of officers in the house, today is especially busy. There is to be some sort of training exercise, and all the ladies are in a state of excitement to watch. Eugenie and Hippolyte are with the younger girls, pulling out silks and shawls, holding brooches up to their bodices and debating the merits of each one.

I set to work in the stable with a bucket, still sick, but also exhilarated by the roiling of my empty stomach and what it means. Eventually, I find a rhythm, the soft whickering of horses and the smell of leather and straw providing a sort of gentle comfort.

It takes hours to finish, and my back is aching when I am finally able to return inside and boil water with which to scald the stink from my hands. At last, I am able to turn my attention to the flowers in the hall. Any wilting heads must be removed to keep the arrangements looking fresh, and new water needs to be put into the vases. This is how I should have been spending my time today, instead of allowing Marie to bully me into doing the stable chores.

"I see you've been promoted, and to a decidedly better-smelling endeavor," says a familiar voice that sends a delicious chill blossoming down my spine.

I peer around the vase, and my gaze lands on the blue-eyed soldier, radiant and impeccably fitted out in a crimson coat and white britches. His smile is unguarded, genuine, as he leans casually against the doorframe. As soon as I realize that I have an audience, my fingers feel slow and clumsy, as if I had never handled a rose before. A thorn catches on my palm, and I let out a little cry. It's not like me to let myself be cut, but my mind was already far away, dwelling on the growing life inside of me and the wicked man that put it there. A crimson droplet forms on my skin.

The soldier moves with the grace and speed of a greyhound. Suddenly he is beside me, my hand in his, gentle and strong. "I caught you unawares," he says. "I did not mean to startle you."

He slowly inspects my palm, holding my hand lightly in his. A little tingle of warmth dances up my arm. He pulls out his handkerchief and dabs away the blood, stanching it until all that remains is a faint red dot.

"There you are. If only all wounds sustained in battle were so easily mended."

I stare at the bloodied cloth in my hand, my heart beating fast before I finally find the courage to bring my gaze to meet his. He is terribly charming, but not in the way that Isidore could be when he was in his cups, like a smooth snake or a practiced courtier. There is an earnestness, a genuine warmth to the soldier's handsome face, and I find I cannot stop myself from staring at him.

"You don't speak much, do you?"

Never have I so desperately wished that I could shake free my stubborn voice. But if I could not speak to save myself when

Isidore cornered me, I cannot speak to the handsome soldier that is smiling encouragingly at me. I shake my head.

He gives me an appraising look. "Yet I have the impression that you have much to say." He directs my attention back to the roses in the vase. "These flowers, they tell a story."

He's fingering one of the glossy leaves, studying the arrangement. He is taller than me, but not a large man by any means. Yet I feel small and safe beside him, his pleasant scent of shaving soap enveloping me. My throat is dry, my palm still throbbing, either from the cut or all the blood that is suddenly pumping fast through my body. Though I'm no longer the subject of his penetrating blue gaze, I still feel the warmth of his attention. "I've never seen such elegance. I know nothing of flowers or the arranging of them, yet I can sense a deep love of beauty within these blooms."

I try to see the roses and anemones through his eyes, through anyone's eyes but mine. Can he truly grasp what I'm trying to say? Do the flowers speak to others as they speak to me? I cannot ask him, of course, but my world expands a little in the space of a heartbeat with the possibility.

The sound of footsteps beyond the hall, and the rest of the world floods back around me. Madame is coming, and the vase still needs water, and that is to say nothing of the dozen or so other arrangements that still need to be seen to.

Cheeks hot, and fingers still trembling, I concentrate fiercely on filling the vases as quickly as possible just as Madame breezes around the corner and stops.

She clucks, her shrewd gaze swinging between us. "I do hope you are not distracting my florist, Captain?"

"I doubt very much such an artist could be distracted by the likes of me," he says easily. "I was just admiring her work."

Any suspicion or displeasure on Madame's part quickly evaporates under the soldier's unaffected smile. "Come to the parlor, won't you? We need another pair for piquet, and there's still time yet before the drill."

I've turned back to my flowers, aware that I am supposed to be no more than a decoration myself. But my neck grows hot, and I feel flustered, a petal falling from my still-shaking fingers. I bend down to retrieve it, only to find myself face-to-face with the soldier.

He picks it up and places it on the little table, brushing my hand as he does so.

"I do wish I knew your name," he murmurs into my ear, before falling into step beside Madame and gallantly offering her his arm.

Sixteen

CORNELIA

BLUE PERIWINKLE: early friendship.

Marching is drudgery, made worse by the poor weather, and what should have been a three-day trip to Paris has dragged out to nearly a week. I have not seen Sophie in that time, nor have I been able to sketch, never mind have anything ready to post. I am still awaiting my payment for my last column, and I begin to wonder if it will even be able to reach me as we are marching.

That night, after the tents have been pitched, I crawl onto my cot and peel off my threadbare stockings and massage my aching feet. There is a muffled sound at the flap of my tent, but when I go out to investigate, there is no one there. Looking down, I see a parcel left squarely in front of me. Carefully unwrapping it, the mouthwatering smell of roast chicken wafts up to greet me. It is dark, and there is no one about that could have left it. Lieutenant Peusol must have stepped away for a moment, and

I wonder if Armand saw his chance to bring me a token of his friendship.

I am too hungry to concern myself overmuch with where it came from. I perch on my cot and devour the chicken, licking my fingers. It's only as my belly slowly fills that I realize how hungry I was, how much the last week of marching has drained me.

There's another rustling outside my tent, and I spring up, certain that it is Lieutenant Peusol come to chastise me for accepting a gift. But when I unfasten the flap, it is not the broad silhouette of my guard but a diminutive woman, a light mist of rain clinging to her wool cloak.

"Sophie," I say, unable to mask the excitement in my voice. "Have you come for linens?"

But of course, she has not, for it is well past dark now, the distant sound of thunder rumbling in the sky. Still, I dare not hope that she has come to see me, and me alone.

"No, I've not come for linens, nor yet to bring you a patient. May I come in?"

I invite her inside and give her a sheepish smile when I catch her eyeing the remains of my meal. "Is that an offering from a besotted admirer?"

I laugh. "Perhaps. I believe from Sergeant Boucher."

She makes a little sound in the back of her throat. "How attentive of him."

Color rises to my cheeks. "Surely you didn't come just to inspect my poor lodgings," I say to her. "Is there something I can do for you?"

She is examining my sketchbook, her calloused finger still incredibly dainty and small as she traces the edges. "It's only… Well, sometimes in the dark and rain, camp can be a dreary place. Lonely, even."

There is another peal of thunder, and her finger shakes. Her whole body is shaking like a leaf. It's all I can do to keep my heart beating steady and even, for she has drawn closer to me. "Even for a self-professed spinster?" I ask, hoping to distract her from the storm.

She gives a pleased laugh, and I feel absurdly proud that I was the cause of it. "Yes, even for a spinster."

Whatever reserve was lingering between us dissipates now, and I invite her to sit on my cot while I pull up the rug and sit below her, cross-legged like a soldier. "Then come, let me be your company. Tell me absolutely everything about yourself, for I am curious beyond all measure."

Sophie tells me of her childhood in Provence, summers spent helping her parents in fields of lavender up to her waist. Evenings filled with stories, told round pots of fragrant curried fish stew from her mother's native island of Guadeloupe. An adored old yellow dog that spent most of the day sleeping but would steal the food right off the table the moment anyone looked away. "How happy we were. But then my mother died, and my father took a new wife. She had no use for me, so I moved on." Her story is punctuated with a cursory shrug that belies the pain beneath. If I were a little braver, perhaps I would reach out for her hand, stroke the soft skin under her wrist. But all my courage has fled before her fathomless green eyes and the adorable upturn of her nose.

"And you?" she asks. "Where do you come from?"

"My father was French," I tell her. The confidence in my voice pleases me, bolsters me to continue. I like the idea of knowing who I am, where I come from. So what if it is a white lie? And besides, I can't very well tell her I am English, now can I? "My mother was a great beauty and from a very ancient bloodline."

I don't offer her anything else, and she doesn't pry. We sit quietly, the sound of rain softly pattering on the tent. She has stopped shaking, though every time there is a thunderclap she gives a little jump. I would not have thought my fearless little friend to be afraid of storms, and I feel guilty that I find it more endearing than anything.

"I never thanked you for helping Jean," she finally says. "So thank you."

"You looked as if you would skin me alive if I had turned him away. What else could I do?"

She traces a lazy circle on the blanket with her finger. "I feel a responsibility for the women here, and some of the men, too." She hesitates, her tongue daintily flicking out over her lips. "May I tell you something?"

My heart beats a little faster, and I nod, my throat suddenly thick with longing.

She grows shy, her hands twining together in her lap. "When I first saw you, tending those plants, I thought you were the most beautiful girl I had ever seen. Too beautiful, too much like a china doll in a fine frock. I've known girls like that, and they are never anything nearly so nice underneath all that powder and finery." She doesn't speak as if she expects her words to shatter me, but there is a tenderness that brings me perilously close to doing so. "But you aren't, Colette. You are selfless and strong. You didn't have to help Jean, but you did."

Though I hardly dare to breathe, I move to sit beside her on the cot. Her hand finds mine, and our fingers lace together. No one has ever called me selfless before, and I can hardly credit that I possess such a noble trait. But coming from her lips, I think that I could endeavor to be a saint for her sake.

"Well," she says, standing and briskly smoothing down her skirt, "I should be going."

I spring up beside her, loath to let her go. "Come back, any-time. You need not have a reason to visit."

As she turns to leave, her shoulder brushes mine and she stills. She smells of soap and sweat and lavender, and I am seized by the desire to take her in my arms, drink in her sweetness. But neither of us move, instead just standing close, suspended in a moment that lingers well past what is proper.

"Good night, Sophie," I tell her in a whisper. She meets my eye and looks as if there's a question hovering on her lips, but then she is gone.

As I lose her to the night, a burning ember to the side catches my eye. A moment later a soldier steps out of the darkness and snubs out his cheroot. "Bit late for laundry, isn't it?"

"Armand!" It seems an age since I have seen my friend in camp, never mind actually spoken to him. His presence is like a cold dash of water to my face after the most beautiful dream, and I am tempted to tell him that I am on my way to bed and cannot talk.

He grins. "I'd thought you'd forgotten me."

"I could never."

He flashes me his disarming smile again, his gaze warm and dark. "I would have come before, but the lieutenant has been keeping you under lock and key, it seems."

"The chicken was a kind gesture, though. Thank you."

He looks puzzled. "Chicken?"

"Didn't you bring me...?" I can tell by his expression he has no idea what I'm talking about. "Never mind," I tell him. "I must have been mistaken."

He doesn't seem particularly concerned with the question, instead nodding off to where Sophie has disappeared into the darkness. "I see you've met the little mother," Armand says.

"Pardon?"

Armand's dimpled grin is bright, though it strikes me as forced. "The laundress, Sophie," he explains. "She's a good girl, takes care of everyone in camp. Some of the men call her the *little mother.*"

Something tells me that Sophie would not appreciate hearing herself being described as a *good girl*, but the thought makes me smile all the same. For all her stubbornness, I can see the tender heart which beats underneath.

"Yes, I've met her." I don't wish to discuss her with him, though. Every moment with which she graces me is a treasure that I want to keep only to myself.

Armand doesn't seem to mind when I don't pursue the subject. He lets out a wistful sigh as he tilts his head back to look up at the dark sky. "Tell me, Colette. Are you glad? Glad that we found each other and that now you are here? I know life in the camp is not so romantic, but are you happy enough here?"

"When I think of the alternative, then yes, I suppose I am glad."

No doubt he thinks that I am speaking of the nunnery or of a night spent on the street. I can only think of my uncle's house and the future that awaited me there.

Catching my hand in his, he lowers his voice. "You must know that I hold you in some esteem. Not just as an artist and friend, but as, well…dash it, as a sweetheart, or something even more."

I am not a prisoner here, and I doubt that Lieutenant Peusol would try to stop me if I engaged in lovemaking with Armand. But I do not wish to fan the flames of this man's desires, despite his charm. Or perhaps it is *because* of his charm, as I know all too well that some men use charm as a weapon or a suit of armor to hide their true nature. He is looking at me with all the fevered passion of a lover, awaiting some invitation from me to continue. "It is late, and you forget I am under guard," I tell him.

I wonder if he can feel Lieutenant Peusol's vital presence the way I can, if he senses my guard waiting like a cat ready to pounce. Armand snorts, a quiet laugh. "Your guard, of course. I will leave you to your rest," he says, finally releasing my hand. "But please, seek me out. Let's not be strangers, not when fate was so generous in bringing us together."

When he has disappeared into the sea of white tents, I return inside and lie down. My mind is still dwelling within the warmth of Sophie's hand on mine, turning over the riddle of how to make her smile at me again, how to make her stay. Yet even as I allow myself to softly drift in the shallows of dreaming, there is a smell of decay, just beyond the edges of sleep, growing stronger the closer we get to Paris.

Seventeen

LIJSBETH

MARIGOLD: loss and grief. Despair.

There is a plate of sweetmeats on Octavie's desk, delicately iced and garnished with candied violets. I turn down the bed—another of Marie's tasks that she has relegated to me—carefully avoiding looking at them, but my mouth waters all the same. My stomach may turn at the sight of anything savory, but it craves sweet things to the point of distraction.

Octavie wouldn't notice if one were missing. She is forever complaining about her figure, and she will probably end up throwing them out or feeding them to her little spaniel. But a brief moment of sweetness on my tongue is not worth the risk of being caught stealing, so I force myself to think of Cook's turnips and pretend that I cannot smell the sugary invitation.

A song finds its way to my lips as I finish and move on to the next room, my arms piled with linens. The reminder of my little friend growing within me is nearly enough to banish the hunger, and I feel light and free. Marie's threats roll off my back like water. I have a friend, an ally.

This is satin, I say to myself as I stroke the pillow on Hippolyte's bed. *It is soft and fine, and someday you will wear a gown of it. You will know only warmth and comfort*, I tell my little friend, though I don't know how I shall make it so.

But my little friend cannot stay my secret for long. Soon my dress will begin to tighten around my hips and stomach. Soon there will be a reckoning, and I will have to choose between the love in my heart for this tiny being or the work that keeps a roof over my head, food in my belly.

"You know, there's a woman in town who can fix that," Marie says that evening, nodding toward my flat belly.

I recoil at her words. She laughs.

"What? The longer you wait, the harder it will be to have it done. Or do you mean to catch yourself a husband?" There is genuine curiosity under the barbed words. Ever since she needled out my secret, she has been desperately trying to guess the father.

I lift my bowl to my mouth, automatically sipping at the tasteless broth. I may promise my little friend all the silks and sweetmeats in the world, but how I will I ever provide any of it? How I will I even keep her? As soon as my condition is known, I will be turned out without a recommendation or character reference. No one will take me on after that. I will have to go to one of those houses for unwed mothers and throw myself on their mercy. They will take my baby, and she will end up just like me, an orphan with no certain future. Eugenie is kind, perhaps she would take pity on me and let me stay until I birth the babe. But then what?

So go my racing thoughts—*I will keep her… I will give her up… I will keep her*—fighting like a tide coming in, only to rush out again.

Until one morning, the decision is made for me.

I am dusting in the downstairs parlor, the sound of carriages in the street floating through the window, when I feel a sharp pain in my middle. I am used to aches and pains that come and go, but this is different. Light is pouring in from the windows. It is a warm spring day, but suddenly a chill descends on me, and some buried instinct makes me want to go find a warm, dark place and curl up.

I hastily untie my apron, pain shooting through me sharp and fast. If anyone catches me, I will say I am going to use the necessary.

I make it to the door when I'm met by the officer with the blue eyes. Despite the pain in my belly and the warm trickle of blood rolling down my thigh, my heart still contracts when I see him.

"I was hoping to find you," he says, softly shutting the door behind him.

I would be ruined if we were to be found alone in a room with the door closed. But right now, that is the least of my concerns. Besides, aren't I already ruined? As if the touch of a man is enough to damn a woman in the eyes of other men.

My mind is sluggish, yet everything in the room is sharp, the colors of the flowers too bright. The soldier says something, but his words sound far away, slurred. Then I realize he is holding something out to me, expectant. Taking my hand, he presses something into it.

It's a little knife, gleaming and sharp, with a pearly handle.

"I saw you cutting the flowers the other day," he explains, his words finally coming into focus. "Your knife was blunt, and it concerned me how easily you might cut yourself."

I blink, my mind racing, my body stiff with holding in the pain. He doesn't know. Doesn't know that I stabbed a man with just such a knife. Doesn't know that I am now carrying that man's baby. How could he? To him, I am an innocent. A good girl who cleans and knows her place. Not a woman who has drawn blood from a man, a woman who got with child and is even now being punished for it.

"All I ask in return is your name."

I can feel his gaze, searching, burning into me. There is a knife in my hand, a handsome man well above my station asking my name, and my unborn child bleeding out of my body.

I want him to have it, to give him the only thing that I have left that means anything, even if it is only a name. I have nothing else, and when this over, I won't even want a name anymore. I don't want to be seen: let me go back to being invisible, for being perceived is torture.

The pain returns, making me cry out with the sharpness of it.

"Are you hurt?" He moves closer, hand extended, and I recoil. I am a wounded animal, and I only know that I must get away.

The knife clatters to the floor, and I run out of the parlor, leaving the officer bewildered, his hand still reaching out for me.

The rest of the day passes in shafts of light traveling across the plastered walls of my room, the pain coming in brutal waves that leave me wishing for death. I am acutely aware of my body, of every twinge, of every failing of what is supposed to be my God-given design.

As the evening light deepens, there is a creak in the hall, and I rouse myself to turn my head away from the hairline crack in the plaster I have been sightlessly staring at. Marie stands in the doorway. She clicks her tongue. "So, it all worked itself out, then."

She lingers, presumably waiting for me to confirm it, but I am too weary, too broken to spare her so much as a thought. I turn my head back to the wall, and eventually the tread of her footsteps fades.

No one comes to look for me as the sun sinks low in the sky and my womb continues to empty. I am alone, utterly alone.

When my body finally surrenders to the pull of sleep, I dream of bloody flowers and a little girl in a tattered nightgown, lost and calling for her mother.

★ ★ ★

I suppose there is some spark, deep down inside of me, that is not ready to be extinguished yet, for in the morning I haul myself out of bed and clean myself and wash my underpinnings as best as I am able. There is no time for me to rest, so I arm myself with thick pads of muslin to catch the blood and go about my daily duties as if I were suffering from nothing more than my monthly courses.

But my mind is faraway. Even with the onslaught of preparations for tonight's party, I cannot stop my thoughts from turning to my soldier. I replay the moment in the parlor again and again, the way he held out the knife to me, the hot knot of pain in my stomach. The look of confusion and dismay on his face as a I pushed away his hand and fled. It is not enough that God has seen fit to tear my little friend away from me—out of me—but he has also exposed me in the cruelest manner in front of the officer, the only other person who has ever shown me kindness.

Eighteen
CORNELIA

MOTHERWORT: concealed love.
Feelings nurtured in secret and brought to light.

"Jean says that his wound is healed."

"That's wonderful news!" I tell Sophie. We arrived at the outskirts of Paris after six days of hard marching. The blisters on my feet have finally started to heal, and I am glad to have a reprieve from the indignities of that mode of travel. Sophie is standing by a great steaming cauldron of water, occasionally stirring the swirling linens inside with a big stick. Her face is flushed from the heat, her sleeves rolled to her elbows revealing her slender arms. When she is finished with each sheet, she hands them to me, and I pin them up on a line. Lieutenant Peusol is stationed a little ways away, watching us from the tree line like a sheepdog might watch his flock.

But Sophie doesn't look as pleased as I thought she might. "What is it?" I ask.

Wiping her perspiring brow, she stops her stirring and faces me. "I saw that wound," she says. "Jean was certain that even if it healed, he would be scarred forever. But not only did it heal, there is nothing to suggest he was ever injured."

The pin I was holding slips from my grasp at her words. "Is that so? I am glad to hear it."

My unconcerned tone does not fool her. "I've seen some of the most awful injuries imaginable, and I have never seen a wound heal so quickly or so cleanly. Most of the army surgeons are butchers." She picks up her stick again and goes back to agitating the water. "You are a good healer, Colette, whatever your methods. And there are many here in camp who would benefit from your services."

As much as I would like to be whatever it is Sophie thinks I am, I'm afraid I must disappoint her. "The camp already has a physician," I point out.

She makes a little sound in the back of her throat. "As I said, the surgeon is a butcher, and the physician is only good for spooning out penny cures. Besides, like Jean, there are people here who can't avail themselves of the surgeon's services."

We fall into silence as we work, every once in a while Sophie throwing me a curious look. I'm not sure how I feel about the moniker of *healer.* There is something about it that brings to mind stoop-backed crones and village midwives. It's really almost vulgar. But then I think of Jean and the satisfaction that came with helping him, helping Sophie.

"You may bring them to me," I tell her finally. "I cannot promise that I will be able to help them, but—"

I don't have a chance to finish, for Sophie has dropped her stick and rushed over to throw her arms around me. For a moment I am too surprised to do anything other than stand there, her wet bodice pressed against me, warm cheek on my shoulder. But then I return the embrace, and I know that I would do anything to be the person she thinks me.

True to her word, Sophie begins bringing me patients that

very night. Mostly it is women seeking help with preventing childbearing, but there are a few men as well with various complaints. I never pry, and for the most part, they never tell me why they have chosen to put themselves under my care rather than that of the army physician. With every ailment healed and person helped, I am filled with a new sense of purpose.

"I think I am in danger of going mad."

Lieutenant Peusol is polishing his rifle and barely spares me a glance as I make my dramatic proclamation. It is a fine day, the sun warm and soft. Now that we have arrived at Paris, everything feels stagnant. While my nights are filled with Sophie's patients, my days are long and empty. I bristle at the idea of charging for my healing services, but I fear that I may have to soon if I cannot correspond regularly with my publisher.

"Mad?"

"I feel like a hound on a tether," I tell him. "I'm not allowed to wander so far as the edge of camp before I am yanked back. I am meant to document flora, yet there is not so much as a daisy that hasn't been trampled by boots on our journey. I cannot help but feel I ought to be allowed some concessions if I am to stay here."

He gives a little grunt without looking up from his rifle. "I wager the emperor has bigger concerns than flowers, at the moment."

"Please, let me just leave camp for the morning. I only want to find some flowers to sketch."

"I can't do that," he says, his rough voice not unkind. "You know that."

The rifle is gleaming in the sun, and I can't help but think that it has been polished and clean for some time now. "What possible trouble do you think I could get into? Haven't I shown myself to be credible?" I ask, skirting the incident with Armand. "Or shall we go find the emperor and ask him what good a naturalist confined to a sea of canvas tents is to his empire?" The lieutenant looks dangerously close to smiling. "Please," I wheedle. "Why don't you come with me? Make a lark of it?"

He snorts, but I'm not so easily put off. "I've never seen you smile. I think perhaps the sky might open and angels descend if you did, and I should so like to find out."

I hold my breath as Lieutenant Peusol slowly puts aside the rifle and levels a long look at me. "We come back by the supper hour," he tells me sternly.

We travel on foot, past the outskirts of the camp and toward the city. If I were not under guard, I would run into Paris, lose myself in the cobbled streets, and search for my mother. But such fancies must be left for another time. To my surprise, I find that I don't mind having the company of the lieutenant, that it feels rather nice to have someone beside me in this unfamiliar place. Lieutenant Peusol is silent, leading me confidently through the countryside and down forgotten lanes lined with elm trees. It is only when the sun has grown quite high that I realize how long we have been walking and how little my body is protesting. My monotonous life in Sussex gave me no tests other than that of my patience for business dinners or village gossip. Now I can see what a fine thing it is to be challenged and find that one is capable of rising to the occasion.

We emerge from a winding lane onto a broad drive lined with overgrown topiaries and exotic trees, at the end of which sits a gracious château. It is a scene that could have been painted on a china dish, a tableau of gently decaying beauty.

"It's beautiful," I breathe. "What is this place?"

"Malmaison, home of the late empress, Josephine. Come." Lieutenant Peusol leads me up to the front of the drive, but instead of entering, we go around the side and out into the back. There is a rose garden, beds of lilies that I have never even seen in books before, and the most exquisite peonies. A castle of a greenhouse peeks out from behind the gently rolling path, though some of the glass has broken, casting it in a rather romantic light with the other follies that are scattered about the landscape.

"Are we trespassing?" I ask the lieutenant as he helps me scramble over a toppled stone wall.

"Probably," he says, rather unconcerned.

I let go of his hand as I find my footing and move closer to gaze at the tropical trees straining against the glass walls of the greenhouse. "Did you ever see her? The empress, that is?" My only impression of Napoleon's first wife was from the caricatures published in England, and she was not portrayed favorably, usually with bad teeth and an overly rouged face.

Lieutenant Peusol comes to stand beside me. "No, but he loved her very much," he says softly. "Even after the divorce, he was devoted to her. Still, she died of a broken heart, they say."

"How terribly romantic," I say with a little laugh, hoping to break the rather heavy air that seems to have enveloped us.

He gives a shrug. "I suppose."

We walk through the overgrown gardens, the only sounds our boots in the weedy gravel, the lazy birdsong above us. I am a voyeur to another woman's pain, her garden a road map of her broken heart. She might have been an empress, one of the most powerful women in the world, but in the end, I suppose she was not so different from my own mother.

A shrub bearing pink flowers catches my eye. "Look!" I squeal as I break away from the lieutenant. I've only ever seen illustrations of this particular variety of camellia, but the delicate layers of symmetrical pink petals are unmistakable. I drop to my knees and take out my sketchbook and lead, my hand nearly shaking with excitement.

When I finally rise, I find Lieutenant Peusol watching me. Color spreads to my cheeks despite myself. "You needn't wait for me," I tell him. "I'll be some time if you'd like to walk ahead."

"I'm at your disposal," he says without taking his gaze from me. "Take all the time you like."

He spreads a thick saddle blanket on the ground for me, then seats himself a respectable distance away on the other side. I sharpen my lead, then fall to sketching. The pink petals remind me of Sophie's lips, soft and inviting. The lieutenant has nice lips, full and surprisingly sensual for a man. I wonder if he has a sweetheart, if his kisses are passionate, or slow and methodical. Does he show her another side of himself that is hidden from me? Does she make him laugh, can she coax a smile from him? For all that he spends his life now only a few paces from me at all times, I know remarkably little about the man.

Gradually my wandering mind quiets. Pages fill, and when I finally look up and shake out my stiff fingers, I find that the lieutenant has moved closer, his pleasant scent of soap just over my shoulder. "What is that flower called?"

I turn the paper so that he can see. "Lily of the valley," I tell him. I show him the dainty stems bearing little white bells and how the roots will grow a network beneath the earth. "That's why it looks as if it's a carpet of flowers, because it is. In the winter, the plants will bear red berries."

I take his silence as an invitation to continue and flip through the pages slowly so that he might see more. What a world apart this feels from the day he held my drawings aloft as I stamped my foot and begrudged him laying eyes on my work.

"The words—what do they…that is…" His brow is gently furrowed as he taps a finger on the page. There is a shade of sadness over his handsome features.

It is a moment before I realize why there is such longing in his eyes. He can't read. I have always taken my literacy for granted, a privilege of my station and upbringing. What a pity that there are those who are denied the pleasure of the written word. I lean a little closer toward him.

"It reads: *Ambrosia is the flower of love, and not just any love, but the sweetest kind—that which is returned.*" Again, heat rises to my face, and again, I feel quite the fool for allowing myself to be moved by the simple act of sharing space with a man.

This seems to break the spell the notebook had been holding over him, and he looks at me as if seeing me for the first time. I would have to be made of stone not to be affected by the awe, the admiration that is writ so clearly on his face. "You wrote that?" he asks.

"I write a few lines for each flower. They have a language, you see. Each one possesses a secret meaning, and a message within. Would you like to try?"

He looks rather dubious. "Speaking with a flower?"

I laugh. "As much as I should like to see that endeavor, I meant writing. Here." I pass him the lead, and he takes it, large fingers gingerly closing around it. "We'll start with your name."

I realize that I don't actually know his given name, that I've only ever thought of him as my guard or a lieutenant. But he is a man, with a name and a history, dreams and secrets.

"Henri," he says.

"Very well. Henri." I help him form the *H*, my hand lightly guiding his. He is sitting very close, a small furrow in his brow as he puzzles over the letters. I see him as a boy, just briefly, born into a world that only values him for his ability to take bullets in the chest for his country.

But of course, he is no longer a boy. He is a grown man who could easily crush the lead in his hand yet is holding it as carefully as if it were a precious newborn. He is a man who is searching for some beauty and enlightenment in an overgrown garden choking with weeds.

When his name is committed to paper, he sits back and studies his work, a small tug of satisfaction on his lips.

I show him a few more words, taking care to sound them out as we trace the letters, but the sun is dropping lower, and a chill has stolen into the air. "I should return you to camp," he says, a note of regret in his words.

"Stay a moment," I tell him as I pluck one of the delicate little white flowers beside us. "May I?" I ask, gesturing to his buttonhole.

He is very still as I thread the stem into the hole and smooth down the wool across his chest. "There," I tell him. "Now you will have a little piece of the empress's own garden when you present arms in front of the emperor."

He stares down at the flower, transfixed. The moment grows warm and expectant, the air thick with sweet pollen. "Henri," I say suddenly, "would you like to kiss me?"

He has gone very still, his gaze still fixed on the flower.

I feel coy and free here in this drowsy patch of evening light in the forgotten garden. Perhaps this is the first time I've truly seen the lieutenant as man, as more than just an impediment to my freedom. Perhaps it is all my thoughts and desires of Sophie, bound up and tangled with the person who is sitting beside me. I feel itchy, constrained under my clothes, desperate for touch. "Well? Would you like to kiss me?"

He finally casts the lead away and sits back, regarding me with something like suspicion. "What is your game, Colette?"

I give him my most winning smile. "I have no game. I assure you, I am completely artless."

He sighs. Rakes a hand through his hair. He truly is handsome. Strong and rugged, but with such a beautifully made face that I cannot stop looking at it. It takes me aback to find that I'm not hungry just for touch but for *his* touch.

"You are many things, but not artless. Do you think because I can't read, because I am a soldier, that I can't possibly have feelings, is that it? That I'm a brute, incapable of understanding?"

"What? No. No, of course not. I—"

"Do you think I haven't noticed you?" His words heat, his gaze smolders. "Do you think it's anything other than torture to be so close to you and not be able to…to touch you? I know you aren't who you say you are. I'm not stupid. But I don't care because I only want to be near you, even if you think little of me or think of me not at all."

His unexpected speech immobilizes me. "Henri… I didn't know. I—"

"I'm not a plaything, Colette." He stands, leaving me a different woman than when we had first sat down together.

"Henri, wait." I wish that I could take back my silly flirtation. I gather up my sketchbook and pretend that Henri's refusal doesn't sting. The flowers, that only moments ago had been obliging as I sketched them, now sing a mocking song as I hurry after him. Henri did not notice that during the course of our conversation the lilies have spread, their petals shimmering with a pearly, unearthly glow. He has not noticed, but I have.

And just as with Anna and Sophie, I am afraid I know what it means.

Nineteen
LIJSBETH

WILLOW TREE: tears of grief.

The sun rises, and life goes on. Marie, for the most part, avoids me, as if my condition might be catching. I am left to do my work, my absence of the previous day attributed to a stomach complaint that confined me to my bed.

Only Eugenie asks once, from across the room as she looks up from her book, "Dear Lijsbeth, you look peaked. Are you quite well?" And what can I say to that? What can I say to this golden young woman who knows only happiness and comfort? So I just smile and nod and continue about my work, and she goes back to her book, placated that all is well within her world.

The days pass with interminable slowness. My little friend is gone, and with her, my only companionship, my only promise of love. Yet I feel as if I were the one to fail her and not the other way around. I was supposed to be her home, a safe haven for her to grow, and I could not even provide that. Perhaps this is my punishment for wanting more than my lot. If only I could be like Marie, hard and sensible, satisfied with the way of the world.

There is only one spot of brightness that carries me through each day until I fall into my bed at night, and that is the blue-eyed soldier. All my memories of that day run together: the blood, the pain, his kindness, the way he looked at me as if he could see into my soul. I almost wish that he had never looked me in the eye or touched my hand so gently, because then I would not know what it is to long for something that I can never have. I tasted just a little sweetness, and now I only know hunger.

I do not see him for several days after, or rather, he does not see me. Whenever Madame has the soldiers over, I am sure to hide away in some other part of the house so that I do not accidentally cross paths with him. I wonder if he thinks of me or if he has forgotten the peculiar little maid who rebuffed his generous gift.

I am sorting flowers in the kitchen when a scream pierces the air and rings through the house. Dropping the wet stems, I rush into the drawing room to find Eugenie, her sisters, and Marie all crowded around something, their backs to me.

"Lijsbeth, is this your work?" Eugenie asks slowly. She steps aside, and I can see Madame's favorite delft vase spilling over with harebells and carnations, willow and amaranth. The flowers have grown tall, so tall that they are almost reaching the ceiling. Around them, a cascade of petals are falling like tears, some scattered about on the gleaming mahogany table. Lichen and dead leaves seem to have sprouted from the very grain of the wood, and the whole effect is one of an overgrown woodland scene, a forgotten temple in ruins. When I arranged it earlier in the day, it had looked ordinary enough. Why, I couldn't even reach that high to place the flowers if I had wanted to. Something has happened to them since I put them there, something that I cannot explain. I give a jerky nod.

"All right, then," Eugenie says with a sigh. "That's enough gawking. The light was low, and Octavie came upon them and was startled. I'll ask Mother what we shall do about it, but for now it will stay." She shoos her sisters away and, giving me one last lingering look, dismisses Marie and me.

Back in the hall, Marie is staring at me, her lips twisted into a frown. She looks as if she isn't sure if she would rather rail at me or run from me.

"There's something wrong with you," she says. "It's not just that you're mute. There's something...in you. I wonder Madame doesn't just throw you out and be done with you. Be a sight easier for the rest of us if she did."

Despite her strong words, Marie does her best to avoid me right up until it is time to climb into bed that night. She crosses herself and pulls the blanket up over her head.

I suppose at least now I don't have to put up with her. But that is little comfort when there is no escaping from myself. Whatever is inside of me is finding its way out, and it is only a matter of time before I am exposed for the strange creature I am.

Twenty
CORNELIA

BRAMBLE: remorse.

My embarrassment, shame, and deep regret from my blunder with Henri stay with me as I lie in my bed that evening. I listen to the camp settle for the night, a rhythm that grows more and more familiar every day, until it is almost as comforting as a lullaby.

But I will not be sleeping tonight. I slip from my tent and go outside. Henri dozes on a chair, the moonlight carving a gentle shadow across the strong cut of his profile. Something in my chest opens from watching him, grows warm and fluttery. The truth, if I must bring myself to face it, is that I did want to kiss him this afternoon, very much so. I never had such an undeniable draw to a man before, didn't know that I was even capable of such an attraction. It is exciting and terrifying all at once, and my only courage comes from the fact that I am too curious not to pursue where this might lead.

Henri opens his eyes. If he is surprised to find me watching him while he sleeps, he doesn't show it. "You're awake," he says.

I could tell him that the sound of roots twisting and feasting on the flesh of the dead is all that awaits me in my sleep. That when I close my eyes all I see is dirt, all I smell is the stench of rot. I could tell him that something terrible is coming, but oh, how my heart is racing with anticipation all the same! But all I say is "It's cold."

He nods, as if this is a reasonable explanation.

"Well," I say.

"Well."

I don't know what I was looking for by coming to him. Perhaps I thought that the moon would soften my hard edges and allow me to be vulnerable or that feeling the cold night air on my face would settle my nerves. The night does take some mercy on me, because I am at least able to cobble together an apology, albeit a poor one. "What I said before. It was…it was not well done of me."

He doesn't say anything, but I press on.

"I did very much want to kiss you. If my attentions appeared factitious, it is only because I was afraid that you would not return my admiration. For the truth is, I do admire you."

Sometimes I forget how free I am, how there is no one left for me to answer to, even if I am confined to this camp. I am not expected to make a good match nor yet even make polite conversation with my uncle's business associates. I am not even expected to work or be a fine lady. I am simply a young woman of little consequence among many others following the camp. But with the roar of cannon fire and drills in the day, and the persistent hum of the flowers, there is a sense of urgency that runs hand in hand with my freedom.

But if Henri feels the same urgency, he does not show it. He just sits, his face a mask of steadfastness, neither accepting my apology nor rebuffing it.

"Good night, then," I tell him when it becomes clear that I will only embarrass myself further by lingering out here.

I return to my cot. A mournful owl calls in the distance. My hand wanders to my locket, tracing the filigree as I curse myself a fool over and over. I didn't realize just how important Henri was to me until I faced the prospect of losing him through my own vanity. I didn't realize that any man could engender such a depth of emotion in me, even if I cannot name the feeling. And as for the flowers that grew and multiplied around us in Malmaison, well, I would rather not examine what that means too closely.

I am staring at the meeting of the tent flaps when there is a rustle of movement, and I sit up to see Henri stepping inside. He doesn't say a word, and neither do I, as he comes to the side of my cot and lowers himself to his knees. His movements are sure and graceful as ever, but there is a hesitation, a question, in his eyes.

Wordlessly, I slide over and lift the blanket in invitation. He removes his saber and sash, and a slow sigh escapes him as he climbs in beside me.

My body gravitates to his, drawn by his warmth and solidness. He has the body of a soldier, hard muscles beneath taut skin, but his touch is gentle, reverent, as he runs his hand up my back and twines his fingers through the hair at the nape of my neck.

A lump fills my throat. "What I said this afternoon… I am sorry, truly."

Henri presses his face to my cheek, gives the smallest shake of his head. "Hush," he tells me.

With my apology accepted, I can at last lose myself to his touch. Our breaths fill the silence of the tent, rasping and urgent, as we kiss away the last of our restraint. Only as I begin to fumble at the waist of his breeches does Henri pull away, his chest rising and falling. "You deserve more than this," he tells me, bracing himself on his elbows, his face a mask of pained restraint. "You deserve a real bed and a man in it who can provide for you. Not a soldier who—"

"Henri." I stop him with a finger to his lips as he searches my face. "I wouldn't exchange this moment for anything in the world."

The words come out small, but they are real. Everything that is happening between us is real, the result of some long-hidden part of me that craves affection and warmth, safety. His slate eyes have stripped away all of my hard-won veneer, and it is nothing short of terrifying to lie in bed naked, with not just my body but my whole heart and soul on display. There are no flirtations, no social niceties to hide behind. And yet, I seem to be enough, the same way that he is enough. It is terrifying, but also exhilarating, like wings have suddenly unfolded from my back, carrying me to new heights.

Kissing away a tear that I didn't realize had fallen from my cheek, he murmurs something low and reassuring against my skin. Then he is finding my mouth, and I am opening to him like a flower. I arch myself into him, demanding as much of him as he demands of me. If I were to open my eyes, I would see that the ground is alive with roses, their petals carpeting the tent. But it is all that I can do to hold onto Henri, feel his arousal crushing into me, and he is likewise too blinded by passion to notice the desperate garden that has sprung up beneath us.

I cry out as he sheathes himself within me, and the twisting roots in my mind withdraw, the cloying scent of decay banished by his sharp, clean smell. I feel myself falling into him, and for a little while, I can forget everything else.

The first light of day is breaking when I open my eyes and turn over in bed. My bedmate is lying beside me on his side, very much awake despite the stillness of his naked body.

"Were you watching me sleep?" I ask.

Henri brushes a kiss on my cheek, the light bristle of his jaw sending echoes of pleasure through me. "How could you expect me not to?" he says.

I push myself up on one elbow. "Lieutenant Henri Peusol, are you *smiling*?"

At my exclamation, his smile spreads wider. It is warm and genuine and beautiful, lighting his entire face. I have never seen him so at ease, so relaxed. "If I had known all it would take was bedding me to see you smile, perhaps I would have seen to it sooner."

"And if I had thought you returned my affection, I would have taken you the first moment I saw you," he says, his expression growing somber and earnest again. "By all accounts you should hate me. I am responsible for your confinement."

He draws a careful line down my shoulder with his finger, and I shiver under his touch. It is frightening to be at the mercy of my own feelings for a man. But Henri is ever easy, and his adoring gaze lets me know that I am still very much in control.

"Hate you? Never. They should not have given me such an amiable guard if they did not wish me to develop a tendre for him."

He grows quiet again, and I can see his mind working. "Was that… Was it your first time?"

Another woman might color at the direct nature of the question, but it seems that I have no shame. "With a man, yes."

He nods, though it is impossible to know what is transpiring behind his plaintive gray eyes. I cannot help but think of Sophie, what she is doing and what she would think of my new bedmate.

"I hope you won't think…" He clears his throat, his somber eyes growing concerned. "I hope you won't think that was all I wanted from you. I won't leave you. Not for anything."

My throat unexpectedly chokes with emotion. I nod. "I know," I tell him. "You are a dear man."

A bugle calls outside, and Henri is obliged to leave to do

his drills. After I wash and dress, I wander outside in search of something to eat.

Armand is lounging by the trestle tables, and he catches my eye. Apparently he is not needed for the drills. I do not very much relish the idea of engaging him in conversation, but he is already making his way over to me.

"Mademoiselle," he says, taking my hand and bowing over it. "The camp has been a drearier place for your absence. What has been keeping you so preoccupied?"

Usually, flirtation and pretty turns of phrase come naturally to me and, with them, a great deal of pleasure. But this morning I find that I do not have the patience or inclination.

"I didn't realize that I had been so absent so as to be noticed," I tell him with a forced cheeriness. "Besides, Lieutenant Peusol would not countenance another excursion, not after our first one."

At Henri's name, Armand grows stiff. "Ah yes, the lieutenant. Was it a trick of the light, or did I see him leaving your tent quite early this morning?"

Something tells me that Armand cannot be put off with lies, or at least not with extravagant ones. "It was no trick of the light. He was assisting me," I say vaguely. I regard Armand, who is methodically tapping his gloved fingers on his arm, his gaze never wavering from me. "Were you watching my tent?"

He flashes me that disarming smile again, except now I see it for what it truly is: a weapon. "Could you blame me if I were? I have a responsibility for you, *to* you. Did you forget that General Guérin will have me disciplined for your behavior if it is anything other than incorruptible? Besides," he adds, "Lieutenant Peusol is a hard man. I don't like to think of you suffering under his watch."

"I thank you for your concern, although I assure you it's unwarranted." I'm already making a point of turning away. Armand was a lark when he was lighthearted and amusing, but I find that I do not care for this new, serious Armand who feels the need to assert his authority over me.

"Of course," Armand says with a little bow. "But you will forgive a gentleman for not wanting to leave anything to chance. So long as you are in this camp, I will be watching you, Colette."

Twenty-One

LIJSBETH

ROCKROSE: determination. The ability to bloom where one is planted, regardless of adverse conditions.

Ever since I can remember, my sleep has always been dark, dreamless. I am too tired at the end of each day for dreams, for anything other than falling into bed and giving in to slumber.

But now when I sleep, I see flowers.

These are not the dreams of a mind preoccupied with work, turning over ideas for arrangements. These dreams feel like a prophecy of things to come, or a vision through a looking glass into someone else's world. And always accompanying the flowers, the face of a young woman, one who I know I have seen before, but from where I cannot place. One night it is an abundance of jonquils, another night mounds and mounds of peach blossoms. I see soft white hands gracefully drawing and sketching, leaving a flowing stream of words and astonishing pictures in their wake.

After a night of particularly vivid dreams of a spiraling arrangement of red poppies and red and white roses, I spare no time in setting out for the flower market and gathering everything that I will need to make my visions come to life. The dreams have made me determined, made me curious. And since there hasn't been a new column from Madame Dujardin in weeks, the arrangements in my dreams will provide a perfect source of inspiration.

My little friend left me a gift, and that is that I am no longer afraid. The worst has happened, and little else in this life matters. I have walked through the embers and come out stronger. There is something inside of me, and I want to know what it is, what I am capable of. I will not hide, will not make myself small. Let Madame Dubois throw me out if she no longer finds my work to her liking. I shall sell flowers in the streets or simply walk into the woods and let myself fade away. I have had the whole world inside of me and lost it, have seen the promise of love and lost that as well.

But as fate would have it, Madame Dubois does not condemn my new work. She marvels that she has never seen such artistry and wishes all of her friends and enemies alike to see the genius of the maid she employs. Yet I cannot explain how the strange flowers seem to grow and twist beyond how I've arranged them.

Marie is glaring at me as I pass by with an armful of flowers. Madame wanted the cobwebs dusted from the high corners of the hall, and as usual Marie had tried to make me do it. "No more of this, Marie," Madame Dubois had scolded when she came upon me precariously balanced on the ladder, duster in hand. "I employ you as a maid, and if I wanted your duties delegated, I would see to it myself. Lijsbeth is only to do the flowers, and I cannot have her constantly muddling about in the yard or kitchen with work that tasks her hands unduly."

"You think you're something special," Marie tells me after Madame Dubois has gone. "You always have, but now you've really gotten all puffed up. I could do the flowers just as well, you know. I did before you came. Madame only keeps you because you're pretty and don't talk."

She grumbles something else until she is obliged to climb farther up the narrow steps to reach the rest of the cobwebs. I pay her no mind, for in front of me a castle in the air is growing. I build the walls with thorny roses, an impenetrable fortress guarding a bruised heart. But then I soften it with sweet anemones, poppies. Blue periwinkles peek out from the little gaps where even the thorns cannot obscure them. In a week or so all the flowers will be dead, the story gone. But while it is here, it is as if I have a voice. As if I matter.

Twenty-Two

CORNELIA

DAHLIA: instability. A dark or uncertain future.

May 31, Paris

The flowers are brighter, sweeter smelling, and it is not because summer has finally stepped into her own and thrown off the last vestiges of a rainy spring. The entire world is painted in fresh brushstrokes now that I look forward to Henri's visits in the evenings. I am content with my rice and onions, content with my blistered feet, content even with the gun smoke that forever hangs in the air.

Yet though my heart is glad, it is not completely full, not yet. Henri is strong and protective, fierce and humble in his love all at once. And he does love me, I am certain of it. He worships me in bed, adores me from afar. But despite the blooming flowers, the petals that unfurl from my fingertips, I cannot allow that I might not still be in full possession of my heart. Every time that he comes to my bed, he peels away a little more of my defenses. I know I should put an end to this before I inevitably find myself hurt and alone, but whenever I find myself in his arms, I am helpless to do anything but give in to my desires and touch him as much as possible.

This morning I have taken my paper and lead to an untouched patch of wildflowers growing on the banks of the river. Whether it's because battle is imminent or because Henri is no longer just strictly my guard, I find that I have more freedom now to do as I please, so long as I do not stray too far from camp.

I've just settled myself on the ground and found a little poppy that I wish to sketch when there is a snap of a twig behind me. I turn, expecting to find Armand following me, but my heart gives a silly little flutter when I see Henri emerging from the path.

"Thought to sneak away?" he asks. His olive skin glows in the sunlight, his gray eyes sparkling.

"Thought to come fetch your escaped captive?" I tease back.

His smile spreads, and he comes and sits beside me. I don't think I will ever be able to reconcile his gentle, careful movements with the uniform that he wears, the saber at his side. He is a beautifully packaged contradiction: gentle, yet strong; quiet, yet intense. I work as Henri looks on, his presence comforting.

I set aside my pencil. "Shall we have another writing lesson?" I ask him when I'm satisfied with the poppy.

He looks up at me, sharp but eager. "I wouldn't want to impose."

"Oh, stop. It's no imposition. Here." I shift over so that he can sit more closely beside me. He smells so good, and I allow myself to lean back into him a little as I pass him the pencil. I show him how to trace the letters of his name again and then mine and Sophie's. He is serious, silent, as I guide his hand and then let him try it on his own. Just like everything that Henri does, he puts his whole self into the endeavor, only showing the smallest sign of satisfaction once he has executed it perfectly.

When he has filled more than two pages with names, poems, and flowers, we lie down, my head on his chest, his arm around me. His fingers lazily comb through my hair. "I'll never tire of this," he murmurs.

I don't think I shall, either. I have always enjoyed attention, made no secret of the fact that I like to be flattered and admired. But with Henri, it is different. There is a profound respect that goes hand in hand with his admiration. And on my part, I think I could spend an eternity with him, and every day learn something new and surprising about him. While he still keeps much of his history to himself, he is a good storyteller and paints vivid scenes for me about the small Norman village he grew up in, the bloody skirmishes that he witnessed in the streets between the revolutionary army and the counterrevolutionaries. About the old man that used to sell finches in the market, and how one day a loose goat ran wild through the stalls, kicked over the cages, and sent a flock of birds scattering into the sky.

With every story, every whisper of his breath against the crown of my head, I feel the flowers opening their petals farther, my heart opening with them. I can try to stanch the flow all I want, but like a dam under pressure, the deluge is coming, and it's only a matter of time before I am swept away completely.

A bugle startles me from my sleep the next morning, and I awaken to bright sunlight filtering through the tent. I stretch, languid and satisfied as a cat that's got the cream. Henri never lingers long in my bed, but today he is not outside at his usual post waiting to escort me to breakfast, either.

"Where is Lieutenant Peusol?" I ask the victualler who is gumming at a spoonful of rice.

She squints up at me with her cloudy eyes. "Don't you know?"

"Know what?"

"The whole camp is gone to the Champ de Mars."

The camp *is* empty, with only a handful of women milling about. "Whatever for?" I ask her.

"'Tis only the emperor come to hold an assembly," she tells me with no small amount of condescension.

I vaguely recall Henri saying that there was to be some manner of gathering today, but I was too drowsy and content in his arms to pay attention to the particulars.

I only have to follow the parade of spectators and I am swept along to the city near the École Militaire. After so long spent marching and in the camp, it feels as if I am stepping outside into some magical new world. The cathedrals and buildings that I dreamed of are now a reality, the energy of the city alive in every tree-lined street. Everyone is gay and excited, singing songs and waving little flags. Someone grabs my arm, and I spin to find Sophie. She is wearing a little tricorne with a cockade, the hat sitting at a jaunty angle on her braided hair. "I didn't think you would come," she says.

"I didn't know that there was to be an assembly. Is it all just to see Napoleon?"

"You do live with your head in the clouds, don't you?" she says, looping her arm through my own and guiding me through the crush. "The emperor is going to sign a charter, and there will be a mass and presentation of arms."

"All this celebration just for a charter?" I had foolishly hoped that all this meant that the coalition forces had submitted to Napoleon, that there would not be any more fighting.

"You goose, it is so much more than that. It is the beginning of a new era. The Bourbons will be banished forever, and France will return to its former glory."

I could care less about charters and referendums, but I care very much about Sophie. She is in high spirits, her eyes shining, her cheeks flushed. We finally reach the Champ de Mars, a large open field near the military school where stages have been erected. Children sit on their parents' shoulders, and Sophie has to stand on her toes just to see. The jubilant crowd swells around us as we push our way as close to the platform as we are able.

Uncle was effusive with his hatred of Napoleon, and it gave him great joy to pontificate on the general's small stature. But even from this distance, I can tell that the man in the black bicorne and purple cloak is no shorter than me and is probably even taller than Uncle.

"Look!" Sophie points to where the troops are making their parade past the stage. The cavalry is coming by, rows of white and dapple-gray horses carrying soldiers with feathered helmets and gleaming swords. The spectacle of it all steals my breath, my excitement only heightened by sharing it with my beautiful friend.

Sophie grins and tosses her hat into the air. *"Vive le Roi de Rome! Vive l'Empereur!"* she cries, her voice joining thousands of others.

And then I see him.

Henri is magnificent in his deep blue coat and red sash, sitting proud and erect on his gleaming bay mare.

"Doesn't your lieutenant look fine?" asks Sophie. I don't bother to pretend that it doesn't please me to hear him called mine.

"Yes, very fine," I answer, my eyes still following the bobbing plume of his helmet as his regiment passes. He catches my eye, and a flash of something hot and jolting passes between us. It is sweet, yes, but it also makes my heart stop in my chest. It makes me question if I have been hasty to let my heart run away from me so quickly. How much of what I am feeling is real, and how much is the excitement, the novelty? The smell of rot fills my nostrils, the scene before me cast in blood. I see flowers growing brown and wilting, putrid and rotten and crawling with maggots. Horses rear up, trampling their riders as bullets fly through the smoky air. But then the vision passes, and I am once again back in the present moment, just one of many in a crowd of eager spectators.

Though we are jostled about in the rowdy crowd, Sophie's lips find my ear. "I said once that you were like a porcelain doll," she says, her voice low. "But you have blooms in your cheeks now, life in your eyes. Love suits you well."

I pull back, surprised by her honest speech. Her lips are slightly parted, revealing her adorably crooked tooth. There is a question in her sparkling eyes, and I am only too eager to answer it. I press my lips against hers. She is soft and eager as she opens for me and tastes like sweet berries. Lacing my arm around her waist, I pull her closer to me. She is everything I have dreamed about, and my heart, already made tender, now completely melts for her.

No one pays us any heed. We are simply two young women swept up in the moment. When I pull away, I expect that Sophie will look angry or, worse, embarrassed. But she only gives me a satisfied smile, as if she has just been proven right about something, and then threads her fingers through mine, leading me away from the spectators.

As I lay in bed with Henri that night, there is an unspoken heaviness that presses in around us. He draws me to him, and I run my finger down the bayonet scar that transects the broad sweep of his chest. I am humming the marching song from the assembly, and the kiss with Sophie, the vision of blood and decay, and Henri all running through my mind. "How grand the spectacle was, and how handsome you looked in your uniform!" I say as a means to distract myself.

I thought this would bring a smile to his serious face, but he seems equally distracted, faraway. "Yes, very grand," he says.

Gently, I turn his chin with my finger to face me. "But?"

"But there is nothing grand about what is to come," he says grimly.

"You think I am an innocent," I tell him, propping myself up on my elbow. "That I don't understand wars or the way of the men."

"You *are* innocent, Colette. In this, at least." He nips my ear, and I allow myself to be soothed back down to the mattress by his firm but gentle touch. I wonder what he would say if I told him of the kiss I shared with Sophie. I wish that I could tell him my real name, tell him who I really am. Would he still want to lie beside me? Would he still be looking at me as if I had hung the moon and stars? But I don't want to spoil the moment or see his rare smile dissipate so quickly. There will be time later, I tell myself.

Twenty-Three

CORNELIA

TRILLIUM: a trinity. Love comes in threes.

June 12

There is a renewed sense of energy and optimism in camp after the Champ de Mars. Napoleon has asserted his right to sit on the throne, and now there is no doubt that he will march to meet his enemies head-on and solidify his empire. It still seems a monstrously bad business that there can be no resolution without warfare, but I suppose negotiation and compromise are not strengths of men. It is incredible, given how much their sex likes to hear themselves talk.

I take my place with my bowl at one of the long trestle tables and listen to the chatter of the men around me. I do not think that I shall ever grow to be fond of rice and onions, but I am at least accustomed to it now.

But today, no sooner do I lift my spoon to my mouth than it turns to ash on my tongue, putrid, sour, and dry. I gag, quickly throwing back a cup of water to rinse the taste from my mouth. I glance about the table. None of the men tucking in around me seem to notice anything amiss with their food. Indeed, no one seems to notice me at all.

Even after I've returned to my tent, the taste lingers in my mouth, soon accompanied by the stench of rot that fills my nostrils. Movement catches my eye, and I watch as the bouquet of daisies beside my bed wilts before my eyes, the white petals curling backward, leaves and pollen falling to the little table. Carefully, I make my way to the rickety table and crouch down to inspect the fallen petals. Though only moments ago they were fresh, they are now crunchy and dry, as if they had been dead for weeks or months. I hastily sweep them off the table to the floor, stomping on them until they turn to dust.

I can no longer ignore that the flowers are trying to tell me something, though what I cannot fathom. Only that death and decay seem to linger around every corner. Perhaps if I had not pushed aside my peculiar abilities with flowers so often as a young girl, I would find now that I could decipher their meaning with more clarity.

Desperate to rid myself of the cloak of sickening sweetness that shrouds everything, I take up my sketchbook and wander some little ways from camp. Henri is busy with his regiment, as most of the men are, now that action is imminent. The sun is warm and mellow, and I find a quiet spot near a little stream that runs clear with daisies growing on the bank. I try not to think of the daisies that I just watched die in my tent. Spreading my blanket, I settle in and try to pretend that it is a normal summer's day in the countryside and not a prelude to war.

"I knew I only had to follow the flowers, and I would find you."

I shield my eyes against the brilliant sun, my stomach giving a little flutter when I see that it is Sophie. "Join me?"

She unburdens herself of her basket and sits down beside me, close enough that I can smell the lye soap on her skin. We haven't spoken since our kiss, though it may be owing more to the fact that we have simply not crossed paths in the last week or so. I continue my sketching while Sophie plucks up some daisies and begins braiding them into a crown.

She concentrates as she twines the stems together, a small furrow in her brow. "You kissed me at the Champ de Mars," she says after some time. "Twice."

My hand stills on my pencil. "You kissed me back," I say, hazarding a sidelong glance at her. The sun warms her rich brown hair shot through with gold, bestowing her with a gauzy halo. I want very badly to reach out and smooth the crease from her brow, but the moment is wound tight, and there is an air of expectancy that makes me stay my hand.

"Have you ever done that before?" she finally asks. "Kissed someone like me, I mean."

"What, a beautiful laundress with emerald eyes and lips like a rosebud?" I tease.

"You know what I mean."

There is no humor in her reply, so I answer her with equal earnestness. "There was someone, once. Yes." I am surprised to find that the thought of Anna passes through my mind like a ghost through a wall, leaving no pain in its wake. "Have you ever thought about a woman in that way?"

Her shoulder raises in a shrug, and I catch the faint hue of pink at her cheeks before she quickly looks away. "No. I never really considered it before, I suppose."

"But now?"

"Now I don't know what to think." Her daisies are in tatters, but she still worries at the shredded stems. "What about Lieutenant Peusol?" she asks.

I feel as if I am approaching a skittish bird, and one wrong movement will send her winging off into the sky. "I am quite attached to him," I tell her honestly.

"If the way that he looks at you is simply *attachment*, then I think love would shake the heavens and open up the earth," she says.

It makes me absurdly happy to hear her say as much, to know that whatever it is that Henri and I share, it is real beyond the confines of my tent. I gently disentangle the daisies from her fidgeting hands and lean close to her.

"You have a lady's hands," she muses, running her calloused fingers over my knuckles. "You heal like a wise woman, but I don't think you have ever worked a day in your life. I wonder who you really are and why you don't tell me."

My heart is in my throat. "Does it matter to you who I am?"

She makes a little noncommittal sound. "It would if you weren't so good. You've helped so many people here at camp."

"If I am good, it is only because of you. I have never wanted to be good before, have never tried."

I am rewarded by her dimpled smile. In the drowsy sunlight, I can feel the love of the flowers for the sun, the birds for the sweet air. I can feel a forgotten emotion blossoming, something that I thought was lost forever shifting deep within me. Beside me, a rose blooms, velvet petals unfurling.

"There is something you ought to know," Sophie says, oblivious to my inner turmoil and the flourishing of the flowers.

At the gravity of her words, my stomach tightens a little. If she tells me that she has another sweetheart or is to go away, I think I should die. "Oh?"

"Yes. I only hope that it… I only hope that you won't hate me once I tell you what it is."

"Who is the goose now? I could never hate you. Never."

She nods, though doesn't look convinced. "Henri and me. We shared something, once."

The knot loosens in my stomach, and I can feel Sophie watching me, waiting for me to say something. "Is that all?"

"Is that all?" she echoes incredulously. "Colette, do you understand what I'm saying?"

I cannot help the relieved laugh that escapes me. "Oh, darling girl, I did not mean to laugh," I say quickly when I see her face. "It is only that I thought you meant to run off with a soldier and leave me." Standing on my knees, I pull her up a little closer to me. "Tell me, did you have feelings for Henri? Did he for you?"

She frowns in thought. "At the time I fancied I was in love with him. Maybe I was. I don't know that once you feel something for someone it ever completely goes away. He makes you happy, and you him." There is the slightest tremble at her lip, and I know that it is costing her everything to pretend not to care. "I am glad for you both," she adds.

"Goose," I whisper, pulling her closer to me. I feel hot inside, restless. Delicious shivers race across my skin as she carefully traces the line of my jaw with her small finger. Nothing else matters except being as close to her as I possibly can, and I slip one arm around her waist, drawing her to me until we are flush against each other. She catches her breath in surprise, but then I am brushing her lips with a kiss and indulging in her sweetness. Once, I would have shuddered to hear myself speak so sentimentally. But then, there was never such a prize as Sophie to be won. "And you make me happy," I tell her, pulling back and tucking a stray curl of golden-brown hair behind her ear. "Deliriously so."

Word comes in the middle of the night that we are to move on Brussels and surprise Wellington at the Sambre. It seems that we have hardly been in Paris and now we are to leave, any time that I might have used to search for my mother all but squandered and forgotten. Within a matter of hours, the camp is dismantled and packed into carts, and we are once more on the march.

The journey to Brussels is cold, wet, and long. Napoleon has ordered the roads destroyed to impede the Prussians and English, and the result is that we must now travel through overgrown rye fields, making our trek twice as difficult. Horses get mired down in the mud, carts overturn, and there is a general air of misery as we tramp on in our wet boots. Henri climbs into my bed at night, tired and silent, starved for physical touch. I know better than to talk about the coming fighting, but there is a tautness in his silence tonight. He is sitting on the edge of the cot, pulling off his boots, lost in some private thoughts. I make light conversation, to which his only contribution is an occasional grunt or monosyllable.

"I would pay dearly to know what is causing that storm cloud about your head," I finally tell him when it becomes clear that he is not even listening to me.

He gives a shrug, though the air radiating off him is anything but indifferent. "Henri," I insist. "What is bothering you? You needn't shoulder everything on your own."

Outside, a thunderclap shudders through the air. "I saw you," he finally says. "With Sophie."

My breath catches in my throat. I must have a conscience, because my heart starts to beat uncomfortably fast. "You weren't meant to."

"No, I daresay I wasn't," he says, his jaw tight.

"Are you very angry?" I do not ask because his answer will change anything, for I would not take back what I did with Sophie. I am only sorry that I might have hurt him.

He rubs the back of his neck in slow consideration, then lets out a frustrated sigh. "No. I couldn't be angry with you, not for anything. Though, my life might be a good deal easier if I could. Do you love her?"

I think of Sophie and her warmth, the gentle euphoria I feel when I am with her. I think of the flowers that were so long absent from my life, blooming at the sight of her. I think of the fierce protectiveness that rises in my chest on her behalf. I can pretend that I am still the cold, pretty doll that used to sit in Uncle's parlor in Sussex, but the truth is, I have thawed, and it is because of Sophie. "Yes," I answer, swallowing past the lump in my throat. "I think that I do."

He nods, his face unreadable.

But my admission has not come without cost. I can feel him slipping away, and I cannot lose him. I rise to my knees, and taking his face in my hands, I turn it so that he must look at me. "Listen to me, darling. It does not change anything between us. You have become so much to me. More than I could have ever dared to dream. I would never do anything to hurt you, and if I seem capricious, please know that it is only because…because I am frightened by what I feel."

His serious gray eyes regard me. He is so beautiful, so perfect. And under those high cheekbones and soldier's body, there is a heart that is gentle beyond anything, a soul that yearns to be loved. Any woman would be lucky to be the object of his affection. So why do I still feel like there is a piece missing?

The answer comes to me in a flash, though I suppose it has probably been slowly building over the past weeks and months. I set out for Paris seeking happiness. When I left Sussex, I thought that I needed to find my mother to know who I was and that would fill the empty ache within me. I thought independence and money in my pocket would make me happy. But the universe was swift in correcting me of my misguided notions. Instead of my mother, I found Sophie and Henri and, for the first time in my life, knew what real happiness is. And now that I have found them, I cannot give either up without shattering that newfound contentment.

"Do you think…do you think that you could love her, too?" I ask, almost too apprehensive to speak the words aloud.

He pulls back, nostrils flaring, and I am not sure if I have insulted him beyond measure or simple shocked him. "Henri, forgive me, I—"

But he does not let me finish. "No, Colette," he says, shaking his head. The tent is too small for him to stand, so he sits heavily on the floor, draping his arms over his crossed legs. I hold my breath as I watch him, waiting for him to decide my fate, our fate. Thunder rumbles, closer this time. It feels like hours but is probably only minutes before he finally looks up, his full attention boring into me. "You will always be first in my heart," he says quietly. "I cannot help it, and I don't know that I can make room for another so quickly. But I loved her once, and I will endeavor to love her again, too, for your sake."

Relief floods through me. I don't deserve this man, but if he can love for my sake, then I can be brave for his sake, too. Falling to my knees to join him on the ground, I cup his cheek, and his eyes close as he leans into my touch. "Colette," he murmurs, a choke that is somewhere between pain and pleasure in the word.

Hushing his anxieties away, I capture his lips in a kiss. He needs no further invitation before he lifts me to the bed, lightly pushes me down onto the mattress and lowers himself on top of me, kissing me all the while. I open myself to him, arching up to meet him and show him that I see his love and that I will do everything in my power to make him as happy as he has made me.

He trails a path of scorching kisses down my body, and my eyes flutter closed. Can it really be so easy? Everything I have ever wanted is being laid at my feet. How different it looks to how I once imagined it would, when I thought that I should die from unhappiness if I could not have Anna as well as my status and my work. Now I only have one dress to my name, blisters on my feet, and an uncertain future. Yet I am happy, content. In Henri I have not just a lover but a protector, something I never thought I needed or even wanted.

My hands are roaming the muscled contours of his back when a sound outside interrupts us. Henri motions for me to stay where I am, and I pull the blanket up to my chin.

Grabbing his saber from where it lies discarded on the ground, Henri opens the dripping tent flaps. He is silent for a moment before stepping aside to reveal Sophie. "What's wrong?" I ask, my heart sinking. Usually when Sophie comes at night, it is because she has brought me a patient. "Does someone need help?"

She shakes her head. "It's thundering. I couldn't sleep."

My nights belong to Henri, she knows this. But seeing Sophie standing inside my tent, so small and stubborn and pretty, makes me want to run to her and take her in my arms.

I look to Henri. I did not expect that his pledge would be put to the test so soon. "Is it all right with you?"

Henri rubs at his shoulder, withdraws into himself. Sophie seems to understand that this is no ordinary question and stays silent, arms hugging herself as she awaits his verdict.

My chest starts to ache from holding my breath as I wait for him to say something, anything. I should not have asked this of him. Of either of them. What if for me to have it all means asking them to sacrifice something? I could still have my beautiful friend, could still have my bedmate. Yet I cannot bring myself to intervene. I suppose I have always been spoiled. As much as the last months have changed me, I am still a young woman accustomed to getting what she wants. But it is too late now, and whether we are ready for it or not, my wants have drawn us all here, tangled us together irreparably.

Finally, when I think the tent should collapse in on itself from the heated tension, Henri turns and holds out his hand to Sophie, who, after a moment's hesitation, places her own hand in his.

Something passes between us, Henri and Sophie and me. I could not name it if I tried, but there is an understanding, a deep respect which I reciprocate with an ardor I never thought possible. *Thank you*, I tell Henri with my eyes, and he gives a grave nod.

Holding out my hand to her, Sophie comes and places her own in mine. But then she turns to Henri, who is watching us with guarded eyes. "I missed you," she tells him.

Henri's gaze deepens as he looks at her. "How it ended between us…" he says. "I… It was not well done of me. I have regretted it every day since then."

Sophie gives a small incline of her head in acknowledgment. She is so proud and small, yet she is holding court like a queen. "We neither of us were at our best."

What happened between Henri and Sophie, I don't know and doubt I ever will, unless they decide to share it with me. But I allow them their space as they make their amends, heal their lingering wounds.

I sit on the bed, keeping my gaze carefully averted while they embrace, murmur some further words to each other. Then Sophie pulls away, leading Henri by the hand. She climbs in, weary from hauling baskets of laundry and wringing out soiled linens all day. I massage away the aches for her, satin skin under my fingers, and soon Henri is kissing along my neck, and we three are complete.

Twenty-Four

LIJSBETH

ZEPHYR LILY: new beginnings and great expectations.
The unpredictable nature of joy.

The city of Brussels quivers with expectation, the narrow buildings leaning forward in their foundations, waiting for a word on the breeze. Wellington's army grows by the day, and it is only a matter of time before Napoleon arrives to meet him. But the excitement that runs through the house today has nothing to do with the movement of armies but the ball that the Duchess of Richmond is throwing tonight. Napoleon could ride bareback into the city and Brussels society would merely raise a brow, then go back to planning and preparing for what promises to be the gathering of the season.

Madame sends me across the street to the Richmonds' lodgings early in the morning to help with the flowers. I am used to being passed about like a basket of eggs, but this time, I am happy enough to go, to glimpse something new other than the four walls of the house which have been like a prison of grief.

The Duke and Duchess have transformed what was once their

coach house into a dazzling palace of light and color. Chandeliers hang between pillars, glittering against the black, gold, and crimson silks that are hung everywhere. A maid is directing a footman, who teeters on a ladder as he struggles to pin a garland of golden foliage above a window. A violinist practices fragments of songs, filling the space with short bursts of music. I could stand here forever, taking it all in, but a housemaid points me in the direction of the kitchen where the flowers are waiting in big buckets, and then I set to work.

Everyone is too busy with their own part in the preparations to notice me, and for once I am glad of my invisibility, the privacy it grants me to grieve even in a room full of people. I fall into a blissful rhythm of fresh flowers and buckets of cold water, soft petals, and leathery leaves. I am assigned two undermaids, who help me assemble the arrangements. Every secret alcove gets a vase, every mantel and windowsill a garland. There is no limit to what I may create, so long as it is grand of scale and impressive in volume. This is a party meant not just to celebrate the English army and its allies but to showcase the Richmonds.

Dusk is falling when I hand off my last arrangement to one of the maids and stand back to survey my work. If the end result is lovely to me, a lowly maid, then I can only imagine how it will look to a society girl in a gown, blushing and eager for a night of romance. For a moment, I close my eyes, pretending that I am one of them, stepping into a glittering ballroom bedecked with flowers and candles, my whole life ahead of me.

"You!"

The brusque voice snaps me from my daydreams, and I turn to find the head housemaid, a stout woman with graying temples and a pinched mouth. She thrusts an apron at me. "What are you doing, standing about? You're needed to help set out glasses."

I blink at the frilly white cloth in my hands.

Another maid who is passing by says, "She's slow, up here," and taps her finger on her cap.

"And? She's got two hands, don't she?" The head housemaid scowls at me as she yanks back the apron, spins me about, and ties it on for me, all before I can so much as blink.

I'm not certain that Madame Dubois meant me to stay on here after I was done with the flowers, but I don't mind. Everyone at the Dubois house will be at the ball anyway, and Marie would just be there to torment me. Besides, I want to see all the fine ladies, and the Highlanders who will be doing a Scotch reel. The apron and cap allow me a degree of freedom to move about the ball so long as I keep up the appearance of being busy.

It must be quite late, because there is no light left in the sky when the first carriages pull up outside. It's strange to see the now-familiar street from the window of the Richmonds' coach house, like seeing the world through a slightly different slant. What looks like my whole world is just another street, another mundane view for them. The glasses set, I watch as a constant stream of guests arrive, officers and generals in coats laden with epaulets, ladies in gauzy silk gowns. The house glitters like a jewel box. Ostrich feathers quiver and dance atop elaborate coiffures. Conversations overlap, made soft and indistinct by the string quartet tuning their instruments.

The Duke of Wellington is announced, and all talking ceases for a moment as he enters. He is younger than I expected, his hair still dark, his form lithe and athletic. His red coat swims with gold braids, and little medals and trinkets clink together as he escorts a young lady down the line. The conversations begin back up again, and I hope that it will soon be time for the dancing.

A few guests remark on the flowers, but mostly it is as if I were never here. I am just a ghost, moving about the house collecting empty glasses and trying to stay out of the way.

"We anticipate action within the fortnight, if not sooner," an English officer says as he passes a glass off without looking away from his friends.

"It will all come down to Blücher and the Prussian forces, and when they arrive. He may yet decide to back old Boney."

A young woman in a pink gown dripping with jewels idly fans herself. "And then what would happen?"

"Why, then we would find ourselves in a very bad way, indeed."

The woman in pink affects horror with wide eyes and fluttering lashes. "But surely it won't come to that. There won't be fighting in Brussels, will there? What would become of us ladies?"

"Madame," says the first officer, bowing over her hand, "you would be most safe with Wellington's finest here to defend you."

The lady titters behind her fan.

"Good heavens, what are you doing just standing there!" The head maid hisses at me and hauls me away by the arm. "You're meant to be working, not gawping at the guests. Now, get away with you."

I'm only too glad to slip away somewhere more private. There is a small gallery overlooking the great room, and I quickly shed the apron and cap once I am out of sight. From here I have a view of the whole ball and can watch as I please, unnoticed and unbothered.

The music finally starts in earnest, and couples begin to take the floor. There are some dances of which I don't know any of the names. Then the Highlanders take the floor and dance their reel, a mesmerizing pattern of spinning tartans. The swelling music of the pipes wind faster and faster, until it is a frenzy of sound and color. I feel something wet on my cheek and find that I have started weeping from the beauty of the scene spread below me. It is not just the dance itself—though, that is lovely as well—but the harmony of the connection between the dancers. They all work as one, each playing their part to create a larger pattern. I wonder what it feels like to be part of something like that, something so beautiful, not to just witness it from above, removed and alone.

"An angel looking down upon the mortals."

The voice pulls me out of my reverie. I spin around to find my soldier emerging from the shadows at the edge of the gallery, his blue eyes sparkling with candlelight. My heart beats like a startled bird as he comes to stand beside me at the railing, his sleeve brushing mine. All my careful work to avoid him and he has found me here, tucked away on the gallery. Yet I cannot make myself move even so much as an inch away.

The reel has ended, and now couples are taking the floor for a waltz in a sea of red coats and gossamer dresses. "They are a pretty sight, aren't they?" he asks, studying the scene below. "Yet the prettiest is not among them." At this he looks at me, and I feel my chest go hot.

I want to tell him that I wouldn't trade all the glittering jewels to be down there in the crush of perfumed bodies, not now that he is here beside me. There are a great many things I want to tell him.

He does not seem offended at my behavior on that day in the drawing room or even curious for that matter. He is just here, solid and warm beside me. And I stand comfortably as if a man has never made me flinch before, as if I have nothing to fear. He feels familiar and safe, which I suppose is danger in and of itself, because I can never have him. He comes from another world, one so different from my own that I can't even begin to imagine how he has noticed me at all.

The waltz ends, and there is polite applause before the musicians take up their instruments again.

"I asked you for something the other day, and you did not give it to me." There's a smile tugging at the corner of his lips, and for a moment it's all I can do not to stare. I have been close to him before, but not like this, not alone. Not without the chance of being intruded upon by one of the family members. Here we are completely by ourselves, invisible to the outside world.

"And now I have a confession to make."

I should be nervous—after all, it is just him and me up here—but I feel only a dizzy sort of excitement as I wait for him to continue.

"I asked for your name, and you would not—or rather, you did not—give it to me. But I have found it out, anyway."

My heart—already racing—beats a little faster. I am completely under his spell, awaiting what comes next.

"Lijsbeth," he says.

My eyes flutter closed, and I take a sharp breath in. I have never heard my name before. Or rather, I have never heard the way it sounds spilling from his lips. It may be my name, but it has never belonged to me, not truly. It is a way for a mistress to summon me, a reprimand. But when he says it, it is as if he is returning a precious gift to me, one that a forgotten mother gave her child long ago.

"I never introduced myself properly. Captain William Norton of the 82nd."

Of course, I already know his name, made a point to learn it and then hide it away in my heart like a jealous magpie protecting her treasure. But now he has told me himself, and my treasure is all the sweeter for being given freely.

If only I had something to give him, some token to show that he is worthy of having occupied my thoughts these past weeks. I flick my tongue over my lips. Close my eyes, let the music and laughter float up around me.

"I d-don't..." My words gutter out like a candle in the wind.

The gallery is safe and small, warm in the golden candlelight. I chance a peek at the captain to see what effect my voice has on him. But he shows no signs of pity or disgust. There is only an earnest curiosity, and I realize it is because he is curious of what I have to say, not curious of what I *am*. His posture is casual, an elbow propped on the railing, a pleasant smile on his lips. He doesn't rush me; he just waits.

I am safest when I am alone in a dark room, door locked, lamp cold. When no one has a claim on my time except for myself. When I know Isidore and his appetites cannot reach me. When Marie is snoring away in her own world. Then, and only then, am I free to speak, and my words unfurl like an uncertain flower in the first thaw of spring. And yet, what have I to say to myself in the dark?

My shoulders relax a little, the invisible vise around my throat loosening. The words slip out like a snake shedding its skin, smooth and quick.

"I d-don't c-care…for dancing."

The captain doesn't say anything, the music below filling the silence. His blue eyes are locked on me. It is too late to take back my words, but I find that I don't want to. I could care less what he thinks of my opinion on dancing, but he has just seen the most vulnerable part of me, and I could not be more exposed if I stood before him without a stitch of clothing.

His golden brows rise, betraying his surprise. But then he is laughing. "Of course you don't," he says, finally wiping a tear from his eye. "Why should I expect anything less from the girl who turns the head of every officer in His Majesty's army, and who makes flowers sing with her fingers? But I wonder if your opinion hasn't been informed by a lack of suitable partners more than anything else."

My shoulders loosen in relief, and I find myself answering his smile with one of my own. The truth is I have never danced. How can one dance with chilblains on their feet and an ache in their back? When does one dance when one's every waking hour is dedicated to labor?

Before I realize what is happening, he is taking my hand in his and leading me away from the rail. His arm comes around me, his hand lightly resting on the small of my back, just below where my apron knot usually falls. He smells of soap and clean sweat, and I want to drink it in, to fill my memory with his wonderful scent forever. But then we are moving, and all thoughts flee from my mind.

I have only ever found myself in one other man's arms before, and I never thought that I would willingly find myself in the same position again. But I feel safe here in Captain Norton's firm embrace, protected. I close my eyes, the music running through me like a purifying stream. I don't have to worry about the steps or where to put my feet; he gently guides me, and I move with him.

Even with my empty womb, I think I have never been happier than in this moment. Have never truly known what happiness is. Tomorrow I will go back to creating beauty that does not belong to me, and he will go back to his drills and card games. But for tonight I am not just a ghost: I am seen, a woman of flesh and blood who can be held.

The music ends, but his hold lingers. His chin hovers just above my shoulder, the gentle exhales of his breath warm on my neck. I should pull away, drop a curtsy, or…*something.* But I don't want to move. I cannot, not when I am so close to touching heaven.

"There," he says, his deep whisper sending shivers through me. "Tell me you don't care for dancing, and I shall consider it a lost wager."

But of course, I cannot tell him, because it would not be true.

He is still close, close enough that our lips could touch with the merest suggestion. "Lijsbeth, there is something I would ask of you." His confidence is belied by the slight rasp of his voice, the smallest of tremors in his hand at my back.

If I were held in the embrace of an angel, I could not feel safer, more content. I should think nothing would ever be able to tear me away from this moment, but there is a ripple of excitement in the dancers. My gaze is drawn past my captain's shoulder, down into the crowd below.

I am hardly the only person to notice the young woman moving like a moonbeam through the crowd. She draws the hungry gazes of men and curious looks from the women, walking with quiet confidence that says she knows she is beautiful and does not care. But it is not her beauty nor the defiant tilt of her chin that is familiar.

I know her the way a rose knows the first light of dawn. I know what her voice sounds like without her having to open her mouth. I know that I have seen that face in my dreams. The locket against my chest is singing, and I wonder that Captain Norton doesn't seem to notice.

But then the spell is broken as a fresh commotion runs through the ball guests. The Duke of Wellington takes the middle of the floor and makes a booming announcement. Beside me, Captain Norton goes rigid.

"Napoleon's army has crossed the Sambre and is advancing on Quatre Bras! We ride at dawn!"

Twenty-Five

CORNELIA

CHICKWEED: a rendezvous ordained by the stars.

I was always impatient in Sussex: impatient for my life to start, impatient for someone new, impatient for a new season to bring with it new flowers. But now I find that time is rushing ahead too fast, that I would do anything to prolong my precious moments with Henri and Sophie. Now that we have crossed the river and are within striking distance of Brussels, there is no time for lovemaking or idle days by the stream. There is only marching, heat, and exhaustion. Fear.

Even if there were time, it would do me little good. The sound of flowers is so loud that it is almost enough to overpower the distant noise of the nearby skirmishes that have broken out between the Prussians and the converging French armies. I can be eating my rice or attending to my sorry toilette, and suddenly the most noxious fumes fill my nose, my lungs. My ears ring from the overlapping chorus of flowers all vying for my attention, and it's all I can do to stumble behind my tent and retch until my body is empty and shaking. I can no longer pretend that all is normal, or even that everything will be all right.

There is little use in trying to sleep tonight. My cot had to be surrendered to the luggage train so that the regiment could travel lighter and faster through the countryside. Both Henri and Sophie are sleeping soundly when I carefully steal from the bedroll we share on the ground now. They look so content, so peaceful. I brush each of their temples with a kiss. There is a meager breeze, and it carries with it the scent of roses and bids me to dress quickly and follow it out into the night.

But outside I find no roses, only a field of cowslip. They bob in the breeze, eager for me to hear them. *In the city. Go to her in the city.*

"Go to who?" I ask the night.

Go to the city.

I don't know what it means, only that I must obey them. There is no one here to judge, to question why a woman can commune with flowers. With my guard asleep in my bed, I wrap my shawl around me and set off through the camp into the night beyond. The way is hard, with the roads leading to Brussels destroyed, forcing me to continue my trek through the rye fields and overgrown byways. Marching in the daytime, we have the men to slash down the fibrous stalks, but now I must navigate them on my own. But I have faith in the flowers, and they reward me by guiding me to an old cow path which runs along the field, narrow but mercifully clear.

I have not been walking more than half an hour when the thundering of hoofbeats approaches behind me. Anyone out at this time of night, on this forgotten path, cannot have good intentions. It could be highwaymen, errant soldiers, or God only knows who else. Too late, I try to scramble to escape the path.

"You there!" the rider calls.

It is no use trying to hide when I have already been seen, so I stand and face him, prepared to defend myself.

"Colette?"

I squint through the dark at the figure on horseback. "Armand?"

Swinging down from the saddle, he lands in front of me. He is dressed in civilian clothes, all black, even a great coat on despite the heat. "What are you doing out here? Are you by yourself?" he asks.

"Of course I am—who else would be with me? I am on my way to Brussels."

He fumbles his riding crop in his hand, nearly dropping it. "Brussels? Colette, you—"

"You cannot tell a soul," I say before he can finish.

"Tell anyone? I… Colette, you are mad." He removes his hat and runs his hand through his dark hair. "What do you want in Brussels? My God, you *are* a spy."

"Really, Armand."

"Well, I cannot think what else would compel you to make such a journey alone in the night, as you have chosen for your path a dangerous territory where fighting is even now breaking out." He has finally regained his composure, and has seemingly grown taller, crossing his arms across his chest like a disappointed father. "There are traps and ambushes about, and a Prussian soldier is not likely to spare a young lady simply because she has taken it in her head to go for a walk in the countryside in the middle of the night. Does your guard know? I daresay he doesn't or else you wouldn't be skulking about like a thief."

In truth, I had not considered that there might be fighting nearby. My only thought had been of following the flowers to the city and not that the roads might not be safe, especially for a young lady traveling by herself.

"Are you quite done lecturing me?" I say impatiently in an effort to deflect from my poor judgment. "Perhaps you could tell me what *you* are doing out here."

Armand gives his crop an impatient flick against his leg and looks cagily off into the darkness. "Officer business" is all that he says.

"Are there any other officers who are obliged to go on this business?" I ask innocently. "It seems you are quite alone and wearing dark clothing. Perhaps you do not want anyone else to know what you're about?"

Armand regards me for a long moment, a muscle pulling downward at the corner of his mouth. But then he gives me a slow smile. "You are too clever by half, Colette. It is business of a most private, most sensitive nature. And you are right, I do not want anyone else to know what I'm about. But as fate would have it, Brussels is my destination as well."

We stand at an impasse, neither of us willing to divulge the reason for our respective errands.

"You've a scratch on your face," Armand says, lightly touching my cheek where one of the rye stalks had cut me. His finger comes away with a smear of blood. He sighs, wistful. "Colette."

He still carries a torch for me. I can see it in the longing glances he throws my way when he thinks I'm not looking, in the way he is even now loath to wipe the blood from his hand. I am quick to seize my advantage. "Take me with you."

"You cannot be serious." He gives me a long look, and I think that I am about to receive another lecture. But then he mutters a curse. "Fine," he tells me, making a point to look as stern as possible. "But once we get to the city, I must conduct my business, alone. We will rendezvous after, and then I am returning you to camp where you belong, and you will not so much as *breathe* a word about what has transpired this night."

I agree, and Armand helps me up onto the horse, then swings up into the saddle behind me. My poor legs and feet rejoice at the reprieve from walking. We ride for several hours through sleepy villages and pastures of cows. I wonder if this is the path that the Grande Armée will take in the coming days. I wonder if the inhabitants slumbering within know that war is coming?

I think of the night of the explosion in camp, the way the air hung heavy with the smell of burnt flesh and hair. In the absence of experience with battle, my mind runs wild, filling in the blank spaces. Uncle's house had paintings of war scenes, full of ancient ancestors in suits of armor with a burning sky behind them. What beauty will artists be able to find when the army comes slicing through the land like a knife through meat, leaving blood and butchered flesh in its wake?

But it has already started. A plume of smoke in the distance curls into the dark sky, the echoes of gunshots ringing out. "The Prussians," Armand says grimly. We skirt wide, traveling through woods and overgrown fields, avoiding the small villages that are even now under siege.

My body is crying out for a soft bed by the time Armand guides the horse toward the first lights of Brussels. The flowers have only grown louder, urging me on. *This way. Just a little farther.* Everywhere, boisterous soldiers in red coats are congregating. Carts lit by swinging lanterns sell ices and sweetmeats to couples strolling through the tree-lined squares. It must be well past midnight, but there is a carnival atmosphere, as if all the soldiers are simply here on holiday. *Run*, I should tell them. *Leave now, before Napoleon descends on your city and kills your men.*

Armand dismounts near a fountain in a quiet square and helps me down. "We will meet here when the church bell strikes two," he instructs me. He hesitates, like he wants to tell me something else, but just warns me to be careful, and then he is gone. I wait until he has disappeared in the other direction before closing my eyes and letting the flowers guide me.

A throng of finely dressed revelers lead me to a gracious stone house overlooking a park, the flowers encouraging me along the way. I don't know where I am, or why I am here, only that there is something within that house calling to me, demanding that I gain entry, by any means possible.

"Stop, mademoiselle," a footman in a powdered wig commands me at the front door. "You must have an invitation." Then, seeing my muddy hem and worn boots, sneers. "You might try the almshouse," he says with a sniff of condescension. He wouldn't dare speak to me that way in Sussex, but now I am beneath the consideration of even a footman. A group of women dressed in pale diaphanous gowns titter as they brush past me inside.

I'm not sure why I thought I could walk up to this grand house in my clothes as they are and expect admittance. But then, I am not thinking, just letting the flowers tug me along like a boat lost to the current. So I give in to it, close my eyes, and allow the persistent flowers to guide me to the back of the house and the mews.

I make quick work, beating the mud and dirt from my skirt and twisting my hair up into a loose topknot. My boots are a lost cause, but with the low sweep of my hem, I am able to hide them by walking carefully. When I slip in through the open stable door, no one notices me.

The coach house has been transformed into a grand ballroom, and it is alive with a party. I move through the house unbothered by the servants who flit about like moths. Every alcove, every nook, is filled with the most extraordinary flowers I have ever seen, urns tumbling them out like jewels, vases crowded with impossibly vibrant blooms. *This way. Come this way, quickly,* they tell me.

Men in red coats and white trousers dance the quadrille, their ladies in gauzy dresses and quivering feathers. Only a few miles away Napoleon is uncoiling like a snake ready to strike, and here the mongooses are at play without a care in the world.

I think of all the days spent mucking through the mountain passes and hard roads, the mean bowls of rice and onions, the blisters and calluses on my feet. Perhaps I was too hasty in my decision that day at the nunnery in Amiens. If I had but found a way to continue a little longer, I might have found a place in the English army, charmed an officer or even a diplomat, and made a life for myself in a city like this, attending balls and wearing fine gowns. But then, I would not know the bliss of Henri's arms holding me to his hard chest nor the sweetness of Sophie's lips on mine.

The whispers of the flowers here are frenzied, like waves crashing one on top of another, over and over. I don't understand what they are trying to tell me, only that I am very close to whatever it is they mean to show me.

And that is when I see her.

The face peeking down from the gallery is small, not a child's face, but surely not a grown woman's either. She cannot be a guest, as she is dressed much too simply, yet I cannot fathom that the saintly little face belongs to a servant. I find myself entranced by her warm brown eyes, the thoughtful purse of her lips. There is a man at her elbow, dressed in the uniform of an English officer. He does not see me as he leans in toward her, his hand at her back, his lips murmuring something close to her ear.

The rest of the ball has faded far away—the glittering lights, the music, even my very reason for being here at all. The chaotic song of the flowers smooths and soars, a melody that has found its harmony. The girl touches something at her neck, a glint of silver in the candlelight. Not once does her gaze stray from me.

I must get to her, find a way up onto that gallery, but there is the unmistakable sensation of someone at my back. Finally breaking my gaze, I turn to see a familiar but unexpected face.

"Armand?" He has shed his dark clothes and is dressed in the colors of the English. "What are you doing here?"

"I might ask you the same question," he hisses, taking my arm and ushering me through the crowd.

He has no time for my concern about the girl on the balcony or why I must stay and watch her for as long as possible.

"Really, Armand, you might loosen your grip on my arm. And why are you dressed like that?"

He gives me a warning look and maneuvers me out of the ballroom into an alcove. Anyone we pass will think us a soldier and his sweetheart, searching for a private spot.

"Well?" I insist once the curtains are drawn about us and the only light comes from the moon through the window. "What are you doing here?"

"What am *I* doing here? I came looking for you."

"And you thought to come dressed in enemy colors?"

"I am not so fortunate to hide in plain sight behind feminine beauty," he tells me, running a longing gaze down the length of my body. "I would be questioned, if not outright arrested. Come," he says, taking my hand, "we must leave before we are discovered."

But I stand my ground, thinking only of the girl on the gallery and her achingly familiar face. "I cannot leave, not yet."

"Colette, this place is ripe with spies and—" he lowers his voice, leans in closer "—and soldiers, with appetites. I'll not let you endanger yourself." He stiffens suddenly, as if entertaining an unpleasant thought. "Have you a beau, among the English?"

"Of course not!"

"Then, what? I saw you staring at something in the ballroom as if you might never breathe again."

I can hardly tell him that which I don't understand myself. "I thought I saw someone, an old friend. Not English," I add.

He doesn't believe me, but Armand will not question me. I can see the hopeful desire that is always present in his eyes, as lovesick as the first day we met.

Appeased, he moves a little closer, so that the hilt of his sword bumps my stomach. I'm not afraid of this man, but I wish now that perhaps I had not been so hasty in my friendship with him.

He lowers his voice. "Will you deny what I feel for you? What I know you to feel for me?"

"Armand." I place a light hand on his chest to distance him and immediately wish I hadn't, as he takes it as license to lean into my touch. "You are like a brother to me. You've done so much for me, and I appreciate every—"

He makes a sound of disgust in the back of his throat. "A brother. I may die tomorrow, and you call me *a brother.*"

"Don't speak like that. You will be—"

"Oh, what do you know of war, Colette?"

My stomach tightens, all the terrible visions and smells that have been haunting me congregating there. "I know that it is an awful thing, that it destroys that which woman has made," I say quietly.

His dark gaze grows stormy. "You are afraid your Henri will not come back," he says.

"I am afraid a great many young men will not come back."

"But Lieutenant Peusol is your beau, isn't he? I've seen him coming out of your tent more than once. Do you know," he says, leaning in again, "I have seen him with the little laundress, too? Do you realize that your lover is not faithful to you?"

"I think that perhaps you should not believe everything you see," I say carefully. "Your concern is unwarranted."

As I watch the emotions flicker across his handsome features in the moonlight, I realize that I do not give Armand enough credit. Under his boyish demeanor lurks a man who sees everything, and I would do well to be on my guard. He might not understand what Henri and Sophie and I share, but he knows that there is something between us, and that is enough to plant a seed of jealousy.

He doesn't say anything, though I can feel desire radiating off him. He could force himself on me in this small alcove, but it is Armand, and I know he will not. As much as he might fancy himself in love, he is not one to take drastic action. A sigh escapes him, and with it I can feel all his disappointment, his frustration.

"Come," he says, "let us return to camp before we are discovered."

News of Napoleon's advance has spread through the ball, a

stone thrown into a placid pond sending ripples. Soldiers, who only minutes ago were dancing a quadrille, are now strapping on their sabers. Tearful goodbyes and farewell kisses are exchanged in the hall. A few young women are still dancing, but all the joy is gone. A tense, funeral air hangs in the emptying room, and no one notices us as we slip out back into the night.

Twenty-Six

LIJSBETH

LISIANTHUS: farewell. My heart follows with you.

No one sleeps that night.

All the high spirits of the ball have dissipated like a dream, leaving a heavy fog of prickling excitement in its wake. Soldiers doze drunk, leaned up in corners, sprawled on settees and chairs. Others have already gone to prepare their kits and say their farewells. More than one sweetheart has extracted a pledge from her beau before he departs for battle. Some of the men who danced so gaily this evening will not live to see tomorrow night.

I wander the house like a ghost, unsettled and unable to sleep. Before, the war seemed a faraway thing, the province of men and their insatiable desires. But now I will be sending a piece of my heart onto the battlefield at first light. Whether I have the right to claim that though, I do not know. Captain Norton spoke no pledges, made no promises. Yet when he was beside me, his kind blue eyes searching mine, it felt like a vow. And whether we have an understanding or not, he has my heart, completely. I think I gave it to him the first day I saw him.

Marie is snoring lightly when I return to our room and climb into bed. Pale moonlight spills in through the grimy window, and I carefully take out the folded clippings from under my pillow I have been slowly collecting. The blooms greet me like old friends, their familiar shapes reassuring. Bluebells for constancy. Hawthorn for hope. I only wish that I had more, that the columns hadn't stopped coming with the onset of war. Though, I think I know why now. I clasp my locket tight, the pressed rose petal within still buzzing with the echo of a song.

In my dreams, the woman with silk-spun hair and clear blue eyes wears the same locket, the same flower preserved inside. When I saw her in the press of the crowd below at the ball, she too wore a locket around her neck. She is not just a dream, but a real person.

I join the ranks of Brussels's sleepless population, my tangled thoughts too full to allow me rest. A dashing soldier leading me in a dance, a face mirroring my own, and a garden full of flowers growing fast and thick, then rotting on the vine.

The peppered tattoo of drums and pipes rings throughout the square as I hastily make my morning ablution. The celebratory air is back as soldiers parade through the streets, marching off to the cheers of the city. Young ladies hang out of windows, throwing down rose petals and little favors. I would have liked to have had one more glimpse of Captain Norton, but I am needed and cannot go outside to see the soldiers off. Perhaps it is better that my last memory of him was his warmth, the clean scent of his soap, his hand on my back. No, not my last memory, just my most recent. He will come back. He has to.

By the time my morning duties are finished, the streets are deserted save for a drunkard hiccupping a broken tune, the red rose petals now trampled and bruised. If I were to follow their trail out of Brussels, would I find myself on the battlefield? Would I be greeted with smoke and cannon shot, screams? Would it be like the hellfire that the minister preaches on Sundays? War feels like a world away, something so terrible and nightmarish that it cannot sit shoulder to shoulder with the gabled houses and clean-swept squares of the city.

The family is breakfasting, and aside from some excitement about the ball, it is much the same as any other meal on any other day. The girls are chattering about the soldiers they danced with last night, and Madame is dissecting the guest list. Eugenie looks pensive, and her plate comes back untouched.

"She's pining about her soldier love," Marie confides to Cook. "She has one, you know. I saw them in the hall one evening, and she even gave him a posy at the ball."

It is a strange thing to share a roof with someone, to know love and heartache, but not be able to give each other comfort. I suppose Eugenie has her sisters for solace and would not need me anyway.

That night, long after everyone else has retired, I stare out the window at the orange roofs of Brussels, the boom of cannons ringing in the distance.

Twenty-Seven
CORNELIA

ZINNIA: thoughts of absent friends. Return to me, my love.

Henri and Sophie are both still asleep when I return, the tangled sheet kicked off them from the heat. I climb between them and roll into Henri's chest, Sophie's warm breath on my back. Many of the other regiments have already pushed forward deeper toward Brussels, but we are staying behind to provide relief when it is inevitably needed tomorrow; Armand had told me when we returned. "Come, Colette," he had said, as he helped me dismount, "will you give me a kiss, for a soldier who goes into battle at first light?" I had brushed his lips with a chaste kiss and seen only sadness when I pulled away.

The possibility, however small, that Henri might not return to our bed tomorrow is too terrible to even contemplate. Henri, Sophie, and I…we only just figured out how we all fit together, who we are. How will we go on if one of us is missing? But this is the price of love, that to be able to experience something so sweet, so pure, goes hand in hand with the risk of losing it. So instead of dwelling on the unthinkable, I let my thoughts run where they will, and inevitably, they lead me to the girl at the ball.

The flowers brought me to her, and though I may not know the question, she has the answers. Pity that Armand should have intercepted me before I had a chance to reach her. Is she English, following a soldier like I am? Or Belgian or French perhaps, simply a guest at the ball? Why were the flowers so insistent that I see her? And now that we are at war, I wonder if I shall ever see her again.

From somewhere in the camp, the sound of a pipe playing floats across the tents. There is a shallow breeze that stirs the grass and leaves, yet fails to bring any relief from the heat. Expectation thrums through the atmosphere. I wonder if it is always thus for soldiers who have chosen a life of uncertainty or if the waiting ever grows easier. Because that is all that it is: waiting to die. Whether tomorrow on a field, or years from now on a soft bed surrounded by their children and grandchildren. Waiting, waiting. Trying to find something with which to fill the time. How I wish I had not spent so much of my time fretting over the vanities of life, pushing away love for the sake of my pride. How I wish I had more time.

I awake stiff with scratchy eyes, my side cold. I sit up, frantically patting at the empty sheets. Henri, he's gone. Sophie stirs from her sleep, a small smile touching her lips before her eyes flutter open. "He left," I tell her. "How could he have left without saying anything?"

Sophie props herself up, yawns and stretches, languid as a little cat.

She finds my hands, squeezes. "It's better this way. Let him go without all the tears. He needs to know we will be all right."

I know she's right, but I still hate it. The supply carts have caught up, bringing with them wives and children that may never reunite with their husbands and fathers. Outside, there is an eerie stillness to the camp, empty tents standing like waiting shrouds. The only residents of the camp now are the women and some crying babes. We greet each other with dark-ringed eyes and empty pleasantries as we move about our purgatory.

Sophie fetches us some porridge, and I sit like a helpless child, poking at it with my spoon. She should not have to take care of me, but I find myself listless and melancholy, like the days following Anna's dismissal. When I have eaten all I can stand of the tasteless sludge, Sophie has me help her collect all the linens we can find and bring them on the carts to a stream for washing. "To be ready for when the men return," she tells me.

I rock back on my heels, the water sluicing off my hands. "Haven't they already all the linens they need?"

Sophie's eyes fill with pity. "For the wounded," she says gently. "And the dead."

The linen falls from my hand into the stream, and Sophie quickly fishes it out for me. We are laundering shrouds. One of these sheets may hold the body of… No, I cannot even bring myself to think it.

After we have hung them to dry, we return to the center of camp, and I quickly wish that I still had something to do with my hands.

"I will go mad if I have to sit here and wait."

Sophie watches me pace about. Rocket fire and gun smoke hang in the air, but everyone is making a pretense of keeping busy, pretending that they do not hear the sounds of war. Pretending that all is well.

"This is part of the life, Colette," she tells me.

"That may be, but I don't have to like it," I snap.

"I daresay there are none here who like it." Her voice is even, but I catch the slight wobble of her lips.

I put my arms around her, rest my head on her narrow shoulder. She smells of lavender and lye, comfort. "Of course. You're right, darling Sophie, as you always are."

We sit in silence for some time, each acting like we don't notice the distant sound of explosions carried on the wind.

"Where did you go last night?" she asks after some time has passed. "I awoke, and you weren't there."

There are some things that I cannot share with Sophie, that I don't even understand myself. What would this beautiful, sweet girl think of me if she knew that I can hear the voices of flowers? Her emerald eyes would turn hard and disapproving like Uncle's. She wouldn't let me rest my head on her shoulder or run my fingers down her arm. I have only just learned to open my heart again; I cannot lose her so soon.

When my silence has stretched too thin and too long, she sighs. "I wish you would talk to me," she says. "I wish you trusted me with your secrets."

"I don't know what you mean," I say, though my guilty heart knows very well what she means.

"I don't expect you to tell me everything, but I can see when something is weighing on you, and it has been that way often lately."

I touch the locket at my neck. It has not stopped singing since last night, a low, persistent hum that rivals that of the flowers. "I cannot tell you that which I do not understand."

She shifts her weight, just a little, away from me. The distance is unbearable, so I swallow my pride. "Do you know," I begin, watching a thin plume of smoke thread its away above the horizon, "I used to think that I would never allow myself to fall in love again, not after I lost someone who I thought had taken my heart with them. I thought I had hardened myself, that I was so above such a fickle emotion. Now I wonder if I somehow cursed myself." I pluck at a loose thread on my sleeve, pretend that I don't care that Sophie is watching me. "How…

how am I to know what there is between Henri and me? And how do I tell him what it is?"

Her hand finds mine, and balance is restored. My throat feels hot, my eyes dangerously close to watering.

"Colette, you can say it for what it is. You love Henri. There is no other word to describe the way you look at him, and he you. We both love you. You have not cursed yourself."

Some of my guilt crumbles, only to quickly build back up again. "And I sent him off to battle without so much as a kind word!"

"He knows. Of course he knows."

"And you, Sophie?" I chance a look at her, the beautiful little sprite who has enchanted me completely. "Do you know that I…that I hold you in the highest esteem?"

"You goose," she says, and though her tone is playful, her gaze is anything but. "You aren't nearly so mysterious as you think." She bumps me with her shoulder, and I pull her closer to me.

We sit and wait. My bottom grows sore and stiff, my throat dry. Sophie's gaze is trained on the dirt road that leads toward Mont-Saint-Jean. All of my dreams and hopes have culminated in this moment, and my chest aches with the weight of it. I only want to see Henri's tall frame, his shy smile, as he comes riding back into camp. I want him to tell us that the battle is over, that it was short and without incident, and that he thought of us the whole time. But it grows later, and soon it is raining.

The rain comes in a deluge of unforgiving sheets, bringing with it despair and gloom. It breaks the heat, but it also soaks the ground, turns roads to mud. Everything is wet and miserable, and time slows to an unbearable crawl.

It is a further two days before the rain tapers off. Some men return to camp, giving contradictory accounts. Wellington has retreated. No, he has pressed his flank guard and driven Napoleon back. No, there is hope that the Prussians will yet not make it in time to relieve the English.

The medics enlist all hands to help with the injured, and I spend hours grinding herbs to make into poultices that provide only comfort where real medicine is needed. Whatever sway I hold with flowers, I call upon them, hoping that I am able to heal all of the horrors that come across my table. I am dressing a shrapnel wound when, as if summoned by my yearning thoughts, a smudge of gray and blue appears around the bend in the road. Soon it is joined by another and another, and a wall of soldiers come streaming back into the camp.

Women rush forward, and there is a flurry of reunions. I drop my pestle and race toward the road, nearly slipping in the mud.

"Colette!" Sophie warns, close on my heels.

"Lieutenant Peusol," I gasp to a soldier who is gripping his arm. Blood dots his temple, and he looks back at me, dazed. "Does Lieutenant Peusol live?"

Sophie has caught up, and she takes me by the arm as the soldier mutters something unintelligible and continues limping along. "Colette, don't. He will come back, or he won't. Let these men pass."

But I cannot accept that. Every dirty face, every stumbling form is cause for my heart to stop. "And what if he's fallen? How long should we let him lie on the field, alone?" I stop another one of the men. "Is it over, then? Have the English been repelled?"

He cannot be above eighteen years of age. He looks at me, confused, then almost with pity, even though he is the one with an eye swollen shut and blood on his nose. "No, mademoiselle. It is but one battle, and the fighting even now rages on."

"Thank God, thank God!" A young woman rushes forward and throws her arms around the soldier. I watch as their bodies collide, the way she shudders with grateful tears as his hands come around her, holding her in a desperate embrace.

My own arms ache with the emptiness. I don't begrudge any of these people their reunions, but it should be me. I want it to be me. Before I know what has come over me, I begin walking, shouldering past the sorry stream of soldiers. I know only that I must go to him, that I can no longer wait for fate to show her hand.

"Colette! Wait!" Sophie calls after me as she struggles to catch up.

"I will not be deterred," I tell her, my step unfaltering even as I struggle against the mud and the crush of bodies streaming in the opposite direction.

I feel her hesitation, feel her weighing the risks. But then she is falling into step beside me, and her small hand slides into mine, squeezing tight.

Twenty-Eight
CORNELIA

LOVE-LIES-BLEEDING: hopelessness.

We smell the death in the air long before we crest the ridge overlooking the battlefield.

The rain has stopped, swept away on a cloud so that God himself may stare down and witness the destruction that man has wrought.

And we bear witness as well. All the conflicting reports that made their way to my ears never could have prepared me for what I see now. Below us, thousands of men are spread out like pieces on a chessboard. Each English regiment forms its own little square, and it is a jarring juxtaposition, the orderly grids in the chaos of cannon fire and billowing smoke. How can there still be so much fighting after hours of action?

I clutch Sophie's hand. We are not the only ones who are watching on this ridge. Village women have begun to congregate, one bouncing a baby on her hip, another mumbling a prayer under her breath. Vivandières dash onto the lines, offering water and bandages, dodging fire and then dashing back. Officers with spyglasses confer on horseback. Sophie hails one down, and he regards us with something between contempt and harried disinterest.

"We are looking for the 4th Chasseurs."

I hold my breath. He will point to some little block of men down below, perhaps one on the edges, and he will say *There, there is your soldier. They are victorious and even now are returning.*

But he only draws back, a frown touching his long face. "I would be sending you down to your death if I told you."

Sophie's hand tightens in mine. "Please."

He points, and I follow his finger.

There is nowhere except safe by our side that I want Henri to be, but it certainly wouldn't be in the middle column that is making a desperate push up the opposite ridge. A cannon shot lands perilously close to the formation, sending clumps of earth flying into the air.

"We cannot go down," Sophie says softly.

"But we came all this way. We must find him. Together we can persuade him to leave with us."

Sophie reaches up, takes my chin gently in her hand, bringing my gaze to meet hers. "And have him shot for a deserter? Or have him risk his life when he sees us and becomes distracted?" she asks. "We'd only get in the way, complicate things for him."

She's right. Sophie is always right, though it does not make it any easier. So we watch. Two women on a hill, overlooking the culmination of one man's hunger for absolute power. I heard one of the soldiers say that this would be the end of it, that once Napoleon took his place back on the throne, that there would be no more battles, that there could finally be peace. But war can never lead to peace. There is always a loser, and men's pride will not allow them to go quietly. Besides, what good is peace if all the good men have died?

"It's in God's hands now," Sophie whispers.

I don't accept that. I close my eyes. I don't accept that I have no power. When my door handle rattled in the night in Sussex, I defended myself. When I dreamed of a way out, I drew for my money. When my heart pined after a brooding soldier and a fierce little laundress, I brought them both to my bed. I have sculpted a life for myself through sheer will and determination. So no, this is not in God's hands. I will not cede what little power I hold to an indifferent deity.

I think of the flowers in my mother's garden and the roots that run under the ground. The dirt that I stand on, that these men fight upon. I think about how I have only stood in my own way by not fully embracing the gift of the flowers. How long I spent trying to tamp down anything unusual about myself, hide it from the world. I could have stood up to Uncle, fought to keep Anna at the house. I pretended that it was out of my hands, but I never truly *fought* for Anna. I could have explored what the flowers were to me on any number of occasions, but I was content not to question the way of things, lest I not like what I discovered.

I close my eyes, shut out the battle and chaos. *I am listening now.*

As if they had only been awaiting an invitation, a thousand flowers sweep into my mind. I can smell their sweetness, feel the velvet of their petals as they caress my thoughts. I have always been content just to heed any warnings issued by the flowers, to let them sing their songs in the background of my life, but now I bid them spill their secrets. Now I ask them to show me what they are truly capable of.

"Colette, look."

Sophie's voice pulls me back from far reaches of my mind. Late-afternoon sun is beating down, and I shade my eyes as I look down.

Flowers are blooming. Not just the patches of cowslips and daises scattered about the hill but the entire valley below us. They spring like a geyser from a well, cascading down and flooding the land. Crimson poppies, blue forget-me-nots, lilies, and violets. It looks as if a giant colorful quilt has been aired out and left to dry on the ground, stretching as far as the eye can see. The air hangs heavy with their fragrance and the smell of wet, fertile soil.

"My God," the officer exclaims as his horse prances nervously about.

Birdsong, which had been stilled by the cannon fire, now fills the sky, and I feel as if I am glimpsing some heavenly Garden of Eden, untouched by man. There is such peace, such joy, in a place that should be only darkness and death.

For a moment the fighting stands still, the cannons silent, the bayonets lowered. The soldiers call to one another in wonder, even across the battle lines. These miraculous flowers have connected every man and woman on the field as well as above it. We are bound together as we bear witness to the beauty. Sophie doesn't say anything, but I can feel her intense gaze on me, and it is too late to shield myself or pretend that I am not the cause of what is happening.

My body trembles, feels at once unbearably light and heavy, as if I am rooted to the ground. But like a breath held too long, it cannot last. The brief reprieve over, blooms shrivel and die, receding back into the earth. The mosaic of colors drains away back into brown and muddy greens. Men rub their eyes, unsure if what they have just seen is real or merely a cruel trick of the chaos of the battlefield.

A pain in my head has been building. I feel as if I were being embalmed, my blood drained out and body packed with petals. Everything aches, feels too full. Now the pain crescendos as light floods behind my eyes, and my legs buckle beneath me. I asked the flowers to show me, to aid me, and they did. But at what cost? The earth rushes up to catch me, a cradle of dirt and petals.

Twenty-Nine

LIJSBETH

SAINFOIN: agitation.
My mind cannot be settled without word from thee.

The first soldiers return in the early afternoon, and with them, a swirling cloud of rumors and conflicting accounts. I watch out the front parlor window with Eugenie under the pretense of keeping her company as she awaits news of her sweetheart. But really, I am searching for a comely, good-humored face, a pair of blue eyes.

Eugenie has aged, grown thin and wan over the course of only three days. She barely eats, barely does anything besides stare out the window, only taking a little broth when Madame's fussing becomes too much for her. She drapes herself on the chaise with an open book of poetry tented on her lap. Wistful, beautiful. What a privilege it is to indulge in lovesickness. What a luxury to feel so deeply and be able to slip away from the world with no consequences.

A long sigh escapes her. "It's Major Reeves, though you won't know who that is," she tells me when she catches me watching her.

I know which one Major Reeves is. He's a very handsome man, with thick black hair and a quick smile under his mustachio. But he also has humorless eyes, and once when he thought no one was looking, I saw him pocket one of Monsieur's pearl snuffboxes.

Eugenie gives another wistful sigh as she drums an elegant finger on the windowsill. "If only he had given me some sort of pledge, left me with some understanding. Mama thinks that he is too low for me. She wants to arrange an agreement with the Richmonds' nephew, but I'm set on a love match. How I envy you, Lijsbeth," she says with a sad smile. "Your life is so simple. You know exactly where you belong and do not have to tax yourself with decisions of the heart."

My hand only falters slightly as I thread an iris into my arrangement. For all her kindness, sometimes I think Eugenie only deigns to speak to me because I cannot say anything back. She sees me as a blank page on which she can write whatever she wants.

"That's lovely," she says, finally coming away from the window and inspecting the flowers I've been arranging. "The petals are like moonbeams. I've never seen flowers so delicate before. They look as if they were painted from watercolors."

The irises do look like moonbeams, I suppose, though I chose them because they are the silver-blue of Captain Norton's eyes when he whispered my name to me on the gallery.

The flowers hold her attention for but a few moments, and then she is back to staring out the window, and I am left with my own melancholy thoughts, the flowers weeping in my stead.

Around noon, a boy brings news of a French victory. Madame becomes hysterical because Napoleon's arrival in the city is imminent, and there are no horses to be found, all of them having been commandeered for the troops. All the bravado and talk of English valor at the ball has apparently been forgotten.

Cook sends me to the market to see about a leg of mutton for some broth for Madame's nerves. A handful of carts display their wares, but most have shuttered or been towed away. A little boy runs through the cobbled square, carrying a fluttering pennant with the bee emblem of Napoleon. Someone shouts a curse at him from a window before slamming it shut. I am debating if I had not better just return empty-handed, when a carriage comes careening through the square, horses frothing at the bit, whipped on by a frenzied driver. I only just manage to avoid being run down and catch a glimpse of a coat of arms on the door before it goes barreling past. Soon another follows it, this time an open-air gig driven by a hatless gentleman. "To Ghent!" he cries as he passes. "Get you to Ghent if you want to save yourself from Napoleon!"

It all seems rather dramatic, but then the roar of a cannon sends me running back the way I came.

I return empty-handed to find that Madame is dosed with laudanum anyway and sleeping. Most of the household has gone next door to watch the developments from the rooftop. If there were horses to be found, Madame and her family would be even now clattering down the street with the rest of society, without so much as a backward glance at their servants.

I roam the house, walking on carpets that are usually forbidden to me, letting my fingers trail over tables that I have no business touching. The flowers in the vases quiver as I pass, the locket at my neck burning. Outside, the cannons continue to roar, as soft shafts of afternoon light filter in through the windows.

Marie is making herself comfortable in the parlor, feet propped on old Madame Dubois's gout stool, eating Hippolyte's bonbons. "What?" she asks innocently. "Soon Napoleon will enter the city and either kill us all or free us from servitude. Why let all this go to waste?"

I leave her to her bonbons. My eyes are tired, my heart heavy. Even used to as little sleep as I am, the last two days have tested me beyond measure. I could sleep in any one of the family's feather beds, but habit leads me to climb the narrow stairs and fall into my own cot. Not ten miles from here, men are fighting for their lives, among them Captain Norton, bravely rallying his men. As I drift to sleep, I fancy I can smell wet earth and sweet violet blossoms, even as cannons ring in my ears.

Thirty

CORNELIA

PERSIMMON: bury me amid nature's beauties.

"Colette! Colette, wake up!"

Slowly, I crack my eyes open and draw in a shuddering breath that feels like stepping back into my body after having been floating in the ether. Sophie is kneeling beside me, her fingers curled into my arm so tightly that it eclipses any lingering pain in my head. When she sees me awaken, she lets out a long, slow hiss of air.

"I thought you had died," she says, a quaver in her voice. "How dare you give me a fright like that."

"Goose," I tell her, though it barely comes out as a croak. But then I remember where we are and why, and the smile dies on my lips. We are at the front lines of battle, and Henri is still somewhere down below, fighting for his life. I struggle to sit up.

"It is over," she tells me. "The battle has been decided."

"Can it really be so?" I think of the flowers that carpeted the valley and for a moment my heart soars. I stopped the fighting. I brought an end to a battle which will decide the war. It is over now.

But then I watch the smoke clearing below us, and my foolish notions are dispelled. Whatever miracle I conjured with the flowers was not enough to do anything of any import. It was simply a brief reprieve, and now the land lies littered with bodies of the dead and dying. It was too little, much too late. What hubris I must possess to have thought, even for a moment, that I could sway the course of history.

The women and officers who had shared our vantage point with us have already left. Sophie is biting her lip, and I finally notice the tears that are streaking her face. "Sophie?" Has she had some word about Henri somehow? Does she know something that I don't?

"It is not just the battle that is over. It is everything. The officer said that the allied forces have cut the Imperial Guard down—cut them all down, like wheat with a thrasher!" Her face is drawn, her lip bloody, and I feel my own heart sink.

"No," I say, unable to accept what she is telling me. "Surely it cannot be so."

"It is truly over," she repeats, rocking with her arms around her knees. "Napoleon might be dead or captured for all that we know!"

I care little about Napoleon, even if Sophie believed that he would usher in a great new age for France. In fact, I think I hate him. I only care for one man.

"We must go down and find Henri," I tell Sophie.

Sophie helps me up, and we leave our vantage on the ridge and go down together. Peace has not brought an end to the chaos. Everywhere Death has tainted the land. Already scavengers have come, while blood is still warm in the bodies of the dead. They pry boots off bodies, inspect medals and sabers. A man in a tattered coat and old tricorne squats beside a body and takes out a hammer, smashing the teeth right out of the skull.

British soldiers, bloodthirsty for revenge, mercilessly cut down any French soldier they still see.

"Don't look," I tell Sophie as much as myself. "Don't look."

Would that this was a nightmare that I could wake up from, that one day I could forget the smell and the way my boots slip in the blood and entrails of the fallen. But everything is sharp and clear and all too real, imprinting itself on my mind forever.

On the hill everything looked smaller of scale, contained. But here in the midst of the wreckage of battle, the dead and dying stretch all the way around us, a never-ending sea of suffering.

Sophie and I agree that we must separate if we are to have any chance of finding Henri. I send her back toward the ridge, while I go in what I believe is the direction the officer on the hill had pointed.

One of the women from the hill has already come down before us and is sobbing into a pile of bloody clothes. It is only when I'm closer that I see the entrails and limbs that were once a body. Acid-sharp bile rises in my throat, and I heave onto the ground.

Everywhere there are men, dead and dying, sometimes only a breath separating one from the other. A hand grips me by the ankle, and I shake it free. I can't stop. I can't look. "Please! Please...help me." The voice is thick and choked with blood. What can I do? What aid can I give to a man who is already halfway to death? I cannot believe that I ever thought I was a healer, that I could help anyone in real need. What can a salve or a tincture do for a man who is cut open, his innards spilling out?

I stumble on. There is too much. Too much blood, too much silence. Too much beauty in the world, too much ugliness. A horse wanders past me, riderless, its bridle trailing through the carnage. When I call to it, it spooks and takes off at a gallop.

Minutes pass—or perhaps it is hours—and I regret parting from Sophie. She is fierce, but she is small, and the scavenging men would have no compunction in taking advantage of a lone woman. What if Henri is not even here? What if he is already safe back at camp, looking for us there? The idea gives me a giddy sort of hope. He will take us in his arms, squeezing tight and kissing our heads. "My girls," he will say in his low, rough voice. "What were you doing all the way at Mont-Saint-Jean while I was here waiting for you?" The happiness will be enough to make us laugh, and together we will plan our next chapter.

"Colette!"

I am pulled out of my castle in the air by a very real voice calling my name.

Sophie emerges through the gathering dusk, resplendent on a white horse, hair loose and tumbling about her shoulders. I think that Death himself must have stepped aside for her, for despite a swipe of dirt across her cheek, she is untouched by the mayhem of the battlefield.

Sliding from the saddle, she lands in front of me, throwing her arms about me.

I return her embrace, tight and desperate. I never should have brought her here. What separates the woman in my arms from the limbs and bodies all around us? She is made of blood and bone, dreams and love. How terribly fragile we are, how precious! I will hold her forever, never let her go. So long as I live, I will ensure nothing comes near her beating heart.

Pulling back, she inspects me, her brows creased with worry. She has not found him, but I must believe that to be good news. He may yet be alive.

"Come," I tell her, reaching for the horse's bridle, "we should go." I cannot ask her to stay here, not when shots are still being fired in last, futile bursts.

But Sophie does not move. "We don't leave until we find him." Her chin is jutted, her emerald eyes hard and determined.

My brave, beautiful girl. I nod, inwardly relieved that she has not given up on him. I let the horse go. Our hands find each other's, and we continue picking our way through the carnage.

Men in tattered coats and no coats at all lean on each other, staggering back to their camps. Any moment Henri will appear. He will be battered and bloody, weary and shaken, but he will be alive. Sophie and I will clean his wounds and bathe him, lay him down and nurse him. He will wince with pain, but when he looks at us, there will be fire in his eyes, and we will know that he will be our Henri once more.

It feels as if night should be drawing in, but the sun still sits low on the horizon, indifferent to the bloodshed below. I suppose not much time has passed, though who is to say? Entire lives have been drawn out and held in thrall of a single breath, only to scatter on the wind. The smell of gunpowder still hangs in the air, but it is beginning to clear. What torture to have to look in the face of each body, what shame we feel when we sob in relief that it is not Henri.

We should not find him. The odds are against us, the sheer number of men, the blood and confusion. Yet when we have nearly reached the opposite ridge, Sophie grabs my arm.

"Colette, look."

Sophie's voice is quiet. I don't want to look down because I know what I am going to see. I swallow past the hard lump in my throat and force myself to lower my eyes.

I let out a little cry as the world shatters around me. His beauty transcends death. I think of the death masks of the great philosophers in Uncle's library, the alabaster white, the sightless eyes. They look vulgar in comparison to my beautiful Henri.

With the smell of death in your nose and blood wicking up through the hem of your dress, the world becomes a darkly uncanny place. Every trilling bird cry, every blade of trampled grass is magnified, brought into sharp focus. A tiny yellow flower bobs in the breeze, just past the reach of Henri's outstretched palm. His hand lies beside the flower, as if at any moment he would awaken and pluck the blossom. I cannot yet comprehend the number of souls lost on this field, the number that may be living still, yet will always carry the scars of this wicked day. But this beautiful man and his untouched hand with calloused fingers, and the bloom that grows just out of reach…that is what cracks my heart and utterly breaks me.

The man with the hammer and bucket of teeth is clambering toward us, and Sophie flies at him, shrieking and swatting at him until he is repelled.

My vision narrows to the tiny yellow flower. Perfect and sweet, a gift of the earth. I am a vessel of sorrow, my tears the water that spills forth. And as I weep, I can think only of the soft brush of Henri's lips, the love that he selflessly offered me. Every half-formed truth of my being, every secret desire unfurls and blossoms. I could paint flowers every hour of every day for the rest of my life and none would match the modest beauty of this one little cowslip amid all the death.

Sophie's quiet sobs have subsided, and she is saying something, though I can barely hear her through my heartbreak.

I look down at my feet where but a moment ago there was mud and trampled grass, only to find that a blanket of flowers has sprouted. What occurred on the hill was but a fraction of what happens now. Every manner of flower springs forth from the earth: yellow cowslip, yes, but also thorny roses, willow boughs, and tangled anemones. The flowers have no regard for the time of year or clime, they only grow and grow, spreading as fast as fire. My empty hands clench around something, and I find that I am clasping a staff of lilies, an offering to the dead, a symbol of peace that is too little and comes much too late. The air fills with perfume, but it is not the sweet scent of a garden on a hazy summer day. It is the stench of rotting fruit on the vine, the decay that followed me these past weeks as we marched toward Brussels.

The valley has grown eerily quiet again, scavengers pausing in their morbid work, the women leaving off in their weeping, as all watch this garden of death bloom around them. There is no disguising that I am the center of this extraordinary phenomenon: the flowers spread from my feet like a bottle of spilled wine, staining everything in their path.

A party of soldiers has come to a stop, their horses pawing the ground and whickering nervously. One of the men alights, approaches me with hand outstretched as if I were the skittish animal.

"Colette, what are you doing here?" Armand has stripped himself of his French colors. His face is wan and tired, but he appears unhurt. He whispers at me as if he is afraid of being overheard. "What is this? Are you all right?"

He tries to take me into his arms, but I push him away. It's not him that I want. It's not him that should be here. Should I not be joyful that my friend has lived? Should I not be grateful that any man has been spared the bayonet today? Yet all I feel is a dark, bitter anger curling through my veins that Armand lives when Henri lies dead at my feet.

The flowers twist upward, spreading fast and blanketing the dead in velvet-soft petals. Vines climb and curl over Henri, reclaiming his body and cradling it more gently than any weeping mother could. When Armand sees that I am the cause, he scrambles away from me as if I were a leper and mounts his horse.

But all the flowers will not bring Henri back. They will not cleanse the blood nor restore the flesh. He is gone, dead from a bullet wound in his side. I know, because the flowers show me. They gather up his memories, his dreams, and bring them back to me through their racing roots. I see him leading his column, shouting at his men to charge. Henri has long since lost his horse and now fights on foot. The drums are beating the *pas de charge*, and there is a deafening chorus of *Vive l'Empereur!* They crest the ridge, an unforgiving volley of British fire meeting them. The man beside him cries out as he is hit, and Henri stops, tries to pull him up. But it is too late for his fellow guard. Henri clambers back up to his feet, levels his rifle at the enemy, only for a bullet to catch him in the side as he turns at the last moment. I see a thousand shards of memories explode through his mind: the bird seller in his village, sneaking off to watch military parades as a young boy, Sophie and I splashing in the stream, passionate kisses stolen in the early morning, light shafting through the tent flaps and dappling our bare skin. I see him fall, never to get up again.

I don't care that he was brave. I don't care that he died fighting for something bigger than himself. What good does that do me? What of Sophie? As my rage slowly subsides to bitter tears, so too do the flowers shrivel and die back, leaving me only with my empty arms and hollow heart.

I shall never love again.

Thirty-One

LIJSBETH

LILY OF THE VALLEY: return of happiness.

"Lijsbeth, will you fetch my wrap?"

Eugenie has finally given up her post at the window, her eyes bright, color in her cheeks. I bring her the wrap, and she takes me by the arm.

"They're back," she squeals, leaning into me as if we were old friends. "We must go look for him."

She does not need to convince me, for I have my own reason for wishing to be there as the soldiers return. We hurry outside and watch the sorry parade that comes limping back through the streets of Brussels. Some of the injured ride on carts, others are carried on stretchers or lean on their compatriots. There are no drums this time, no fluttering standards or rose petals. The women that watch out of the windows have no songs left to sing, their breath having been spent praying for their lovers to return.

"Is it over, then?" Eugenie rushes to ask a soldier with a bandage about his head. "Have we won?"

"Buonaparte has been repelled!" he exclaims. "The Prussians came in from the flank, and by Jove, we've sent the little man scurrying back to Paris!"

This information does little to satisfy Eugenie. "And the 82nd? What news of the 82nd?"

I don't hear the man's answer, for at that moment, I see my captain coming down the street.

He appears like the sun breaking free of the clouds on a stormy day. When he sees me, his face opens into a brilliant smile that even the dirt and mud cannot disguise. He quickens his pace, then runs the rest of the way and scoops me up, mindless of the sling on his arm. My heart flies up into the cloudy sky, my burdens falling away from me like broken shackles.

"Lijsbeth. My own, dear Lijsbeth."

I bury my face in his neck, the scruff of his unshaven jaw prickly and real, oh so very real, against my own skin. The rough wool of his coat smells of smoke and earth and just a little of his soap. Even my most desperate, wildest dreams could not have prepared me for the sheer joy and relief of this moment. Yet I have no right to him. There is a family back in England that is sick with worry for news of their son, their brother, and perhaps even their fiancé. And I, a maid with nothing to my name, am the one holding him. I am the one whose tears of relief are flowing down my face. He holds me tightly as if he is drowning, squeezing my ribs so tight that they feel as if they would break, and oh, I would welcome it. Break me until I am nothing but blood and bone, love and flowers. I know that I am just the first person that he recognized, that this doesn't mean to him what it means to me. But what does it matter? It *is* me.

He loosens his hold on me, but only a little. His face is alight with wonder. "Do you know, I saw you. It will sound mad, but I saw you, out there in the smoke and cannon fire. An angel in white, carrying a staff of lilies."

His finger runs down my jaw, and I lean into his touch. I don't know what he's speaking of, but I don't care. I am near him, and that is all that matters.

"And the most incredible thing happened. I don't know how, but..." He searches for words, but I hardly hear him. My arms are still twined round his waist, my cheek against his chest. I could listen to his heart beating forever. "There were flowers," he continues. "Everywhere. I would think it was the result of some sort of battle mirage, if not for the fact that other men told me they witnessed the same thing. Why, just as the French were charging, the ground seemed to erupt with flowers. I never saw anything like it. I—"

Whatever he was about to say is lost as Eugenie finally catches up to us, her shawl falling from her shoulders. "Captain Norton! You've come back to us!"

She stops when she sees me, a faint crease in her brow, but I cannot bring myself to step away from my captain. "What news?" she asks.

"Vanquished," he says, his face a picture of weary triumph. "We have vanquished the French, and Napoleon is defeated."

Another soldier sees us and breaks from the procession to come join us. "Did he tell you? Our own captain is a true hero. He ran under enemy fire to drag a fallen comrade back behind the line. Saved the man's life and showed true valor, our captain did."

Captain Norris looks embarrassed, clears his throat uncomfortably. "It was only what any other man would have done," he says.

"And Major Reeves?" Eugenie asks the man. "Does he live? Was he very brave?"

The soldier demurs that he hasn't heard about any particulars but is certain he saw the major and can confidently say he lives. This seems to be enough for Eugenie who sags in relief, her eyes swimming with happy tears.

Throughout this exchange, Captain Norton has not left my side, though he has loosened his embrace, and I wonder if it's because of Eugenie.

"Oh, but your arm, Captain!" Eugenie says, finally noticing the sling. "Won't you come inside where we can tend to you? Take tea with us. Mama will want to serve you herself."

Even now, when blood soaks his clothes, and the air hangs heavy with the acrid smell of smoke, propriety must be observed, social niceties extended.

"You are too kind, but I must decline. I am… I have other matters to tend to." I look up to catch his steady gaze trained on me. My stomach floods with warmth.

Eugenie's mouth tightens, but she manages a smile. "Of course. You will join us for dinner as soon as you are recovered. We will be quite eager to have the hero of Waterloo. And when Major Reeves returns, we shall make a party of it."

He gives a gracious nod, and I wait for Eugenie to leave us alone, but of course, I am not to be given such a consideration. "Lijsbeth, come along," Eugenie says, her hand outstretched. Her smile is warm, but her tone reminds me that I am still a servant.

Reluctantly, I step away from my captain's side, immediately feeling empty and lost.

"Actually, I would beg a moment with Lijsbeth. Please," he says to Eugenie. Before she can respond, he's guiding me to a quiet spot out of the traffic and next to an empty cart. Cupping my face with his good hand, he looks into my eyes, and it's all I can do to return his gaze without melting right into the ground. "Circumstances have not been kind to us," he tells me, his breath warm on my ear. "But there will be time now." His gaze drops to my lips, lingers there, and he seems to be debating something with himself.

He seems to finally break out of whatever spell he was under and gives me a regretful smile. And with that rather cryptic message, he steps back and executes as low a bow as his arm will allow, before rejoining the stream of soldiers and disappearing around the corner.

Thirty-Two

CORNELIA

HEMLOCK: all is lost. Death.

Dusk draws close, and lanterns bob across the field as scavengers continue their grotesque search for trophies, and gravediggers come to bury the dead. We have no need of the latter's services; the flowers reclaimed Henri, drew him back down into the earth. He is safe from the scavengers now, guarded by thorns in his hallowed tomb. It is a cold comfort.

"Where are you going?" Sophie calls to my retreating back. "Camp is back the other way. We need to get back before the British come for prisoners."

"I cannot go back, not when Henri will not be there." I know that Sophie is in pain, too, that I am only bruising an already broken heart. "Don't look at me like that," I say, my voice hoarse.

"Colette, please."

But I cannot go back to that camp. I knew it the moment I saw Henri's lifeless eyes, felt his cold hand. All my hopes and dreams died in this valley of blood and dirt. I should have known better.

Didn't I learn anything after Anna left? I thought that I could open my heart, love, but just like Anna, Henri abandoned me.

There is only one thing for me, and that is in Brussels. The remaining flowers on the field are no longer voices humming quietly in the back of mind as they used to be; now they scream at me, urge me on like a reckless rider whipping a horse. They want me to find *her*, the girl from the ball.

Sophie hurries her step, places her hand on my arm. She is warm, but even the warmest touch cannot thaw a frozen heart. "Where will you go?"

"Does it matter?" My freedom should be sweet: after all, I have no guard anymore, nothing to keep me tethered to the army. How cruel an irony it is to finally be free.

The obstinate set of Sophie's jaw tells me the answer before she does. "I'm coming with you."

"Sophie, no." I stop, distancing her with my hands on her shoulders. "What I must do, I must do alone."

"I loved him, too," she says, her hands fisting into her skirt.

"Perhaps you did, but not so deeply as me." It is a cruel blow, but the cruelty feels good. Anything besides the aching emptiness feels good. I turn and continue through the carnage, following the mass exodus of soldiers and prisoners streaming toward Brussels.

Sophie's footsteps stop, and for a moment I am swept with the urge to go back and take her in my arms. But even if I wanted to, the flowers are drawing me along, giving me no peace until I follow them. *This way this way this way*, they sing.

The road is clogged with soldiers and horses, carts of the injured and bodies being transported for burial elsewhere. I walk alone with my thoughts for some time, until I hear Sophie jogging to catch up with me. "You are like a bad penny," I tell her crossly.

"Maybe, but I know better than to let you make rash decisions when you're in pain. Be vexed all you like, but I'm coming with you. Besides, the English will be looking for prisoners," Sophie says, lowering her voice as she takes my arm.

"What need have they of two women? Besides, I speak very good English. They will not even know that we are French."

Sophie doesn't look convinced. "You think that as long as you tilt your chin and take on that lady air of yours, they'll tip their hats and let you be on your way. But these are men who saw their friends fall today, are still bleeding from French bayonets."

I pick up my step, refusing to waste my time exchanging barbs with her.

She matches my pace, remarkably fast for someone so small. "You are fickle, Colette. Only an hour ago you were holding me as if you couldn't bear to ever let me go, your eyes so full of love that I thought we should be closer than ever. And now, even after all the death and loss, you would leave me behind."

I tuck my chin down, pretend that her words don't sting me like nettles, and plow ahead. I hate that she is right, and it only proves the more that I am unworthy of her. If I keep moving forward, if I lose myself in the overpowering stench of bodies and the overlap of voices, I can outrun the guilt and overpowering grief. I can give myself over to becoming no more than a leaf in a current.

But Sophie will not let me go easily. "Colette! I know you can hear me."

The sound of horses approaching spares me from responding. Not frightened horses wandering riderless through the field but horses being guided directly toward us. A handful of riders draw up beside us, a lantern held aloft against the gathering dusk. Suddenly the road is empty, all the soldiers and carts far away, leaving us alone.

The riders greet us in French, but their red coats and English accents give them away. A tall, thin man with dark side-whiskers is the first to speak. "You are with the army, yes?"

Sophie spits on the ground.

The men exchange looks, and I move to put Sophie behind me. I know that look in their eyes. The officer signals to his men, and before we can run, they are sweeping us up onto their mounts.

Sophie puts up a fight, scratching and kicking. "Hellcat!" exclaims the man with the side-whiskers. He chuckles, easily pinning her arms, but her eyes are filled with fire. As for me, I have no fight left in me. I only hope that they do not hurt Sophie.

Another rider joins us. "What's this?" he asks. His voice is rich, deep. Familiar. But in the dark, I cannot make out more than a high-cheekboned profile and dark hair.

"Two camp followers," explains the first officer. "Out past their bedtimes."

The new man draws up nearer, and the others rein in their horses in deference to his unspoken authority.

"And you think to have a little fun before tucking them into bed?"

There is some good-humored laughter from our captors. But the man's gaze never wavers from me, and the poppies at the side of the road are screeching in warning.

"This one," he says, pointing a gloved hand at me. "Bring her to the city. Blücher and the Prussians are on a bloodthirsty spree, and I want her alive. You're not to touch her, though. Do you understand?"

"Yes, Major" comes the grumbled chorus. "And the other?" one of the men asks, gesturing to Sophie. She has gone pale, motionless, as she watches the situation unfold.

The major shrugs, already wheeling his horse about. "I've no use for that one."

A jagged cry escapes my throat, but it's no use. The last thing I see of Sophie are her wide, frightened eyes as her captor clamps a hand over her mouth, and then I am borne away, carried in the opposite direction.

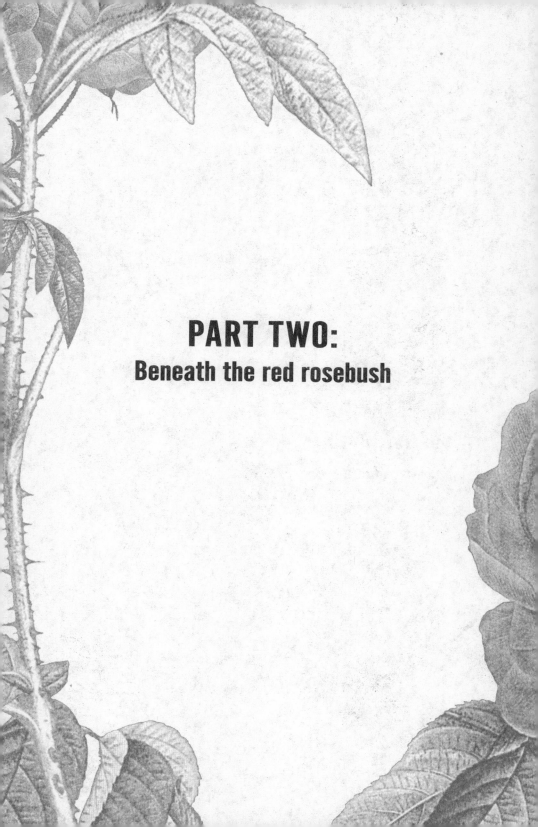

PART TWO:
Beneath the red rosebush

Fade, flow'rs! fade, Nature will have it so;
'Tis but what we must in our autumn do!
And as your leaves lie quiet on the ground,
The loss alone by those that lov'd them found;
So in the grave shall we as quiet lie,
Miss'd by some few that lov'd our company;
But some so like to thorns and nettles live,
That none for them can, when they perish, grieve.

Edmund Waller

Thirty-Three
LIJSBETH

PETUNIA: anger and resentment. Revenge shall be mine.

A slaughter has occurred, and our little lives go on just as before. Contrary to Marie's predictions, nothing has changed. Napoleon did not enter the city on laurels and free all the servants, ushering a new era of enlightenment and equality. This was not a revolution but one last strangled cry of a desperate tyrant. I still wake before the sun rises, hauling buckets of water into the kitchen. I still go to the flower market, though the squares and avenues are full of men awaiting surgery, and I must pick my way carefully through the sea of stretchers and blankets that fill the city. I still wait with bated breath as I go about my work for a glimpse of my captain.

Though he made no grand declaration of love or promises on his return, Captain Norton is alive, and that must be enough for me. Any enthusiasm on his part to see me was surely the result of a temporary rush of goodwill after surviving the battle. He will return to his homeland, and I must content myself with the memories of our dance and the way he held me so tenderly.

It is just Marie and I in the house today, and old Madame Dubois upstairs sleeping away. Eugenie and her sisters have donned aprons and gone out into the streets to assist the wounded, tearing strips of linens, serving tea, and reading books aloud. It feels wrong to go about my work when there are men still dying right outside the door, but the house must still be run, and pretty shows of charity are reserved only for the young ladies.

Marie has been throwing me sly glances all afternoon as I cut roses in the kitchen, and when she finally goes to dust in the parlor, I breathe a little easier. Madame is holding a dinner tonight for the remaining officers and their wives, and I work quickly, in case Captain Norton will be here.

"Lijsbeth, come quick," Marie says breathlessly, poking her head through the doorway. "There's a dead mouse in the cabinet in the parlor giving off a foul air, and you're the only one small enough to crawl in and get it." Marie gives me an impatient scowl. "Well, don't just stand there staring!"

Even though Madame has told Marie time and again that I'm not to do other chores, if I'm the only one that can get the mouse, then it will have to be me. I reluctantly set aside the roses and follow her to the large cabinet in the parlor. She steps back and gestures inside. "Go on, then."

I don't smell anything, but Marie is holding her nose as if she might expire on the spot. It doesn't feel right, but I duck inside, eager to be done with it. The cabinet is dark and warm, much too warm. Marie could have fit easily in here, but I have fallen for her trick to do her dirty work. I take a deep breath in, but there is no foul odor. Instead, there is the whiff of soap, and under that, sweat. And that is when I realize that I'm not alone. The handle clicks behind me, and my breaths start coming shallow and fast. She's locked me inside. I bang my hands against the door, but it's locked fast.

"No need for all that," says a masculine voice. "Marie said you were shy but willing enough."

The man chuckles. It is a cold, unpleasant sound with no trace of humor in it. "Major Reeves," he says. "You probably do not remember me, but I saw you the night of the ball. You looked so very pretty in your blue frock, with the candlelight shining on your hair. Captain Norton monopolized your time, but I vowed I would avail myself of your company at the first opportunity."

I need to tell him that there's been a mistake, a terrible mistake, but my throat is tight, and my words won't come out. A strangled grunt is the most I can manage. A hand roams up my leg, hot breath on my neck. I have no knife to protect myself.

He murmurs something that he probably thinks is charming or reassuring, but I hardly hear him. It's hot inside, too hot. I close my eyes, try to get a full breath. Life is not fair. It has never been fair, and it is a lesson that I learned long ago. But it is as if the true depth of the injustices of the world have finally become clear. The air clogs with the smell of roses, overpowering and thick.

I am not the only one who notices the sudden onslaught of scent.

"What is that?" Major Reeves pulls back from me. "I can't breathe. There's—there's something about my neck."

He is gagging, clutching at his neck. In my mind I see the thorny vine winding about him, see the way the dagger-sharp thorns pierce his skin, drawing blood. The man before me is not just Major Reeves but also Isidore. He is every man who has ever taken a liberty with a woman, who has thought only of his pleasure and not the girl that he has inflicted pain upon. He is the embodiment of all that is corrupt in his sex.

It is coming from me, though I could not say how. I can feel it, growing from some deep, hidden place within me.

"Help—" he gasps, his words swallowed by a desperate gurgling sound.

I couldn't help him if I wanted to. My hands are behind my back, my nails digging into the wood of the cabinet's door. But it's not helplessness that keeps me from reaching out, because I don't feel helpless. I feel strangely powerful, and despite whatever is happening, it sends a thrill through me to know that I am the cause of it.

Just when I think that there can be no air left in his chest, there are clipped footsteps and the rattle of a key. "Really, Marie, I don't know what you think is—"

The door swings open, and I fall out, Major Reeves behind me, his hands still clutching at his neck. My eyes squinch tight against the flood of light in the parlor. I can think nothing except that he will surely die if the vine is not cut. But when I am finally able to open my eyes again, there is no vine or roses, only pricks of crimson blood that dot his throat, as if some invisible thorns have pierced him. His face is purple, his eyes bulging, as he takes a gasping breath. I scramble up away from him.

Madame Dubois stands with the key in her hand, her eyebrows flying up to her graying roots. "Major! Are you all right! What in heaven's name has happened?"

Even if he could speak, I doubt the major would be able to explain what has just occurred. Slowly, his color returns, his breathing becoming more even. He takes a few more rasping breaths, then stumbles away, upsetting a table on his way out.

Madame watches in wonder, mouth open. Finally, she drags her gaze to me, a horrid sort of understanding passing over her face. "Lijsbeth! What is the meaning of this?" She knows that I cannot answer, and indeed I give her no reply. "I did not think you capable of such licentiousness, especially not after all my charity. Alone with an officer! I wonder that Madame van den Berg did not warn me about you."

I want to tell her that it's not what it looks like, but even if I had the words, what exactly *is* it? Whatever just happened was surely caused by me, but I am completely lost as to how or why.

Eugenie steps out from behind her mother, her face very pale, her eyes brimming with unshed tears. She is still in her apron from tending to the injured soldiers in the street, still pristine aside from a swipe of blood on the skirt. I watch as her heart breaks right in front of me, betrayal flowing into anger, then unspeakable sadness, before she turns and flees.

Madame is giving me a droning lecture about the indecency of my behavior. I do not think that my shame could be any greater, but then there is the sound of voices, and Eugenie has returned with Captain Norton. She catches my eye, triumphant but sad. It is the first time I have seen the captain since his return. I thought that perhaps we would come across each other in the house at some point, snatch a few lovely moments of quiet privacy with each other. My stomach turns over on itself, and I wish that I was anywhere else, even back at the van den Berg house. Anywhere but here, under the captain's piercing blue gaze.

"Is everything all right?" Captain Norton asks, quickly surveying the upset table and cabinet door standing ajar. I turn away so that he cannot see my face. What would be worse, that he believes me to have been compromised with the major, or that I have some strange and unnatural power that caused vines to grow from my mind?

"Nothing to concern yourself with, Captain," Madame says shortly.

"Lijsbeth was caught with Major Reeves in the cabinet!" Marie is giddy with the excitement of it all.

"Marie!" Madame scolds, but the damage has already been done. Eugenie has begun to look faint again, and Captain Norton assists her to the chaise. I watch them as I wonder why Marie doesn't like me, why at every opportunity she has gone out of her way to see me fail. As if reading my mind, she slants me a superior look.

"Before you came, it was my job to do the flowers. You showed up, and everything was handed to you. Now I'm made to do all the dirty and rough tasks, with no hope of moving up."

I stare at her. That's all? It's hard to imagine Marie surrounded by flowers or even having an eye for beauty at all. She seems determined to see only the ugliness in the world and to spread it.

"And if I were the one doing the flowers, it would have been me that had caught Captain Norton's eye," she continues, her wistful tone turning hard.

I steal a glance at the captain, who, along with Madame Dubois, is leaned over Eugenie. He seems determined not to acknowledge me, his body pointedly turned away as he speaks in low, soothing tones to Eugenie.

"Now you'll be ruined, and he'll want nothing to do with you," Marie continues.

"Girls."

We both stand up straighter at Madame's voice, though I feel as if my knees might give out at any moment.

"Marie, return to the kitchen. Lijsbeth, go upstairs and gather your things. You are going back to the van den Berg house immediately. I don't care how good your work is, I will not tolerate this sort of indecency under my roof. You…you are a *harlot*."

My stomach knots further. As soon as it becomes a reality, I regret thinking that I would rather be there than here. I can't go back, not for anything in the world. What if Marie somehow pieces together that Isidore was the father and tells him? Then what will happen to me? Through all these racing thoughts, knowing that I've compromised myself in Captain Norton's eyes is somehow the worst part. He will return to England, and the only memory that we shared will be tarnished. And without that, what did we have?

At this, Captain Norton finally stands from where he had been administering salts to Eugenie. He looks between Madame and me, his usually good-humored face grave and serious. "I take exception with that language, Madame."

Madame's mouth drops open, and it would be comical if not for the fact that my future is hanging precariously in the balance.

"And furthermore," the captain continues, "it is not necessary to turn Lijsbeth out."

Madame draws herself up. "Are you presuming to tell me how to run my household, Captain?"

"Madame, I would never. But you see, I have an interest in this particular maid."

"You and everyone else," mutters Marie. Madame looks skeptical.

"Does Madame van den Burg have any claim on Lijsbeth? Any outstanding debt?" he asks. His posture is casual, one arm in a sling, the other lightly resting on the hilt of his saber, but he exudes a quiet sort of power that has us all under his spell.

Madame huffs. "Well, not that I know of, but—"

"Never mind," he says before she can finish. "I don't care if she does." I cannot explain the sensation that comes over me when Captain Norton trains his beautiful eyes on me, the smile that lights up his face. He comes to stand before me, taking my hands in his own.

"What are you doing?" Madame asks, voicing my very own question.

"Why, isn't it obvious? I'm offering for her. I want to marry Lijsbeth."

He turns to me, his blue eyes dancing. "You'll beg my pardon for not asking you first. *Would* you like to be my wife?"

My broad smile must be answer enough, because he returns it with one of his own. "Good," he says. "Very good." He is still holding my hand in his, his thumb lightly grazing the smooth skin under my wrist.

Marie's anger seethes off her like steam from a kettle, while Madame is at a complete loss for words. "Captain, I really... that is...you can't think to..." Madame's gaze sweeps about the room, then lowers her voice to a hiss. "She's a *maid*."

"Yes, thank you, Madame Dubois, I am well aware of that.

What I was not aware of was the fact that your opinion was one which I was obliged to take into consideration."

Madame sputters, and I bite the inside of my cheek to keep my smile from spreading too much. I feel dizzy inside from the series of the events that one moment saw me compromised with a man, to feeling some strange power from within me unfurl, to now being betrothed to the person I esteem the most in the world.

"Lijsbeth was with child when she came here," Marie blurts out.

My face goes hot, and the silence in the room is stifling. Eugenie finally rouses herself to sit up and look at me. I drop my gaze to the floor, ready for Captain Norton to withdraw his offer.

But he only turns soulfully concerned eyes on me. "Is that true?"

I manage a nod, my throat choked with tears. Is it not enough that I lost my child, but that it may now be the reason that I lose the happiness that is almost within reach?

"Why didn't you tell me?" he asks, his voice gentle, but not without concern. "Never mind that now. It doesn't change anything, unless—" He curses under his breath. "We will talk later."

My shoulders unhunch, the warmth returning to my stomach. There will be a later; he will not abandon me. I don't know how I will be able to explain what happened to him, but it must be enough that I will at least have the chance.

Madame is bemoaning the trials of finding good help to Eugenie, and Marie finally admits defeat and leaves, but not before throwing me a look that could scald the skin right off me.

There are arrangements to be made, and Madame grudgingly agrees that I will stay in the Dubois house for the sake of decency until the wedding takes place.

I accompany the captain outside, finding the courage to offer him my hand. In the courtyard, he raises it to his lips, imparting an achingly sweet kiss on my wrist.

I want to be with him now. I don't care if we live in a tent or a battlefield with bullets flying over our heads. I just want to be with him and fall asleep knowing that he is truly mine. This all feels like a dream. My legs are still shaking from what happened in the cabinet, and now I am a soon-to-be married woman. "W-when?" I ask, the question too burning to stay trapped inside my throat.

"Soon, Lijsbeth," he tells me, running a gentle thumb down my cheek. "Everything will be well. Just a little longer, and then we will be together." It is easy to fall into the depths of his fathomless blue eyes, to lean into his strong touch and allow myself to believe that happiness is within reach.

But of course, if life has given me but one lesson by now, it is that few things are simple, and fewer still are guaranteed.

Thirty-Four

CORNELIA

HORTENSIA: you are cold.

I am brought to the city's courthouse, which has been taken over by British troops and houses prisoners of war awaiting transport to England. If my captors know on what charges I am being arrested, they do not share as much with me. The ride is a silent one, and undignified as I bounce in the saddle, trussed with my nose against a soldier who reeks of sweat and gunpowder. It seems a lifetime ago I rode with Henri in just such a fashion. The memory sends a hot pang of grief and anger surging through me.

We follow a never-ending train of soldiers, supplies, and weapons streaming into Brussels. I see French soldiers being led like dogs on ropes, kicked and whipped. There is no humanity in peace, apparently. Anger and resentment from the war has turned men's thoughts only to revenge and cruelty. My stomach turns at the thought of where Sophie could be right now, what they could be doing to her.

The city is like a battlefield itself. Injured men on stretchers and blankets fill the squares, crying out for a surgeon to take mercy on them and amputate their rotting limbs. A putrid stench fills the air. The occasional gunshot rings out, though it is impossible to tell if it's merely celebratory or something more sinister.

I am being led up the broad marble steps of the courthouse, picking our way through the wounded men that are strewn about, when I catch sight of her. The girl from the ball is distracted, or even in distress, her large eyes worried as she pushes her way through the traffic of returning soldiers. Then she stops, looking about, as if she can feel my gaze on her.

We lock eyes, a moment suspended as precariously as a dewdrop trembling on the tip of a leaf. This time there is no swelling music, no riot of flowers like at the ball to denote the importance of the occasion. My escort jostles me roughly, and the girl is lost from my view.

I don't have time to meditate on who she is or why we have crossed paths twice now. The courthouse is filled with English deserters and French prisoners and a few other women sitting among the soldiers. "Peddlers of flesh," my guard says, leaning down to whisper with sour breath in my ears. "They'd thought to make themselves mistresses for Napoleon's marshals if he had won but now find themselves bending over for a franc to any soldier, English or French."

We pass the miserable women, and I am led deeper into the courthouse, past overcrowded rooms of men in urine-soaked clothes. "Where are you taking me?"

"To the magistrate."

"I am to be tried today?" I have hardly had time to process that I have been arrested for some unknown crime, and now I am to be tried already? "On what charges?" I dig my heels into the marble floor. "I demand that you tell me before I go another step!"

He looks amused. "That's not my business. My business is to deliver you up to the magistrate and nothing more."

He grips my arm tighter and pulls me along past women with petitions clamoring for entrance and into a room with wood-paneled walls and high windows that let in drowsy slits of sunlight.

A haggard-looking man in a wig and black robe is signing papers and shooing away the rest of the petitioners from his great desk. He raises a weary brow when my guard marches me in.

"I've no time for more women petitioning to have their husbands released," he says, barely glancing up before going back to his papers. "If she's a harlot, put her with the rest."

The guard coughs. "No, sir. She's neither a petitioner nor a harlot. Or maybe she is, but 'tisn't on that matter which she's been brought in."

The magistrate gives a weary sigh and waves the guard over, leaving me to stand in the corner. They confer in harsh whispers, and the magistrate looks at me anew, his eyes sharp and troubled at whatever the guard is telling him. "Yes, yes," he says finally, dismissing the guard with an impatient wave.

"Are you going to tell me on what charges I stand?" I ask when it is just the old magistrate and I alone in the room.

"You will address me with the respect due to an officer of the court of England," he says in accented French. "And it is not my habit to bend to the whims of a camp follower." Nevertheless, he leans back in his seat and looks at me. "You are suspected of conducting espionage against the British Empire."

The absurdity of the charge almost makes me laugh, but then I see the gravity on his face and check my tongue. "With all due respect, sir, I am not a spy."

"No? You were seen by several officers at the house of the Duke and Duchess of Richmond the night of a ball. Perhaps you thought to charm some poor soldier out of sensitive information and bring it back to your camp."

My mind races. The true reason for my unbelievable trip to the ball is not something of which I can easily convince this man. "Armand! Sergeant Boucher can clear my name, could clear it immediately," I tell the unimpressed magistrate. "I simply went to visit a personal friend."

"The word of another French soldier will not help your case, young lady. And then there is the matter of the major's allegations."

"I'm not acquainted with any major."

"Well, he knows you. You will stay here until you can be accommodated by the next transport ship, and then you will be tried in England."

Before I can speak another word in my defense, he calls for the guard, who appears and leads me away by the arm.

The mystery of the allegations aside, I am too weary to dwell too long on this new turn of events as I sink down onto the mean straw mattress on the floor. I have, at least, been given my own private quarters and am not subjected to mixing with the men. It is tempting to nurse the pity I feel for my situation, but a dirty room in a Belgian prison seems a fitting end to this charade I have been playing. I am neither a healer nor an artist. I am not a Frenchwoman with a shadowy and exciting past. I am a vain girl who fancied herself in love and have only a broken heart and a dead lover to show for it.

I have hardly closed my eyes when there is a sound at the door, and then a face is peeking in at me through the little window.

Despite my aching body and weary mind, my stomach does a little flip at the sight of her. Sophie is a ray of light in this dark and inhospitable place. I spring up. "What are you doing here?" I ask.

"I followed you after they let me go and slipped in with a group of petitioners." She is whispering, looking back over her shoulder, and I know that we do not have much time.

I clasp her fingers through the bars. "Last night... That is, they didn't hurt you, did they?" She looks tired, and her face is smeared with dirt, her beautiful hair shoved messily under a cap.

Sophie shakes her head, but I catch the frown at the corner of her lips. "I know how to take care of myself. It will take more than a couple of English brutes to rattle me. But never mind me—what will become of you?"

I wish I could reach through the bars and take her in my arms. She looks so small, so fragile, even with the determined glint in her eye. "They will take me with them, back to England," I tell her.

"On what charges?"

"It is unclear." This doesn't seem like the time to tell her that there are yet more charges than just espionage apparently being brought against me, from some mystery officer.

She stares at me for a long minute, and I shift my weight under her hard gaze. "Colette, have you even asked?"

"I suspect that I am to be a trophy. And as the English were victors, I am a spoil they are entitled to take. No one here will speak for me, and really, all I could hope for would be a quick death if I were tried here."

"Death?" All the color drains from her face. "What are you *talking* about?"

"I assume the penalty for espionage is death," I tell her. If I am able to speak about my position candidly, it is only because it still feels so very unreal.

She is still studying me, as if trying to read some riddle on my face. Finally, she swallows, nods. "I'll follow you," Sophie says quietly.

Only a week ago I would have been deliriously happy to hear her say that, but now my stomach plummets at the thought. "No, you will not. You'll stay here and forget me and go on with your life."

"As if I could forget you!"

There is dirt under her fingernails and blood still on her

clothes. I wonder if she has dwelled at all on what happened on the battlefield, the writhing sea of flowers that reclaimed Henri. I wonder if she has finally seen me for what I am. But it doesn't matter, because I will not have her become a casualty of my peculiar abilities.

"I wish you would," I tell her. "I can bring you nothing but heartache. You deserve a safe life, an easy life. If I am found guilty, then I will not have you put through the pain of a trial and death sentence. Go to France, start again. Please, Sophie."

She stares at me for a moment that grows long and thin, the sounds of women wailing and men shouting filling the silence. When she finally speaks, it is low and determined. "Henri died, and it was a terrible thing. I loved him as well, and I will never be whole again. But I did not die on that field, and neither did you. There is love between us, and it is a crime to sever it for the sake of some self-imposed punishment. Because that's what this is, isn't it? You're punishing yourself for Henri's death. But Henri would not want you to go on like this, and neither do I."

Guilt settles heavy in my chest, but I did not grow armor around my heart in Sussex for nothing. "You do not know me, Sophie. The real me. Colette is not even my real name. There are things that I did before I met you for which I deserve to be punished."

She stares at me in disbelief, and it takes all my strength not to let her see how much it costs me to tell her this. If only she would just let me be.

"I refuse to believe that," she says.

"And what would you have me do?"

"I would have you fight!" Her voice rises, and she quickly glances behind her shoulder into the hall before lowering it again. "I have followed you everywhere—into the heart of battle, to prison, and I will follow you to England, but I will not follow you to your death simply because of your own misplaced sense of guilt. Fight for *me*, Colette, if you will not fight for yourself."

A tear slides down her dirty cheek. It would be so easy, so natural, to reach out and swipe it away, feel her warmth under my hand. I am unused to seeing Sophie being so vulnerable, to glimpse the tender soul that resides behind her carefully constructed walls. I don't like to think that I am the cause of it. Pulling back from the window, I let her hands fall from mine. "Guard!" I call. "Please come take this woman away!"

"Colette!"

"I told you—that is not my name." I don't know what comes over me. I don't know why it feels so good to be cruel, to see the effects of my words. But I cannot stop myself. "You shouldn't have come here. You should have gone back to camp and your old life. I told you to leave me at Mont-Saint-Jean, and I wish you had listened."

I turn swiftly, but it is not soon enough, and my last glimpse of Sophie is seeing her heart break as she is led away.

Thirty-Five

LIJSBETH

DOGWOOD: quiet endurance.
Our love shall overcome adversity.

Madame has cleared out a little room in the eves previously used for storage and given it to me as my own until I am married. I sweep away the cobwebs, and pin up an old lace shawl on the window that Eugenie gifted to me when it no longer suited her. My flower column clippings are too precious to even put on the walls, so they stay instead under my pillow.

My newfound privacy could not come at a more opportune time. It is all I can do to carry on as before and not lose myself in the memories of what happened to Major Reeves when we were in the cabinet together. All of the strange dreams, the visions, even the incoherent whispers that I hear from the flowers...all of that can be easily explained as a product of my overworked mind and body. But how can I explain what happened in the cabinet?

As I sit in my bed in the little room, I force myself to go back to that day with Major Reeves and remember exactly what was going through my mind as he began to choke for air.

If there had not been those pricks of blood about his neck when we tumbled out, I might have thought that it was my imagination. After all, he could have panicked in the small space and thought that he could not get air. But it can be no coincidence that, as I thought of thorny vines twisting about his neck, such marks would actually appear on him.

So what *was* I thinking as he began to choke? I was frightened, certainly, and desperately wished to escape. But there was something simmering beneath those primal instincts, and that was anger. Anger at my situation, at my own defenselessness. Anger that circumstances had again delivered me up to the mercy of a man who saw me as only good for one thing. I have never been content with my lot. Oh, I bear it, as I must. But that does not mean that I accept it.

With only the light of the moon slanting into my room, I lower myself to the floor, sitting with crossed legs. I close my eyes, slow my breath. It is not hard to draw on the reserve of anger within me. I need only think of Isidore, of Madame van den Berg banishing me from the nursery to the kitchen. I think of the days, weeks, months, years of my life that have been given over so that others may live more comfortably. I think of my origins and how I will never know where I came from.

I think of all these things and more. And as I meditate on the injustice of it all, there is a vibration, starting in the ground but working itself up my body until it is in my fingers. I feel light, yet somehow tethered to the earth, an extension of some old and powerful network.

My heart beats in time with the vibrations thrumming through me, my anger surging, until I am shaking with it. It reaches a peak, and when I open my eyes, I find that a small white chrysanthemum has appeared in my hands.

The air deflates from my chest as I turn it over in my fingers, too stunned to be fearful. Aside from the effervescent shimmer of the petals, the little bloom looks as ordinary as any flower at the market.

The full brunt of what I have just created settles on my shoulders. There is something inside of me, and it is beginning to seep out through the cracks in my heart. Outside, a city scarred from war slumbers on, unaware that a nameless young woman has just spun magic in this little room. What else might I be capable of? What else might I accomplish if I only knew the workings of this extraordinary gift? From now on, every night after the rest of the household is asleep, I take out the clipping from under my pillow, trace my fingers across the illustrations of flowers, and practice widening the cracks of my heart.

My bucket does not seem so heavy the next day or the trimming and stripping of flower leaves so monotonous. I am certain I look mad, grinning as I go about my work. When I go to bed at night, I no longer have to worry about Marie tormenting me, and I'm able to practice, quietly discovering what is inside of me. How to train it so that I am able to communicate with a single flower, spun up from nothing more than my latent desires. My dreams are warm and sweet, filled with promises of what is to come with Captain Norton. Any day now he will come to make me his wife. I will be protected and loved and safe and so, so happy.

Yet there is one thing that keeps me from slipping completely into the bliss of my daydreams. I have not forgotten the girl from the night of the ball. Her face no longer fills only my dreams but my waking moments as well. I would be lying if I said I never gave my origins any thought. For I do often wonder who brought me to the orphan house and left me there. The token around my neck makes me think that I did have a mother, one who perhaps loved me very much and wanted to have me back once she could take care of me. But she never came, or if she did, I was already gone, spirited away to the van den Berg household to be a companion to a lonely little boy.

My feet are light upon the cobblestones as I browse the flower market. I carry a secret with me as I inspect the roses and hothouse flowers. I am *betrothed*. I am *somebody*. I may look like just another little maid with a basket on her arm, but I share the love of a man who is all things goodness and bravery.

I feel the locket quiver at my neck before I see her. The flowers sway in their buckets, leaning toward the courthouse. I never gave much thought to the old stone building before, though there are those who treat the trials and hangings as a sort of sport, always coming to watch and delight in the misery. Of all the places I thought I might catch a glimpse of her again, it wouldn't be here. But there she is, a splash of a violet dress and golden hair against the sea of uniforms on the steps.

"Mademoiselle, have a care!" The flower seller scrambles to catch the bundle of stems that have fallen from my hands as I move toward the great marble steps in a trance.

Her dress is mud-wicked, and her hair is tangled and loose. Yet she walks with her head held high, as if she were a princess being escorted to her palace. She pauses, as if sensing that she is being watched, and turns to look over her shoulder. This time there is no mistaking the jolt that passes between us. Her eyes find mine, and her lips open in surprise, petals parting to the sun.

The roses in my basket are singing, their petals trilling in the breeze. A crowd has assembled. Women are rarely tried, and I suppose the spectacle of so fair a prisoner has drawn the interest of everyone from soldiers to passersby. There is some jeering, but mostly curious stares.

And then she is gone, whisked inside by soldiers in red coats. Disappointed, the crowd quickly disperses. I stand a moment longer, unable to drag myself away while the roses' song begins to fade.

Captain Norton visits that evening.

Some of my euphoria has slowly dissipated over the course of the day. What seemed like a precious secret has lost some of its luster as I go about my work, anxious both to learn the identity of the girl at the courthouse, as well as secure a date for my wedding. Every moment that Captain Norton is not with me is like torture.

But my excitement quickly returns as soon as he enters the drawing room. "There she is." His good hand strong on my waist, and his kiss on my brow are almost enough to draw me away from my tumultuous memories of what happened in the cabinet and the mysterious woman in the square. When he pulls back, a frown is touching his lips, and his gaze rakes over my work dress. "I say, you aren't still working, are you?"

I don't know how to tell this man who has ridden into my life on a golden chariot that I have no other choice but to work until he comes to release me from my bonds of servitude. He has offered me no wedding date, no plans beyond the next day he will visit. It is a wonder that the earth beneath my feet doesn't fall away when I think about all the things that will change now that I've accepted him.

Madame Dubois, Eugenie, and Octavie are across the room, ostensibly to work on some piece of embroidery but really to act as chaperones. Madame raises her brow from behind her hoop. "So long as Lijsbeth lives under this roof, she must earn her keep. I am not in the habit of running a boardinghouse, Captain."

"I see," he replies coolly, before moving closer to me and stopping just far enough way to maintain propriety. "I cannot move you into my apartments, not with my landlady and us not married," he says, his voice low and warm, apologetic. "We could make a quick business of it, but you deserve more than a register book and a priest. You ought to walk an aisle strewn with rose petals and have orange blossoms in your hair." He touches a stray lock near my ear as he says this, as if envisioning the scene. "I would take you back to England with me, have it done there, the proper way. My father is a hard man, and I can't say he'll be pleased with me bringing back a foreign bride, but my mother and sisters would attend, stand up with you at the altar. Would you like that, sweetheart?"

My head swims, visions of having a new family, a big wedding in a church. "You have s-sisters?" I manage to ask. This man, whose eyes I have memorized, whose hand upon my arm feels as familiar and comfortable as my own skin, is still a stranger to me.

"Yes, I have four sisters, which is altogether too many when you are a young boy and only want a companion to shoot arrows with. But rest assured, they will all fall in love with you immediately, just as I have."

Looking up into his handsome face, I can see the hope on the edge of his lips. But I can also see the effort it takes to conceal his lie. He is too kind to say it, but I know what he is really thinking. He is thinking of how he will return from war with a maid on his arm and how disappointed, if not angry, his family will be. He is wondering if he is risking his inheritance for me. Madame's reaction is only a fraction of what his own family's will be when they realize how far beneath him he has stooped to take a wife.

I want to tell him that I don't mind a quick ceremony or cramped lodgings with a disapproving landlady, but then I think of the young woman at the courthouse. I must know who she is, and that will take time.

"It won't be long now, I swear it. I have a small amount of business to take care of here in the city, and then as soon as I receive my orders, we may go."

So I return to my work, no more a bride than I was this morning, and no closer to learning the identity of the young woman at the ball.

Days pass, then a week. I feel my joy, my hope slowly slipping through my fingers each day that I fail to find her. Captain Norton—William—visits me in the evenings, and Madame has grudgingly given me an hour off after the family's dinner in which I may have use of the small parlor. His visits are sips of sweet water, meted out to a parched flower, but it is only enough to keep me alive, not to bloom.

I am sweeping up dead petals in the drawing room one morning while the family lounges about, some of the girls reading, the others decorating bonnets. "Look at this!" Hippolyte is sitting with a newspaper in her lap. "There's a woman in custody of the British, claiming to be Madame Dujardin."

The girls spring from their seats and gather round, reading over her shoulder.

"A ploy," Madame speculates, "borne of desperation. The author of those columns is a highborn lady. You can see it in her manner of writing."

Eugenie doesn't seem so certain. "Madame Dujardin *did* stop writing months ago. Could it be possible that it really is her?"

Eugenie catches me listening and scowls, snapping the newspaper shut. "Come," she tells her sisters. "Let's go for a walk." I am still not forgiven for my encounter with Major Reeves. Never mind that I spared Eugenie a miserable marriage to a brute. But whether she meant to or not, she has just given me the greatest gift I could ask for.

I now know who I must look for.

Thirty-Six

CORNELIA

ROSEMARY: remembrance.

The scent of lily of the valley wakes me from my fitful slumber.

I turn my head on my pillow, waiting for Henri's face to come into focus, for the warmth of Sophie's breath to touch my cheek. But all that greets me is a damp wall and a spider scuttling perilously close to my nose. The light in my room is thick and dusty, a hopeless, miserable air permeating everything.

A belligerent guard informs me through the window in the door that I have a visitor, and I sit up, my body protesting. I didn't realize I was still allowed the privilege of receiving visitors, and I will wring Sophie's neck for coming back here. But the footsteps coming from the hall are different, more hesitant, and a moment later a shaft of light in the shape of a young woman appears at the window.

I upend my pitcher of fetid water as I bolt to my feet. Soft chestnut hair, a gentle demeanor, great, soulful eyes. She is not the angel on a pedestal like the night of the ball but a real woman, though one who looks like she has just stepped out of a painting by an old master. Her movements are small and shy, but she meets my gaze squarely. She is the calm of a morning dewdrop, sweet and pure, and so familiar.

"You." It's the only greeting I can manage, and it comes out in a whisper.

"I saw you at the ball," I say when she still doesn't speak. "And the other day in front of the courthouse. Do you speak Dutch? French?"

She nods to both but doesn't offer anything more.

"Why have you come? Who are you?"

In reply, she produces a sprig of rosemary from her cloak and hands it to me through the window. The guard is preoccupied with smoking his cheroot and does not seem particularly concerned.

I take it, unsure what this ruse is. But no sooner do my fingers close around the stem, then the breath is knocked out of my lungs. I feel faint and adrift, as if I have awakened inside of a dream. The images that flood my mind are hazy and unspool like a tapestry coming undone. The voice that accompanies them is clear and familiar, yet the young woman's lips never move, I am sure of it.

I see myself through her eyes—no, not her eyes: her *mind*—hazy images of my head bowed over my sketchbook, hours spent in the garden. My journey from Sussex to Dover to Calais, and then Amiens. It is impossible to parse what is a long-buried memory and what she has just shown me through the sprig of rosemary. Tiny footsteps running through my uncle's house—our uncle's house—chased by a beautiful woman with rich chestnut hair and a golden laugh. A solemn little girl who never spoke. Then my mother disappearing and my little sister being sent away by my uncle. It all must have happened before I was even five years of age.

The rosemary falls to the ground as a light bursts behind my eyes, its fragrant leaves scattering through the straw. I don't ask how she can make me see her thoughts through the flower. It seems inconsequential in light of what I've just learned.

"You're my sister." My words come out in a breath of amazement. "But I don't… I didn't have a sister." Except, of course, I obviously do. I was not my mother's only child. "My mother—our mother—do you know where she is?" I ask her, possibilities whirling through my mind.

My breath tightens in my chest as I wait for her to answer. But she only gives a sad smile that tells me she has no more answers than I do.

"Well," I say briskly to mask my disappointment, "I shall just have to be content with gaining a sister, then. What is your name?"

"Lijsbeth."

It is the first, the only, word that she has spoken aloud. "Cornelia Shaw, and sometimes Madame Dujardin, or Colette," I tell her. "Lately of Sussex, and now as you see me here. I could tell you how I came to be in this sorry state, but it seems you already know more of me than I know myself."

She bows her head. At some point throughout this extraordinary exchange, we have moved closer, taken our hands in each other's. There is so much to say, so many questions to ask, yet we both seem to be content to just be near one another, to revel in the great discovery of the other's existence.

"I wish we had met in better circumstances," I tell her. "What a sorry creature you must think me."

Again, I am met only with silence, and the impression that she can see through all of my thickest armor to the parts of me that I have tried so long to keep hidden. The tender parts and frightened parts. The guilty parts.

The sound of raised voices and clumsy boots in the hall shatters our reunion. "What do you mean, she has a visitor? Are you mad! The woman is a dangerous criminal, and you're letting every sundry maid off the street come and take tea with her, giving her who knows what opportunity to pass along English intelligence."

Lijsbeth hears him, too, the merest ghost of a sad smile flitting across her face. It isn't fair that I only just found her, and now she must leave. But if I could not bring myself to let Sophie stay, then what right do I have to ask that of Lijsbeth? What claim can I make over this young woman, of whose existence I only just learned?

I can just see the guards striding down the hall toward the door, fury in their eyes. "No, don't hurt her! Wait—"

But my sister is too fast. She dodges them, and then, like a startled bird, she is gone.

Thirty-Seven

LIJSBETH

LINT FLOWER: I feel my obligations. Fate.

The clock in the parlor is ticking, a crisp, unforgiving sound that punctuates the awkward silence.

Captain Norton—*William*—sits with an untouched cup of tea on his knee, while Hippolyte acts as indifferent chaperone on the other side of the room.

I should be happy. I *am* happy, but not completely. How can I be when I have found my sister, but she sits in prison? I knew as soon as I saw her that we were bound together in some way, but it was the flowers that sang her name to me, drew me along, and gave me the strength to find her.

This is what has been building inside of me. Cornelia is the reason that I hear whispers in the flowers, and indeed I wonder if it isn't *her* voice, whether she is aware of it or not, that has been quietly guiding me all these years. In her I have found not only a sister, but perhaps a key as well. She could tell me who I am, where I came from. Why I have never belonged. But what if it is better not to know? What if I have found her only to lose her again?

Captain Norton sits with his ankles crossed, sipping his tea, and making polite conversation to fill the silence. By now he must be used to my quiet spells, but the silence is particularly heavy today. All I can think of is that I cannot go with him to England, not while my sister is in prison. And while I desperately want to tell him about Cornelia, I cannot when Hippolyte is here, casting sour glances in our direction. My words wouldn't come out, and besides, what would I say? But then, if I told him, perhaps he could put in a word for her and have the charges dropped. He *is* a decorated war hero, after all: his word must have some weight to it. Or would he have to decline, putting his country first? I am terrified to learn if there are limits to his affection. If my sister is to be helped, it must be I who helps her.

I surface from my churning thoughts to find William watching me with tender concern. "Lijsbeth? Is everything all right? You look a hundred miles away. I was just saying that we should be able to travel within a fortnight."

My words pile up in my throat, and it is as if I am back to the first day we met. I shake my head. I should tell him, about Cornelia, about the baby, about everything. He is to be my husband and is already the other half of my soul. But what if he changed his mind? What if he saw me only as a scheming opportunist? He would wash his hands and be done with me, and his good English family would be only too glad.

"There, now." William sets aside his tea and comes to kneel beside me, his back to Hippolyte so she cannot see the tender brush of his finger on my cheek. "Though I only want your happiness, I would be lying if I didn't also want to be with you as soon as possible. I thought you were eager to leave your position, but perhaps I misjudged the situation. If it is time you need, then time you shall have. We will wait as long as you need and then be married here, in Brussels, and travel to England together as man and wife."

I sag in relief. A few more days to plan, to get my answers, and save my sister as well.

Hippolyte clears her throat and stands. My time with William is over, and I spent it worrying and drowning in my own thoughts. He gives me a formal bow, then brushes my ear with a kiss that sends shivers down my body and makes me want to reconsider everything and just go with him now, tonight.

I spend a sleepless night fruitlessly wondering how to help Cornelia. I cannot petition the court nor can I enlist a lawyer. But what bothers me above all else is the look in my sister's eyes when I had first come in, before she knew I was watching her. She looked defeated, bereft of hope. I wonder if she even wants to be saved or if she has accepted her fate, whatever that may be.

No one is awake to stop me when I slip out of the house first thing in the morning and steal to the courthouse with the seed of an idea.

But my efforts are stymied as soon as I arrive and the guard who admitted me the other day shakes his head. He is Belgian and had seemed kind, unlike the English soldier who had tried to throw me out.

"You cannot see her, mademoiselle," he says.

I crane my head to see over his shoulder, as if I could somehow see all the way into the bowels of the building, and he seems to take pity on me. "It's no use, mademoiselle. She is not there." He glances about and then leans down, as if imparting a secret, and my stomach drops at his words. "She's been transported. Back to England."

I walk into the little church an orphan with nothing to my name besides a locket and a lost sister and leave Mrs. Captain William Norton. It is a small ceremony, witnessed only by a couple of William's men and the minister. When we emerge into the hot summer air, arms linked, I feel no different except that now I have a thin gold band on my finger and no longer have any need to worry about my future. I am still as full of love for my captain as the first day I met him. I am still aware that there is something inside of me that marks me as different, and I still cannot name what it is.

We leave directly for Calais, and then on to Dover where we board a crowded stagecoach. Our journey is shared with other soldiers returning home, some with arms in slings, some with no arms at all. Some are eager to engage William in conversation and relive the glory of the day, but many seem just as glad to give him a knowing nod, then slip into silence.

Our first night on English soil is spent at an inn along the turnpike. William apologizes for the small room, but it is warm and snug with fresh bedding, and a little window that looks out over a peaceful field of grazing sheep. It is our first time alone since the ceremony, and my heart begins to beat faster as bedtime draws near.

William brings dinner to our room, great tin platters of unfamiliar food that he apologizes for, yet tastes better than anything I have ever eaten.

"Tomorrow the journey to Portsmouth will not be so long," he tells me, smiling, as I yawn after my plate is cleaned. "You did very well, my brave girl."

I color at his words. Any intimacy which I felt with him before our marriage seems to have vanished, replaced instead by a shyness that renders me practically immobile.

My apprehension only deepens when the time comes to turn down the lamps and make ready for bed. William disrobes down to his breeches, unaware or simply unconcerned that I am watching him from the bed with guarded curiosity. I'm not so naive that I don't know what a man's body looks like; after all, I saw Isidore undressed more than once as children, and then later when Monsieur van den Berg would supposedly forget to shut the door to his chamber.

But I have never seen *William* in all his beauty before. And he is beautiful. Perfect, even.

And I am…not. I am too small, with calluses on my fingers and cuts and chilblain scars healed over and opened again from scratching in the dry, winter months. I am unsure of how I appear to others, and I have never thought to look at my body fully in a looking glass. But worst of all, I am broken and used because of Isidore. I thought I had left him in Brussels, but now he is in this room with us, crowding my husband and me.

"Dear one." I look up to find William beside the bed, regarding me with concern. "Your lip is bleeding."

I touch my lip to find that I've bitten the skin clean off while in the throes of my despondent thoughts. William dabs away the blood with a cloth and then sits beside me, the mattress dipping so that our bodies are separated by only a hair's breadth.

He takes my hand in his, idly rubbing my cold fingers until the blood is circulating in them again. "I don't presume to know what troubles you, but it is only natural that you are apprehensive about tonight."

I'm already biting at my lip again, unable to bring myself to look at his concerned blue eyes, the kind inclination of his head.

"Lijsbeth, will you look at me?" His gentle demand bids me to finally meet his gaze. "We are together, and God willing, we will be together for the rest of our days and nights. There is no rush, no imperative to do anything that you aren't willing and ready to do. Do you understand?"

I nod, because it is he who does not understand. I could put him off tonight, could put him off for any number of nights and my dear William would not complain. But the truth is, I do not wish to put him off. I dearly want to be close to him. If only Isidore and his shadow were not here with us.

My stomach roils, the words piling up in my throat. But

every minute that I don't tell William everything, is a minute that widens the space between us. "There was—there was a b-baby," I whisper.

There is a catch of breath from beside me as William goes still. "Yes, I remember something about that," he says. There is no censure in his voice, but neither is there understanding. "I was very sorry."

How do I tell him that I abhorred the father, was sickened by the act, but very much wanted the resulting baby? Is there a way to say such a thing? My cheeks grow wet, and William murmurs a sound of surprise and pity as he tenderly brushes them away.

"Y-you did not…d-did not ask who the f-father was," I say.

His hand stills on my cheek, but only for a moment. "I did not think it my place," he says evenly.

He has every right to ask, but because he is William and he is good, he has not. The ensuing pause tells me he is choosing his words carefully. "If you had a lover, I do not fault you. I was not looking for a paradigm of chastity or maidenly virtue in a wife. Only a good heart and a gentle soul."

This does nothing to stanch the tears, both because of William's sweetness and because of the truth of the circumstances around which the child was conceived. "I… He was not m-my lover. He was…he was…" My misery eclipses my words, lodging them deep within my chest. I wish there was a flower that I could place in his hand that would gild the ugly edges of my story, explain it all.

Understanding dawns on William's face, and it is only in the drawn-out silence that I notice the crackling of the logs in the grate, the way the rest of the world has hushed for me to tell my secret.

Uttering an oath, he pushes himself up and paces about the room as I shrink into myself. I shouldn't have told him, even this much. What can it possibly accomplish? Isidore is hundreds of miles away, and the baby is gone. I had thought not telling William was torture, but this is worse.

When William catches sight of me, he breaks off in his pacing and comes to kneel beside me. "Lijsbeth," he says. "If I appear angry, just know that it is not with you." He rakes a hand through his hair. His eyes have gone stormy and dark, and despite his assurance, he looks capable of violence. "I would go to any lengths to protect you, to take back what has happened," he says, his voice husky. "I wish I could face the blackguard with my pistol, but I don't think it would do much good, and what's more, I don't think it would bring you any sense of peace. So just know this, Lijsbeth, my wife. You will never know fear or pain, so long as I live. I take my vow of safeguarding both your body and your soul with the utmost seriousness. I love you as you are now, and I will love you forever, no matter what is to come."

I gaze at him as he awaits some word from me. It is too much. My heart is not capable of holding so much love, and I want him to take away all the lingering memories of Isidore and my life in that house. He looks surprised when I rise on my knees to wind my arms around his neck, but then he is leaning into my kiss, and we lower to the bed. He only pulls back once, a question in his eyes, and I nod. Because, yes, I am certain. I want this more than anything.

Cold air is seeping over my body.

I pull the blanket tighter around me, instinctively clinging to the last precious moments of rest before I must get up and begin work. My senses are slow to catch up as I awaken. I am in a dark, unfamiliar room, and there is a not-unpleasant ache between my legs. Drowsy memories of being rolled in William's strong arms drift through my mind. But when I reach to my side, I only find empty sheets.

William.

It is dark outside, the distant sounds of ship horns carrying through the night. He cannot have left, can he? Gathering up the blanket, I wrap it around my shoulders and go to look for my husband.

I find him in the tiny parlor that adjoins our room, head propped up on the arm of a threadbare chaise, his legs draped over the other side. His nightshirt is open at the throat, and he looks as if he tossed and turned a good bit before finally finding slumber.

The wood creaks under my feet as I stand there, confused and hurt. Do the English not sleep in the same bed as their wives? Did I do something wrong after all? It was so lovely, and I truly thought that we had looked into each other's souls as we held each other. But perhaps I was wrong.

William mutters something in his sleep, then turns farther into the side of the chaise. Cold and lost, I return to bed, alone.

Thirty-Eight
CORNELIA

TANSY: hostility. I declare war against you.

July 1815

England clamps her greedy hands around me like irons, her slate-gray sky smothering me, the sooty buildings of Portsmouth opening wide like rotten teeth, ready to swallow me whole.

I did not think when I made my escape six months ago that I would ever return, but even if I had planned to, I would like to think that it would have been as a successful woman, one with *something* to her name. Instead, I am shuffled off the ship in shackles, along with the other prisoners, and put onto carts that bear us to the gaol.

The view from Portsea Island is drab and endless. The sound of the metalworks rings ceaselessly through the day, replaced at night by drunken brawls and ships scraping against the docks. Days pass with no word on the date of my trial. Time has ever been the enemy of young women, depriving us of our youth and beauty, our only currency in a vain and uncaring society. In the absence of pretty diversions with which to fill the time, my mind is forced to dwell upon all manner of unpleasant things. Will I be hanged? Or shot? Will it hurt?

My morbid thoughts are interrupted when the cell door swings open, revealing a guard. "It's time," he tells me.

"Time for what?"

The guard, a burly man with a red face devoid of humor, runs his sleeve under his dripping nose. "For your trial."

I spring up. "I had no warning!"

"What, did you think that you was sitting here for an audience with the king? Come on, now."

As a woman, I am used to the world expecting me to cede control of my future, but this is beyond the pale. Now I am a prisoner, too, and I don't even know what the next day brings.

"Anne Boleyn at least did not have to suffer such indignities," I murmur as I reluctantly follow his broad back.

"Your trial is set to be the spectacle of the year," he tells me as he leads me down the dark hall. He says this as if I were throwing a ball and all of the *bon ton* of London have come. As if I should be flattered. "Soldiers is delaying their returns home just to come see you. Was even a story about it in the papers last week."

I am transported by cart over the bridge to the Crown Court on the mainland. "Where the murderers are tried," my guard gleefully informs me. Throngs of people stop to watch us pass, some jeering and throwing rotten cabbage, others waving and shouting my name. "Told you," he says.

The journey is short, the air outside brisk and wet. Still, it is fresher than my cell, so I breathe it in, savoring what little illusion of freedom it grants me. Then quickly, much too quickly, we arrive at the courthouse.

A crowd has already gathered on the front steps, and I am ushered inside amidst more shouting and jostling. Someone reaches out to try to grab my hair, another spits on my cheek. My guard does not seem in a hurry to reach the door.

At last we are inside, but my relief is tempered with what is to come next. The courtroom is much bigger, much more intimidating than I could have imagined. Everything is high, from the judge's seat to the jury's bench to the marble statues that line the gallery, looking down with vacant indifference. I take my place in the box where I am instructed and wait. I wish they had allowed me some time to make my toilette. I look half-mad with my hair matted, and the world is not kind to madwomen.

Every seat is filled, with more people overflowing into the back of the great room and onto the gallery above. The judge, a hoary old man with rheumy eyes and thin, drooping lips, calls the court to order.

"Cornelia Shaw, do you know of what you stand accused?"

I start at hearing my name—my real name—from him. "Your lordship, I have sat in a wretched cell these past days, with no word on any—"

He waves me off, hardly bothering to look up from his papers. "You are being tried on suspicions of treason, as well as a number of other complaints brought by a number of accusers."

It seems along with my name, my nationality has been discovered, and with it the charges of espionage have become treason charges. I do not have a chance to fully sit with the implications because the judge is continuing.

"The list of charges is lengthy, and I do not have the inclination to list them out piecemeal, so we will begin with the witchcraft charges," he says.

I nearly fly from my seat. "Witchcraft?"

"Miss Shaw, you will be quiet or you will be escorted from the courtroom and not have the privilege of being present at your own trial."

It's all happening so fast. There is no one to speak for me, no one to explain what is happening. I sit in shocked silence as a young man in uniform I am certain I've never seen before is sworn in and begins to testify against me.

"Private Joseph Liddell of the 52nd," he informs the court. "I fought at Waterloo and was present when the Imperial Guard charged and was consequently broken." There is an appreciative hush in the courtroom at his words.

"And what did you observe on the battlefield that day?" the judge asks.

The young man tilts his chin up. He is dark-haired and has a slight cleft in his chin. Not unhandsome but with an inflated air of importance. Whoever he is, I decide that I don't like him, not least of all because he is testifying against me. "Your Lordship, I observed bloodshed and chaos that day. I observed both the most heroic of men and the most cowardly. I observed the glory of Britain and the fall of Napoleon. But the most extraordinary thing that happened on that field was not found within the province of men." He pauses, perhaps for effect, or perhaps because he is genuinely trying to find the right words. In either case, he has a rapt audience, as everyone in the courtroom sits on the edge of their seats, waiting for him to continue. "I saw the earth spring forth flowers, an entire field of them, in the space of naught but a minute. And in the middle of those flowers was standing a woman." He turns to face me, pointing a finger. *"Her."*

The judge scratches at an old pockmark on his chin. "You are saying that this woman was responsible for growing a garden in the middle of battle?" His watery blue eyes squint at me, as if he cannot reconcile the anecdote with the woman he sees before him.

"I am saying," soldier says testily, "that it was witchcraft and nothing less."

"And how can you be certain that the defendant was responsible for this—for this phenomenon?"

"Because she was not like the peasant women who had come to pick and scavenge, nor was she come to help the wounded. She stood like a statue of some Roman goddess of war, letting out the most awful scream, and from her feet sprang the flowers."

If there is anything to be grateful for, it is that the judge does not seem impressed with the fantastic nature of this testimony. There is some rabble from the crowd, and then the soldier is thanked and dismissed before the next witness is summoned.

My body stills, everything in the courtroom fading away except the man making his way to the stand. I almost do not recognize him. He has exchanged his blue uniform for a crimson red coat, his collar starched and crisp. He is handsome as ever and carries himself with that swagger that I have come to know, yet there is shame in the way he avoids my eye.

The judge asks him to give his name, and he presents it as Armand Boucher, though his accent is different, more aristocratic than I remember.

"And what is your rank in His Majesty's army?" the judge asks.

Armand looks unsure, almost worried. "I am not, strictly speaking, ranked," he says.

"Yet you wear the regalia?"

"Yes, it was deemed unsafe for me to continue wearing the uniform of my countrymen after I was recruited to provide intelligence to the English."

The judge does not seem impressed. "You might have worn civilian clothes." He gives a weary sigh. "In any case, continue. How did you find yourself in the service of the English?"

Armand clears his throat, shifts slightly in his seat. "I ingratiated myself with General Guérin, which was easy enough as our fathers were students together at the Sorbonne. Whatever intelligence I was privy to as a result of this alliance, I passed on to the British army."

The judge regards Armand as if he was mangy rat, and I am tempted to agree. "Very well," he says. "How did you come to be acquainted with this woman?"

Armand has finally brought himself to look at me but quickly cuts his gaze away. He clears his throat uncomfortably several more times. "I was doing some reconnaissance near Amiens when I happened upon a young woman in the garden of an old nunnery. Gentlemanly conduct compelled to ask after her welfare. I noticed that she was dressed in a violet dress, so I asked her if she was a lover of violets and—"

The judge raises his hand to stop Armand. "A lover of violets? And what is the significance of that?"

"It is a commonly understood indication among the French to ascertain if one is a supporter of Napoleon."

At the fallen emperor's name, there is a chorus of booing in the courtroom. The judge calls for order.

"I recognized her as English immediately," he says. "She seemed unfamiliar with her surroundings, and her French was not nearly so good as she thought."

Of all the accusations leveled against me, this one stings quite a bit. Oh, but I hate him.

"She was easily convinced to join up with the men assembling to support Napoleon on his return and—"

The judge pinches the bridge of his nose, looks weary. "Were you often in the business of recruiting for one army while informing for the other?"

Color touches Armand's high cheekbones. "No, Your Honor. It was only… I found her quite an extraordinary young lady, and I, well, I thought to impress her. She is a gifted artist and naturalist, and I knew that her talents would be prized by Napoleon, should she ever reach his attention. I thought that in the future, she could prove quite a valuable asset." He pauses, turns to address me. "My feelings, while born of an ulterior motive at first, were true," he says quietly. "If you had only seen me as the man I am and not simply a boy in uniform, this all might have turned out very differently, for both of us."

"You are not to address the defendant," the judge reminds him.

Armand gives a short nod of contrition. "I came to regret my interference in bringing her on," he continues. "It soon became evident that she had ulterior motives herself for being in the camp. She entertained late-night callers and partook in strange activities with some of the more unsavory characters there. I took it upon myself to interview some of these individuals, though there were some that would not speak to me, either due to some sense of gratitude toward her or embarrassment on their part."

He produces a list from his pocket and begins to read. It is a litany of everything I did in the camp but cast in the darkest of shadows and held up as proof. The charges of witchcraft and espionage dovetail nicely, until they become one and the same.

She would often go a-gathering herbs.

I saw her grow flowers with her mind.

She healed me without medicine, using only her hands and herbs.

She would often disappear from camp for hours at a time.

I am relieved, at least, that Jean does not number among my accusers. But I wonder what it is that makes men so cruel. Surely a bruised ego cannot solely account for such anger? Is it not enough to shed blood and conquer the world but they must also see a woman who only ever tried to do good brought to her knees? Their domination must be total, their sovereignty complete.

The judge thanks Armand and dismisses him, and soon the next witness is taking the stand. He is some officer of the English army, corroborating Armand's claims about my work as a spy. It is all so ridiculous, so beyond the scope of reason. I hardly pay him any attention, and then yet another witness is called.

There is something familiar about the man, but I cannot think where I might know him from. He carries himself with the authority of a military man and is wearing a coat heavy with medals. There is a sharpness to his profile, an assessing glint in his eye. I have seen him before, I am sure of it, and when he speaks, the timbre of his deep voice is familiar.

"What is your name, and what is your complaint against the defendant?" the judge asks.

I sit up a little straighter, my pulse quickening.

"My name is Major Josiah Reeves of the 82nd, lately of Chichester, Sussex."

"No." The word slips from my mouth before I can stop myself, drawing attention from some of the men on the jury.

He is rather stouter about the middle than I remember him, and it does not appear that he suffered overmuch during the war, for he looks to be in good health. All the same, I can now see the cruel twist to his lips, the unfeeling light in his eyes that sent me running to France all those months ago.

"And how is the defendant known to you, Major Reeves?"

"I had an agreement with her uncle, but Miss Shaw did not uphold the terms of the engagement. Indeed, she took the most extreme measures to ensure that her uncle could never manage her affairs again."

The judge leans forward in his seat, and any remaining murmurs die away in the courtroom as he asks the major to explain himself.

"After our first meeting, I found the young lady in question to be immensely spirited and hoydenish. I was insulted when she dismissed me out of hand, but her uncle assured me that she was simply still warming to the idea of the match and that he would bring her 'round. He begged that I would call the following day after he had spoken some sense to her." The major's gaze slides over to me. "Well, I returned the next day, and neither he nor his niece were anywhere to be found."

My pulse is racing hot in my ears. All the secrets that I thought I had left buried in Sussex are poised to spill out in front of an audience hungry for my demise.

"Was it unusual for this man to make arrangements, only to break them?" the judge asks.

Major Reeves shrugs, drawing out the gesture. "I never knew Mr. Shaw to renege on his invitations nor yet be forgetful of his engagements. But that is not why I took it upon myself to enter the house and search it."

By now every person in the room is holding their breath, tipping forward in their chairs.

"You searched the house?"

"I did. I thought it strange that when I called, there was not even a maid to admit me. I found the door to be unlocked, so I let myself in. That is when I knew that something of the most heinous nature had occurred."

He is looking me dead in the eye as he recounts this, and I am sure that only I can see the triumphant glint there. I know in this moment that all the stories about him were true, that he delights in the torture of young women.

"How did you know that?" the judge asks.

"Well, for one thing, the blood on the steps."

A ripple of excitement runs through the audience. I have not moved in my seat so much as an inch since he began speaking. My ears are buzzing, and I desperately wish that I had a cup of water, for I feel as if I should surely faint.

"And?" the judge prompts.

"It appeared that a struggle had occurred, as I found several pieces of furniture upended in an upstairs chamber and there was blood on the floor. I followed the blood into the garden, where it appeared to me that the ground had been disturbed. I returned with the local magistrate who agreed that something was afoot and had the garden dug up."

"Can you tell the court what you found in the garden, Major?"

Major Reeves gives a sad smile, but one that still shows the sharpness of his white teeth. "Your Lordship, I can."

Thirty-Nine

LIJSBETH

SNAPDRAGON: your tongue delivers only falsehoods.

It takes a further two days by stagecoach to reach the city of Portsmouth. Our lodgings here are temporary, as William explains that he has some business in the city before we continue on to Hampshire where his family resides. "Perhaps we will even go to Brighton, visit a proper seaside town. I'm afraid there is not much in the way of entertainment suitable for a young lady here," William tells me at breakfast the next morning. Nonetheless, he gives me some pocket money and bids me not to stray too far from the inn while he is conducting his business. He says nothing of why he leaves me in bed each night to go sleep on the uncomfortable chaise alone. There is nothing in his good-humored demeanor that even suggests that he thinks anything is amiss. As for me, I find myself too embarrassed to question him. He gives me a cheerful kiss goodbye, then leaves for his business in the city.

I hadn't known what to expect of an English city, and I do not find much outside the walls of the inn to occupy me. Aside from a few streets with colorful houses and clean-swept steps, most of the city is full of naval machines and transport ships, dirty alleys and hungry faces. I wonder where in England my sister has been taken, and if every city is thus or if she is somewhere more hospitable.

The streets are like mazes, and I walk without direction. I am certain that, if I can just find some flowers, they will guide me to my sister, show me a glimpse of where I might find her. I keep walking in the hopes of coming across a garden, but after the better part of an hour, I have only gotten myself hopelessly lost in the bowels of the city.

As thick clouds begin to roll in off the harbor, I not only despair of never finding any flowers but of even finding my way back to the inn. My English is not very good, and I dare not ask any of the women that are lounging against the stone buildings or the men that hurry out of the alleys, adjusting their breeches and avoiding my eye.

After what feels like an eternity, I emerge into a cobbled square. It is not neat by any means, but at least there are no buildings overhanging it, blocking what little daylight there is.

There are a few carts set up, and a young boy selling some sort of etchings catches my eye. "First witchcraft trial in over a century!" he calls to me, his English so strange that I can hardly understand him. "See the treasonous Witch of Waterloo!" He thrusts an etching at me. "Only a penny, miss. Don't miss your chance to own a piece of history!"

I give him his penny and study the smudgy paper. I cannot read the words underneath, but the picture is what arrests me. It is a crude sketch. The artist has given her long, unkempt hair and wild eyes, but I still recognize my sister.

I am torn between relief that I have found her so easily and terror that she is being held on such charges. Is England really such a backward place? Do they really try women as witches here? Perhaps I misunderstood the boy, and she is not on trial for witchcraft. But then, what?

He is still hawking his wares to passersby when I approach him again. He gives me a wary look. "No returns, miss."

I shake my head, pointing to the picture, then gesturing *Where?* He gives me another incredulous look, then points up at a great hulking building, where a stream of people are pushing their way up the steps. I take a hard swallow. Folding the paper, it joins my other clippings which I keep safe in my pocket.

"Good luck!" he calls after me as I follow the traffic to the courthouse, squeezing myself into the crush.

Inside, there is hardly room to breathe. I shoulder my way to a spot near the front of the upper gallery between a woman peering through opera glasses and a man with a notebook.

The trial is already underway. Standing at the witness box, a handsome young man with black hair is recounting his recruitment of Cornelia into the service of the Grande Armée. Cornelia is dressed only in her smallclothes, having probably not been able to pay the garnish to keep her clothes when taken into the jail. Though she sits serenely, I can feel the anger seething behind her indifferent facade. This is the man who appeared at the ball and led her away from me that night, and whoever he is, I like him no better than I did the first time I laid eyes on him.

His testimony completed, he is dismissed, and the next witness is called.

I sit up straighter, certain that I misheard. But then there he is, striding in, sharp and handsome in the same uniform that I used to watch for in the Dubois house.

William states his name for the court when instructed. As he turns to take his place, he catches my eye, momentarily stumbling over his words before quickly catching himself and continuing.

"And how came you to be acquainted with the defendant?"

He clears his throat. "She came to be known to me in the course of my work as a correspondent with Armand Boucher."

My vision swims. I double over, as if I was feeling the sharp pain of losing my little friend all over again. The perfume and stench of bodies around me is too much, and I wish that I were outside, even if the polluted air reeks of dead fish. But I cannot leave my sister, so I force myself to stay and watch.

"Though I never met her, Sergeant Boucher told me of a system she devised in which flowers were used to pass communication to the English," William continues. "She wrote a popular lady's column which provided the basis of the code. Men's sweethearts were recruited to pass the flowers along, thus bringing the message to the enemy."

"And this...code, it was used to pass along English secrets?"

"To the best of my knowledge, Your Lordship."

It is ridiculous. How can my husband believe that? How could anyone think that a lady's column could be used in such a way? From what Eugenie and the other girls explained to me, all the flowers had only the most general of meanings, tailored to situations like dances and courtship. What could the army possibly think to communicate with them?

William's testimony completed, he steps down and then another witness is called. This man also wears the regalia of the English military, his coat heavy with medals and epaulets. Though I would not be able to say why if asked, there is something about him that makes me squirm a little, as if it were me who he was staring at with those pale blue eyes instead of Cornelia.

My heartbeat kicks up, and my palms go clammy as I suddenly realize that I know this man. He has shaved his mustachio, but Major Reeves is every bit as repulsive as when he had his hands on me in the cabinet. Judging from Cornelia's narrowed eyes and high, tensed shoulders, she knows him as well and thinks just as little of him.

Major Reeves begins to speak, and I watch as my sister's hatred simmers and distills into something else. It seems an emotion so foreign to her that it takes me a moment to see it for what it is: fear. The spirited woman who was unperturbed by prison and battle is afraid of this man.

He is telling the court how Cornelia had been promised to him in marriage and how she rebuffed him. But then the questioning takes a morbid turn.

"Can you tell the court what you found there in the garden, Major?"

"Your Lordship, I can."

My throat is dry as parchment. The man standing beside me has ceased his scribbling and leans forward, hanging on the major's next words.

"The fresh remains of the late Mr. Shaw buried in a shallow grave beneath a lavender bush."

For a moment all sound in the courtroom ceases. The major is smug as he allows his words to find their mark. Meanwhile, Cornelia's face has gone three shades whiter.

Then an uproar erupts. My sister stands accused not only of witchcraft and treason but murder.

In vain, the judge tries to call the court to order. England might have been spared the Reign of Terror, but the people here are just as hungry for a reckoning. And Cornelia, with her cool demeanor and aristocratic background, provides the perfect scapegoat.

The man with the notebook begins feverishly sketching her again, giving her long lashes to go along with her full lips and breasts, which he spends extra time emphasizing. "The Temptress of Sussex," he tells me with some glee when he catches me watching him.

The judge has finally brought the hall to order with threats of contempt, and the questioning resumes. Major Reeves is accommodating and gracious, expanding on points when asked, and deferential when addressing the judge or jury. Cornelia, in contrast, looks wild with her unbrushed hair and grimy smallclothes, her expression one of pure contempt.

"Why has this crime just come to light now?" the judge asks.

"Your Lordship, when I informed the local magistrate about my terrible discovery, we agreed that it would be best to keep the information confidential until we could locate Miss Shaw. Not knowing her whereabouts, we feared if she were to learn that we had discovered her crime, that she might flee farther abroad. Arrangements were quietly made to lay poor Mr. Shaw to rest with dignity, but beyond the sexton, the magistrate, and me, no one else was informed. And as he had no male issue to which to pass his fortune, there was no need for a reading of Mr. Shaw's will to be made public."

"It has certainly made for great deal of excitement in the court," the judge mutters, not wholly pleased about the matter.

"And I do apologize for that, Your Lordship. It was never my intention to create a scene. You see, when we received our orders for the Continent, I had to abandon my search for Miss Shaw, and I never expected to find the very same in Belgium, just miles from where we were stationed. It was there that I learned of her...proclivities and disturbing habits. I thought it best to see her transported back to England and brought to trial under good, English laws."

Cornelia is standing, making a pitiful attempt at smoothing out her petticoat. For all that I don't know my sister, I feel as if we have been living like two trees growing beside each other, their branches never touching but connected by a deep network of roots. Could she really have killed someone? And her own blood, no less?

But in this moment, I know. I know that it does not matter if she killed him or not. If she did, she must have had good reason. What other recourse are women given but to use their wits? Who will protect us, if not ourselves? My knife might have just as easily found Isidore's heart as his shoulder, and I could have found myself in the very same position as my sister.

The sounds of the courtroom begin to fade. Everything that is spilling from Major Reeves's mouth is lies, all lies. He is just like Isidore, putting on a face of charm and innocence in front of his mother and then turning around and committing the vilest of crimes. Why can no one else here see it? Why do they all hang upon his every word as if he were an authority on the minds and motivations of women? I want to stand up, to shout that he is a liar. I want his vile accusations to clog in his throat, choking him. My sister is not a murderer. She could never hurt a soul, I just know it.

It's getting hot inside the courtroom, and I feel dizzy, a strange ringing in my ears. I look about to see if anyone else is feeling the heat or notices that anything is amiss, but they are all too trained on the vignette below. Oh, but the major looks smug as he lavishes detail upon detail about Cornelia's crimes.

Then, something happens.

He pauses for a moment to clear his throat, but his coughing only intensifies. The judge asks if he needs something to drink before continuing, and Major Reeves only shakes his head. But the coughing does not subside, and soon he is gasping for air.

Something is very wrong. The major's face is turning purple, his mouth gagging open as if he cannot get a breath in.

After a prolonged moment, it becomes apparent that he is not going to stop gagging. "Major? Someone call for a physician!" the judge orders.

Something red is protruding from between the major's teeth, and I am not the only one to notice it.

"There's something in his mouth!" cries the woman with the opera glasses.

Everyone's voices are far away, and I cannot do anything except stare. It's a rose, deep red, its head blossoming out of the major's mouth.

William rushes over, slamming him on the back to try to dislodge the flower. But the thorns are dug in deep, and it will not budge.

Blood is pouring forth from the major's mouth now, and he falls to the floor, his body stiff and jerky as he convulses. William finally gets purchase on the flower and is able to pull it out, but not without tearing at the flesh of the major's tongue and throat. The major screams in agony.

He will never tell another lie again.

I finally start to return to myself, the ringing in my ears fading and my body once more solidly anchored. Women have fainted, and the judge's wig has slid off, his bald head beaded with perspiration. "Take the prisoner away!" he is screaming. But no one seems to be willing to touch her, to even get close to her, so she stays in her little box. Her face is a mask of apathy, but even from this distance I can see her pupils flare as she watches everything unfold.

"Do you see?" The dark-haired soldier who was testifying when I came in has reappeared, standing in front of the crowd. "She is a witch!"

"Miss, are you all right?" Dazed, I look up to see the man with the sketchpad peering down at me. He gestures to my hands, and I find they are bleeding, a hundred little pricks of blood, as if I had been clutching the stem of a thorny rose.

"Is—is it o-over?"

The man looks at me with my bleeding hands, my strange accent and stutter. “I daresay it is now. She’s just proven herself a witch and a murderer.”

Forty

LIJSBETH

OLEANDER: betrayal.

They have all but decided that Cornelia is guilty. It is only a matter of drawing it out, of making it look as if they have given the matter some consideration before sentencing her.

And Cornelia, more than anyone, seems to understand this. She watches the jury confer in hushed tones with the stoic detachment of Joan of Arc. It takes them but a few moments to reach their decision.

"How find you in the case presented before you?" the judge asks.

"Your Lordship, we find the defendant guilty on all the charges brought against her."

It should come as no surprise, but still, the words slice through me like a knife. Guilty. Guilty of murder, of treason. Guilty of being a woman and possessing that which men covet.

The judge takes pleasure in his sentencing. "Cornelia Shaw, as seen by the evidence presented here today, you are found guilty of those most contemptible, most evil of offenses: treason *and* murder."

The crowd erupts, their bloodthirsty appetite finally sated.

"You are hereby sentenced to hang by the neck until dead," the judge shouts over the din of the courtroom.

William is nowhere to be seen. Everyone is falling over themselves to be the first to see Cornelia led away, but I push my way through the crush with single-minded determination, only knowing that I must escape this building.

Outside at last, I double over, wretch out my empty stomach until I'm gagging with pain. The sharp sea air cuts into my lungs, forces me to understand that this is not some dream, nor some strange vision. This is real, all of it.

"Lijsbeth!"

William is pushing through the crowd that has spilled out the steps. I pretend I don't see him and continue my charge out into the square. Everything is dark and gray and wet. I want to get away from this evil place, go somewhere beautiful and safe. But no such place exists; the closest that ever did was in William's arms.

William easily catches up to me. "What are you doing here?" he asks, taking me by the hand. "Please don't tell me that you walked here from the inn. Come, I'll find a hack and—" He looks down. "Good God, what has happened to your hands?"

I snatch my hands out of his grasp. How can he be so casual when he has all but been the one to drive the final nail into Cornelia's coffin? He spoke against a woman who has clearly been badly used. I did not think my William capable of it.

"Lijsbeth, please, tell me what is wrong."

My anger is burning so brightly that I don't think I will be able to get the words out. "C-Cornelia Shaw is m-my sister."

William's face falls; his mouth opens and closes. "What?" I can see the full implication of my confession settling over him.

"I didn't know. I had no idea she was your sister, that you even *had* a sister."

Because, of course, what *does* William really know of me? How many of my silences does he simply fill in with assumptions? I had thought that our souls were sympathetic, that we did not need words to bind us together, but now I realize that I was only what he wished me to be. He knows that I was a maid, and that I was badly used. But he does not know the depths of my terror at the van den Berg house. He doesn't know that my favorite color is blue or that I used to name the mice that lived in the kitchen walls and cry when the cat killed them. He doesn't know any of the little things that have made me the woman he claims to love.

It is all too much. I am in a strange country with nothing except my husband, and now, I cannot even trust him. He will not share a bed with me, will not admit that there is something about me that repulses him. And whether he realized what he was doing or not, he has betrayed me, stolen my sister from me. I turn to go.

"Lijsbeth, please, wait." He reaches for me. "Let me explain. I—"

There are no words profound enough to express what I am feeling. If I had flowers at my fingertips, I would bind them together in an arrangement that spoke of betrayal, heartbreak, and despair. So instead, I wrench the ring from my finger and throw it at his boots, wishing that it would crack open the cobbles and swallow me up.

"Please, this changes nothing between us! I did only what duty demanded of me, both in my regiment and the courtroom." He does look truly remorseful, his brow pained, his eyes searching my face.

Words are bubbling up, choking in my throat. I can feel the flowers in my mind, ready to spring to my defense. I don't want to hurt William, but it's unfair that he keeps speaking, keeps trying to explain himself, when he knows that I cannot respond.

He must sense this, because he puts his palms up in surrender. "I won't say another word. Please, just come home with me. There are pickpockets and other unsavory characters about. This is no place for a lady."

I don't care about any of those things. William has no idea what my life used to be, for if he did, he would realize that there is only one thing I am scared of, and it has already happened.

There are a thousand things that I want to say, but I can only manage to get a single word out.

"Bastard."

Forty-One

CORNELIA

AMARYLLIS: pride. I shall not bend.

She was there today. My sister was at my trial.

I didn't see her, but then, I didn't need to see her to know that she was watching me from the gallery. Just like the first time we laid eyes on each other at the ball, she watched me from above like some sort of guardian angel.

And she is an angel, I am convinced of it, an avenging angel. If flowers seem to betray any love harbored in my heart, they spring from her in anger, like hornets rattled from their nest. I wonder where her anger comes from, how she harnesses it.

A sigh escapes me as I look out the narrow window into the gray city beyond. I wish she had not come, had not expended herself on my behalf. I have resigned myself to my fate. Why cannot everyone else?

"I will take my meal now," I inform the guard through the door. I may be brought low, but I shall never be low enough not to attend to whatever necessities I am still able. They have taken my gown, denied me any small comforts such as a hairbrush or mirror. If food is all that they will allow me—though moldy and mean it may be—then I shall take every crumb from them. The guard laughs at my demand.

"You'll eat when you're told. Besides, there's someone here to see you."

Since coming here, I have learned that the guards have little compunction in the way of using me as a means to make a bit of money and will occasionally admit a curious spectator. I have had more than my share of leering men who are happy to pay a shilling to see the Witch of Waterloo or whatever ridiculous moniker they have bestowed upon me now.

But the man that the guard shows in now is not some ghoul off the street nor yet even a stranger.

I had not noticed how comely he was in the courtroom, with his blue eyes and amiable complexion. He is the picture of a good English boy, proud and brave and eager to serve Crown and Country, though there is a shadow that lingers just behind his eyes. Would that I never had to countenance the attention of an Englishman again.

"I've seen you before," I tell Captain Norton before he can extend a greeting. "Not just in the courtroom but in Brussels at the ball. I suppose you thought that passing encounter made you authority enough to testify against me? Tell me, were you able to ascertain my character just from that one glance across the room? Or perhaps you have come to gloat?"

"I have not come to gloat," he tells me, and he does look rather beaten down, dark circles under his eyes, a tightness at his mouth. "I have come—I have come on behalf of someone. Someone very close to you."

I gesture to the bench that serves as the only other seat in the cell, but he declines.

"Well? Must I drag every word out of you? It was *you* who has come to intrude upon *my* solitude. Who is this mystery person on whose behalf you have come?"

"Your sister."

I fold my hands at my waist so that he cannot see the sudden tremor that has seized them. I feign casualness. "What of her?"

"She is my wife and I… I love her. Beyond all measure and all reason. I would not see her hurt. And I fear that my testimony has hurt her, very much."

"I only just learned of her existence. What makes you think that I care anything at all for her?"

He gives me a sardonic look. "To know Lijsbeth is to love her. Don't insult us both by pretending otherwise."

I let out a little sigh. "Very well. And what would you have me do? Pen her a letter begging her forgiveness on your behalf?"

"You?" He looks surprised. "Why, you need do nothing. I will see to it. There is always something that can be done, some paperwork that can be held up or some bureaucrat who only needs a little convincing with the appropriate incentive."

I am less convinced by his rosy view of English justice. "You testified against me."

"I had no choice in the matter, but allow me to beg your forgiveness all the same."

I suppose for his own conscience, he must return to Lijsbeth and tell her that he did everything in his power to help me. And what does she think, I wonder, now that she knows the truth about me? Is she glad that we found each other? Or does she regret learning that she has a murderess for a sister?

We slide into silence. Captain Norton adjusts his helmet under his arm, looks uncomfortable. "Did you—did you really kill that man?"

"That man? The man who did unspeakable things to me since I was a child? The man who sold my sister, his own niece?" I meet his eye. "Would you blame me if I did?"

The captain has the decency to look contrite. "No, I suppose not," he murmurs. "Do you know anything of Lijsbeth's life after she left England?"

I look at the captain, closer now, and see the fine lines around his clear blue eyes, the knot of worry tightening his jaw. "I am hardly the person to ask. I only just reunited with her. Surely you know more of her than I do."

He finally sits, placing his helmet beside him on the bench and letting out a great sigh as he braces his elbows on his knees. "I should, shouldn't I? I'm afraid that I have been a poor excuse for a husband."

"If you came here to feel sorry for yourself and smooth matters over with your wife, Captain, then I am afraid I cannot help you. Now, you will excuse me, but I am tired from my ordeal and would like to rest."

I speak as if I had a choice in the matter of who calls on me, and how long they stay. I am not a lady with a parlor; I am a prisoner sentenced to hang.

But the captain nonetheless stands, taking up his helmet. "Of course. I thank you for your time."

Turning to leave, he stops before he has even reached the door. He tilts his head slightly at me, considering. "You saw what happened in the courtroom today."

I could ask him of what he is speaking, but there is little use in pretending. "I did."

"And at Waterloo. Was that—was that truly your doing? The flowers?"

There is a gull outside, wheeling and crying. I follow its path through the window, allowing the silence to grow long.

"Were you there?" I finally ask him.

"I was."

"Then, you saw for yourself. Tell me, what did you think when you saw the bloody earth pour forth flowers?"

He hesitates, his throat bobbing. "I thought that God himself was responsible," he says, his voice low and earnest. "I thought that perhaps I had died and was in Heaven."

I let out a bitter laugh. "But it was not God. God did nothing to stop the slaughter." I come away from the window, meet his gaze squarely. "If I told you that it was born of love, that it was solely a reflection of one woman's love, what would you say?"

The lines at the corner of his eyes soften. "I would say that your love was very great."

"Ah! But what good is love if it has nowhere to go? All the flowers and love and tears could do nothing to save…those men," I finish, unable to say Henri's name out loud. The captain looks down at his boots. "I see you have no answer," I tell him, bitterly triumphant.

"It is a hard question you put forth," he finally says. "But I would say that it was not in vain, that love is still the most powerful thing in this world, more powerful even than—no, let me finish," he says when he sees me opening my mouth to argue, "—more powerful even than emperors and cannons and death."

"And yet, I am in a cell with a noose days away from my neck, my lover dead."

"Do you really not see, Miss Shaw?" He takes a step toward me, his blue eyes bright. "You have a sister that loves you, and I am sure other people as well. You ask what the point of love is if it has nowhere to go? I ask you, what is the point of living if not to love? Would you rob your sister of the love she has for you?"

I flinch, thinking of Sophie. "I wish she wouldn't, for I certainly do not deserve her love."

He heaves a sigh, threads his fingers through his hair. "I see that you are determined to have your way in this," he says. "I will leave you to your rest now." With a short bow, he turns to leave.

His hand is at the door when I stop him. "Captain, you did not ask me if the roses in the courtroom were my doing as well. Are you not curious about my answer?"

He pauses, looking back at me. "I just assumed..."

"It was not me," I tell him. "I think you should speak with your wife. Learn who it is you claim to love but do not even so much as seem to know."

Forty-Two

LIJSBETH

BITTERSWEET NIGHTSHADE: the truth will come to light.

Dawn in England is not so very different from Brussels. Some days are cloudy and dark, some wear sparkling mantles of pink and lavender. Birds sing, and the sound of carts lumber to life down the streets. But then the cries of seagulls and the rancid salt air soon follow, and there is no longer any mistaking where I am.

After running from the courthouse, I came back and took refuge in the bedchamber, bolting the door from the inside. William arrived shortly behind me, and I listened to him pleading with me through the door, until he finally gave up and retired to the little parlor. Though my heart was breaking, it gave me time to plan.

I take my leave of the inn, before even the scullery maid has lit the fires, stealing out past William who is awkwardly sprawled on the settee, still in his coat and boots. I slip out into the lane, the brisk air nipping at my cheeks. I ask the first person I see how to get to Sussex and am dismayed to learn that it is not a town but an entire county and will take the better part of the day and several coach changes to get there.

Any romantic fancies I had about William are inconsequential now. He betrayed me, betrayed my sister. His family would never have accepted me, and I suspect the novelty of taking a Belgian servant as a wife would lose its luster once we reached Hampshire. No, there is nothing for me here and potentially everything in Sussex.

My small savings, comprising my work earnings as well as pin money from William, are only just enough to get me coach fare, and even then, I must walk the last hour of the journey. Even though I don't know what town I'm going to, I need no map; I can see it perfectly in my mind, feel the garden pulling me toward it, and the flowers guide me along the way.

My blistering feet and parched throat are forgotten when I finally come upon the stone gate climbing with rose vines. I have seen this house in my dreams, felt the soft breeze sweep in off the hills, and heard the toll of the village bell ringing in the distance. Though named Hill Cottage, it is a large house, gracious and stately against the backdrop of rolling green.

The hedges are overgrown, the fountain dry, and it looks as if it has not been lived in for some time, but the gate does not squeak when I push it open. Since there is nothing for me in the house, I make my way around the side, stepping over brambles and using the stone wall to steady myself.

Though I have never stepped foot here, I could find my way with my eyes closed. The back of the house opens up to an expansive view of gently rolling hills, and though the garden is in want of weeding and care, it is still the most beautiful thing I have ever seen.

Birdsong fills the late-afternoon air as I take off my boots, unpeel my stockings, and let my feet sink into the loamy dirt. I am exhausted from my journey, but the sun warms my face, and something blooms deep within me.

My locket is singing, vibrating like an excited child. The tarnished silver has become so much a part of me, warm and familiar in its weight against my chest, that I sometimes forget that it is there at all. But my hand strays to it now, and it opens with a click.

The rose petals within, once papery and translucent, blush with vibrant color. They grow darker as I wander the gravel path toward the far end of the garden, like a botanical compass pointing north.

It leads me all the way to the back wall. Crouching, I brush away the dead branches and leaves until a tangled rosebush is revealed, crimson petals stark against the dirt. Violent red, the color of blood, of my soldier's coat, of my little friend's untimely end.

"Miss Cornelia, is that you?"

A woman is coming out of the house, wiping her hands on her apron. She stops short when she sees me, her mouth falling open. "Holy Mary," she says, the color draining from her ruddy cheeks. But then a big smile is cracking her face, and she is waving me to her. "Bless me, but you look just like her! Well, come here, child, and let me see you."

I'm given no leave to recollect myself or finish my exploration before she is folding me into an embrace that squeezes my ribs and threatens to suffocate me.

She pulls back to inspect me, her wrinkled eyes softening further. "You won't remember me," she says. "You were just a babe when the master sent you away. A black day it was for this house. Betsy Patterson is my name, and I'm the head maid here at Hill Cottage. Well, now the only maid since Mr. Shaw left us. But never you mind that. Come inside, come inside. We must get you warmed up with a proper cup of tea and summat to eat. Look at you! Why you're just a little slip of a thing, aren't you?"

Linking her arm through mine, she leads me down the overgrown paths, away from the rosebush which is still calling my name. Mrs. Patterson prattles on good-naturedly, asking about my journey and where it is that I have come from. I throw one last look back into the garden where the roses are waving to me in the breeze and then follow her inside.

Mrs. Patterson settles me in the kitchen, and I watch as she clatters about making tea and a plate of sandwiches. The dutiful servant in me feels strange sitting while someone else is working, but my body is too exhausted to rise and help her, so I allow myself to be fussed over. "You'll have to excuse me, going on," she says. "You've no idea how lonely a soul gets in a house like this with naught but the mice for company."

Pressing a warm cup into my hand, she settles heavily on the creaking bench opposite me and pours out another cup for herself.

"I bargain you'll be wanting to hear about the family?"

I nod, still dazed from this sudden turn of events, and she is only too eager to oblige. "I don't know how much you remember, but after your mother left, everything went to the devil. Mr. Shaw found himself guardian to two very young girls. He never wanted children, wasn't the kind of man to look kindly at the follies of little ones, you know. Oh, but I begged him to keep the both of you together. Cornelia was already five and such a little beauty, and it didn't take much to see that she could make a good marriage on her appearance alone.

"Now, that's not to say that you weren't pretty in your own way, but you were only three, and such a little thing. Never said a word, and such a serious little face! Mr. Shaw didn't know what to do with you. He claimed that he brought you to a charity house and that he would send for you when you were older. I don't believe it was ever his plan, and when I learned he'd taken you to an orphanage across the Channel, I had John the butler write a letter to get you back, never mind what the master would say. But when they wrote back, they said that you'd been taken by a Belgian family as a companion for their only child. Oh, I did try to find the family, but they wouldn't tell me, and as I can't write nor read, there was naught else for me to do."

My cup trembles in my hands as my history is laid out before me, all the terrible details that I so longed to know. There was never a loving mother who tearfully took me to the orphanage, hoping to collect me one day. My own uncle sold me off, and that was that.

"You still are a quiet one, aren't you? And what of your mother, you'll want to know about her. Oh! What a beauty she was, and kind. Too kind for this world, I think. The master used her badly. Took her for a wife when his brother, her first husband, died. They'd been married but oh, a year perhaps, when he died. Mr. Shaw had always coveted her, and she being a widow had no one to protect her. But for all that he coveted her, he used her ill. Got the two of you off her and then didn't want anything more to do with her. Perhaps he would have been kinder if one or both of you had been boys, but it was girls he got. He took his hand to her, and I don't know what else. Who can blame her when she ran off to Paris to be with her soldier love? Though, I will never understand how she could leave you both with Mr. Shaw, knowing the kind of man he was. I hope that wherever she is, she at least knows peace."

My cup clatters to the table, tea spilling. "F-father?"

Mrs. Patterson looks at me. "Oh dear. Oh, my poor child. Did you not know he was your father, and your uncle as well?" Mrs. Patterson tuts and insists on cleaning up the tea while I sit, too stunned to move.

"Miss Cornelia ran off some months ago now. And it's a good

thing she did, too." Mrs. Patterson leans in. "You'll have heard about the discovery in the garden, by now? It was a bad business, it was. Major Reeves walking in with the magistrate like he owned the place, digging around in the garden. But all that is over now, and Mr. Shaw is laid to rest in the village, God rest his black soul." She crosses herself. "What was I saying? Oh yes—that the house is yours, should you want it. Mr. Shaw didn't have a will, and no male issue. Now, Mr. Reeves—that is, the major—he thought it might come to him. But of course, there was no understanding with Miss Cornelia, and she has not come to claim her inheritance, either. Well, I am sure I've said more than my piece, and now I've gone and upset you. Listen to me, prattling on like a hen!"

"M-Mrs. P-Patterson, will you excuse m-me?" I push back from the table, leaving her with her mouth compulsively opening and closing.

Back in the fresh country air of the garden, I can finally breathe again. I take great gulps of it, bracing my hand against the cool brick. The sun is starting to sink, a cold edge returning to the air. Could this really all be mine? Would I even want it? Surely it must be up to Cornelia to claim it as her birthright. But she is in prison, sentenced to death. And I am a married woman with a husband awaiting my return, even if I have no intention of returning.

The rosebush in the back corner beckons me, promising me respite from the tumult of my thoughts if only I will come a little closer.

Kneeling on the ground, I cup one of the blood-red blossoms in my hands. Such a red I have never seen before, deeper than blood, fathomless as a ruby.

My darling girl. The voice comes from the petals themselves, singing within my mind. *Come, my own little love. You are returned home, and I can now show you the truth. I whispered it to you all these years, searched for you in every blossom, every thorny stem. But we are now reunited, and you shall know all.*

I choke on a sob at the sound of the voice, for this is my mother. It has never been the flowers nor even Cornelia. All these years, it has been the voice of my mother calling to me, using the flowers as a means to find me, to guide me.

Everyone believes that our mother ran off to Paris. But my mother is not with her lover or on some sunny foreign shore. She is dead in the ground, buried beneath the flowers that are even now speaking to me. On the other side of the path is the disturbed dirt where my father was buried and exhumed. I knew it as soon as my fingers touched the rose. The soil mingles, my parents' stories twining like tangled roots.

Will you hear my story? she asks me. *Will you stay a moment and learn where it is you come from? My darling girl, my own little love.*

How can I deny such a request? I should be afraid, but listening to her words feels like falling into the warm, motherly embrace of which I have dreamed all these years. So I open my heart and let her story spill into me like water rushing from a dam.

The images come fast and sharp into my mind. *"Is it not enough that you have trapped me in matrimony?" my mother demands of him. She is small of stature, but there is a fierceness in her eyes. Behind her cower two little girls, hands clasped, holding each other tightly. They have heard the fights between their uncle and mother before, but this time it is different. This time there is a current of dread that permeates the air.*

The man's lip curls. "You, madam, came freely enough. I take no more than a husband is entitled to take. Your willfulness is what earns you such reproof, and you would do well to see your daughters don't inherit your obstinate spirit, else I should be forced to beat it out of them as well."

"Go to your room, girls," she instructs. The girls don't move, but then their uncle roars at them, and they run back upstairs, peering down from the balustrades on the landing.

He has threatened her girls for the last time. If he means to strike them, he will have to go through her first. And that is just what he does.

Perhaps he did not mean to hit her so hard that she reeled back and hit her head on the corner of the marble table. Perhaps not, but then again, he is a strong man, and he does not seem particularly perturbed as he watches the blood ooze out from her thick gold hair.

He buries her in the garden. Less questions that way. It's not a pretty business, but there it is. When anyone asks him what became of his young wife, he tells them the same story he will someday tell his own daughter: that she ran off to be with a soldier. "And a good riddance," he will add, hatred still simmering behind his eyes.

They are his daughters, but he has never felt any affection for the two little girls. Burdens, that what girls are. Dowries and dresses, seasons in London, that's what he can expect after raising them and keeping them under his roof for years. The older one is pretty, and he has seen an intelligence in her that makes him think he could at least get a good marriage for her, one that would benefit his business schemes. One is more manageable than two. The younger does not speak and is perhaps deaf, too. He will take her to the poorhouse, let them find a place for her. Really, it is a kindness of him. He's not equipped to care for a simpleton, and she will be given charity and good, honest work. He only feels the smallest twinge of guilt as he leaves her on the steps and feels her eyes on him, the same eyes of her dead mother's. But then he remembers the strange way that he once saw her mumbling to a flower until it sprouted thorns, and he hurries his step. Her mother was like that, too. There had always been something odd about her, the way she took to the garden and would talk to herself for hours, her lips moving with no sound coming out. No, he won't be responsible for another young woman who seems to commune with the very Devil himself.

I take a shuddering breath, force myself to keep watching as the images flicker, move forward in time. *A young woman with golden hair moving through a dark house, carrying a teacup in her trembling hands. It is Cornelia, grown. I can feel the painful thud of her heart against her ribs as she finds our father sitting at his desk. He regards her with surprise that quickly shifts to wariness. "I have brought you your tea, Uncle."*

"Finally making yourself useful, then." He watches her place the cup on his desk, then scowls. "Well? What are you doing standing there? Get out of here."

She drops a demure curtsy and turns to go. Just as she is about to pass through the door, she gives one last glance over his shoulder, assuring herself that he is drinking the tea.

Every day for the next month, she brings her uncle his tea. And every day, she mixes a tiny amount of powder into the liquid.

She had been ready, had been preparing her escape for some time. It was only when the suitor came that she realized how quickly she must act if she were to avoid a lifetime of beatings such that her mother had endured. Her uncle has been growing thinner about his jowls, and a racking cough often shakes him in the evenings now. With any luck, it will not be much longer.

But her ministrations will not have the chance to complete their job. Her uncle must have heard her moving about the house, because he comes to her door, just like when she was a small girl and he would force his way inside.

Perhaps if he had not come to her door that night, she would not have run. Perhaps the nightshade would have killed him in a few months' time and his death would have been ruled the result of an apoplectic fit. But she does not have a few months, and regardless of her uncle's vileness, he is her guardian. Without him, she will be more vulnerable to the man's suit. No, it must be now.

I can feel the weight of the brass candlestick in her perspiring hands, feel the painful thud of her heart against her ribs as she swings her bedchamber door open and meets him face-to-face. I can see the surprise, then fear in his small eyes as he realizes what is happening. The crack of his skull makes bile rise in her throat, but she brings the candlestick down again—just in case. When she is certain that he will not draw another breath, she drags him from her chamber down the hall, and out into the garden. He is still a large man, despite the effects of the poison, and it takes her the better part of an hour to maneuver his body outside.

She wipes her arm across her perspiring brow, leaving a streak of dirt. She is beautiful in the moonlight, her yellow hair glowing like a halo as she sets to digging. She hums while she digs, as if she were embroidering a pillow or arranging a vase of flowers. It was not supposed to end like this, but it has, and she cannot be sorry. The grave yawns open in the moonlight, awaiting its offering.

When she is done, she pats the earth flat with the shovel, then spits on the fresh grave. "You don't deserve to rest among my mother's flowers," she says. "I hope you rot."

How melancholy the dawn draws, bruised light and damp air, as she washes and dresses, taking care to pin her hair with every comb that might later be pawned if needed. She studies her reflection in the mirror and then, as if sensing that I am watching her over her shoulder, smiles.

The memories rush out of me in a deluge, and I gasp, curling my fingers into the dirt to steady myself. My dear mother has shown me all the stories, all the pain, that have shaped the course of my life. I scramble to my feet. I do not think I can bear to carry the sorrows of so many lifetimes.

"You're not leaving already, are you, dear?" Mrs. Patterson has come out of the house, her brow creased with concern. "Did you find what you were looking for?"

I nod. The only thing worse than the knowing is having to tell Cornelia the truth about what happened to our mother and who our uncle truly was. How cruel the world is for not giving us even one golden memory of our mother to carry with us. How cruel that our separation came so young, and with it, so much blood and loss.

Despite Mrs. Patterson's pleas to at least stay the night, I know that I must go. There is nothing for me here now, and I don't think I can bear to spend another moment around the ghosts that haunt this place. I walk slowly out through the gloaming and begin my journey back, still weak from the first one. My heart is weary, and I long to run to William, to bury my head in his shoulder and unburden myself, but then I remember that he is simply a stranger who proved himself untrustworthy, and that I am truly alone.

Forty-Three

CORNELIA

PENNYROYAL: flee away.

Sometimes when I awaken in the morning, before the guard comes with the slop bucket, or the miserable cry of the beggar boy rings through the empty streets, I fancy that I am back in a field in France, sun warming my face as I lie in the grass with Henri and Sophie. We are tired and perhaps a little hungry, but we are together. Sophie and I pick flowers, and later I give Henri a reading lesson. As the sun dips, we gather together, my head on Henri's shoulder, Sophie's in my lap. But then, inevitably, the deplorable reality of my situation resurfaces, and I remember what I have done. Henri is dead, and Sophie hates me, and I settle back into my punishment.

I think, if I were to be given the chance to begin over from that night in Sussex, I would not do a thing differently. Everything I did led me to Henri and Sophie, and I cannot regret that, even if I now carry a heavy load of guilt. I have loved and experienced more in a single year than many people do their entire lives. Captain Norton was right, in that one respect, at least.

A key fumbles in the lock, and I grab a loose stone, ready to defend myself against another clumsy advance by my guards. But it is a different man today, and he has someone with him.

I let the stone fall to the ground. "Lijsbeth!"

Now that I have been sentenced to hang, I am not supposed to receive visitors, but I see her press a coin into the guard's hand.

The frail little creature that stands before me looks as if she has not eaten or slept in days, but there is a determination in the jut of her chin, a flinty resolve in her sad brown eyes.

"Will you sit?" I ask her, more worried that she is at the point of fainting than I am of extending any social nicety.

She slides, more than sits down, onto the bench, and I rush forward, afraid that she will fall. I wish I had something to offer her, more than just moldy bread or a cup of fetid water. "Rest a moment," I tell her, as I help her down.

Nodding, she closes her eyes. Her breathing is labored, her lips dry and burned from sun. When she takes my hand, I can feel every small tendon and bone.

"Your captain came to see me," I tell her once she is settled, and her breathing steadies.

She looks up at me, sharp, a question on her lips.

"He loves you," I say, taking her small hand in mine again. "He thinks me a murderer, yet he came to try to secure my release, for your sake."

Her lips part farther, and she struggles to get up. I gently press her back down for fear that she will overexert herself.

"What? Did you not know that your husband adores you? He is a good man, as far as men go. Though, he apparently was not successful in his appeal, as I am still here. Just as well—I am at peace with my circumstances."

With nothing else to impart, I wait for her to gain enough

strength to tell me why she has come. Silence settles around us, as gloomy as the sky without.

"I've b-been to Hill C-cottage," she says, surprising me with her voice.

"What? When?"

She doesn't answer, instead pulling out a delicate rose from her pocket and presenting it to me on the palm of her hand.

I would recognize the crimson bloom anywhere. "This is from the garden. You were just there? Why? Have you traveled all the way there and back alone?"

She looks as if she wants to say something, though it is hard to tell if it is her manner of speech or grappling with whether to divulge a secret. In the end, she says nothing, instead relying on the flower to speak for her.

Pressing the bloom into my hand, she curls my fingers around it, and then I am hearing her voice. *I want you to see what I saw. I want you to know that whatever our uncle did to you, you were justified in your actions. But dying for it is not the answer. Will you throw away your life because of your misplaced sense of guilt? You are not alone, and it is selfish not to think of those who love you still.*

And here I had thought myself past the sin of vanity. This little sprite has cut me down quite neatly. "It is not as simple as that," I say, exercising my authority as older sister.

She unloops her locket from her neck and opens it, showing me the red petals within that match my own. *When was the first time you realized that there was a language to the flowers you drew? When did you realize that you hold the key to it within you?*

I'm not sure if she expects me to answer her or not, and indeed, I wouldn't even know how to answer. She continues.

There is someone that you love, someone that yet lives. I've seen her in the flowers, felt your love for her. I once had someone I loved, and I would have done anything to keep them, but I lost them all the same. My heart was shattered, and I felt empty. But we must go on living—what else is there? And so long as we are in this cold world, we will go on with or without love. If you are lucky enough to have someone who you love, wouldn't you rather go on, if not for yourself then for their sake?

"You are very wise, little sister, but you forget that I do not have the luxury of choice. I am to die in two days' time, and there is nothing else for me but to make my peace with it."

She tosses me a stormy look. *If you do not have a choice, it is only because you have decided that you would not fight long ago. What made you pick up a pencil for the first time and sketch a flower?*

The change of subject surprises me, but I humor her. "It was a primrose," I tell her, remembering it as clearly as if it were yesterday. Uncle had given me a dressing-down after I had spoken out of turn at the dinner table, and I was in the garden nursing my pride. It was growing dark, and on a whim I plucked the little pink bloom and brought it inside with me. That evening when I was supposed to be reciting my Bible verses, I wondered if I couldn't do something to preserve the little flower. It seemed such a shame that it should only live for a short time and then be lost entirely. I suppose it gave me some sense of control.

"But when I picked up the pencil and began to commit the bloom to paper," I tell her, "something came over me. It was as if I could hear the soul of the flower. I could feel what it was to grow from the darkness, reaching for the light. I could feel the nourishing rain thrumming through my roots like blood. I knew then that there was something inside of me. I'd always known, but then it became impossible to ignore." Though, to ignore it I tried. I tried to bury it deep inside me for fear of what the world would think of me, for fear that it would make me unworthy of love.

What do you think would happen if you were to let it out?

The question makes me uncomfortable, forces me to acknowledge that there are parts of my soul that are as yet uncharted. But I have no time to meditate on it, for the guard has come to show Lijsbeth out.

My sister stands, grabbing my hand and holding it tight. She looks at me with large, pleading eyes, her unspoken words hurried as she continues.

I heard the testimony, saw for myself through the flowers what happened at Waterloo. Glancing at the iron-barred window, she turns back and gives me one last meaningful look before the guard takes her away. *I should think that if a battle can come to a standstill because of a deluge of flowers, anything else could likewise be accomplished.*

Forty-Four

LIJSBETH

RED CARNATION: alas! My poor heart. All is lost.

Outside the gaol, the sky has grown dark and heavy, letting out a torrent of rain that needles down my back. A weary mule is whipped on as it trudges through the mud. Little boys, faces stretched thin with hunger, beg pennies from passersby, then steal soggy loaves off carts when they are denied. Perhaps it was a blessing that my little friend was spared a cruel life such as that.

My heart should be light knowing that William tried to atone for the part he played in my sister's sentence. Yet all I can think of as I put my head down against the rain and wind is that it doesn't matter. He cannot save her. Only Cornelia can, and I fear that my sister does not want to save herself. It seems impossible that I should only have just found her and am now poised to lose her already.

My body is weary, spent with the effort of communicating myself through the rose. I search my pocket before remembering that I used my last coin for a private audience with Cornelia. The rain drives harder. It has been a hard two days of travel, with little to eat and no time to rest.

My fight with William seems inconsequential now as I think about our rooms and the fire that is probably in the hearth. Is he wondering where I am? Or has he figured that I chose my side between him and Cornelia? Perhaps he is relieved that he is no longer responsible for me. But my stomach still twists with guilt as I think of him waking to find me gone.

I could still go to him. Didn't I tell Cornelia to fight? Didn't I tell her that she must cling to life, strengthened by the promise of love? Why can I not rouse myself now to live by my own words? But life seems so very grim with the thought of losing the sister I only just found. William is likewise better off without me. He deserves an English wife, one who understands his country and him. One who does not cause flowers to spring forth from her in anger, choking and maiming. A good, gentle wife, who will bear him the children he deserves. Not someone broken, who could not even carry a baby.

Spots of light flicker behind my eyes as I stumble down the filthy street, narrowly avoiding a hack as cold mud splashes my face. Someone yells at me to mind myself, and there is some snickering laughter. But I can only lurch on, heedless of anything other than the fact that once I stop, I will not get up again.

When my body finally cannot carry me any farther, I sink to my knees in a muddy alley, simply another invisible face in a sea of poverty, just as it has always been my destiny to be.

Forty-Five

CORNELIA

DATURA: witchcraft.

There is no pride the night before you are set to die.

There is no pretension, and there is certainly no vanity. The noose hangs in the courtyard below, the rain and wind stirring it in a macabre dance. All of my hubris and determination flee now that I find myself alone in the night with my thoughts. I had thought that I was prepared for this, that I could meet my death with quiet fortitude. But I find that I am not, I cannot.

All I can think of is Sophie's visit in Brussels, the devastation on her face as I cut her free against her will, and knowing that I was the one responsible for it. What have I done, and how can I make it right? Whether I like it or not, my sister's words have found their mark.

What do you think would happen if you let it out?

Lijsbeth is wrong. Though I love her dearly, she is wrong. An enchanted field of blooming flowers could not save Henri. It could not stop the flow of blood or the violence of men. Whatever strange power—or perversion, as Uncle called it—is useless when faced with the cruel realities of the world.

Nonetheless, I raise myself from the straw mattress, my bones protesting with the dampness. Some Good Samaritan has paid for a Bible to be placed in my cell, but I have never prayed to God before, and I doubt he would want to hear from me now. Instead, I go to the window and wrap my fingers around the cold metal bars and let my eyes drift closed, the salty air washing over me.

Since I was a little girl, I have taken for granted hearing the whisper of flowers, been content to take any guidance they might offer, so long as it did not interfere with my carefully maintained aura of control. Their constant chorus has been a background to my life. But it was not until that day at Waterloo that something within me sang back.

I let my mind wander, to all those places both pleasant and dark, that have filled my life these twenty-two years. Henri sharing a drowsy afternoon with me in a forgotten garden. Sophie's crooked grin when I pulled her into the river. The slant of sunlight in the summer evenings in Sussex. Anna's berry-red lips, slightly parted, when she would dress my hair at night. The heavy footfalls of Uncle coming up the stairs. The sting of a backhanded slap. The stream of men constantly coming and going from our house, eager to have an audience alone with Mr. Shaw's pretty niece.

My fingers tighten around the bars as the memories come faster and sharper. Days spent in the garden, learning the secrets of the flowers. Rosemary for remorse. Mandrake for horror. Fennel for strength. Trefoil for revenge.

I can smell them, even through the putrid night air of the prison. I am the flowers, rooted and defiant, growing toward a smothered light. My love is strong, has always been strong. It was me who was frightened to recognize it for what it was.

I think of Lijsbeth, her quiet fortitude, and the way she made

Major Reeves choke on thorny roses. Was it done out of love, or anger? Is there a difference between the two? How can you not be angry with a world that treats love as a frivolous pastime but war as the pinnacle of civilization?

At Waterloo, I was hardly aware of what was happening. But now, I am calling for help. I am opening my heart and letting everything that I have held inside for so long spill out. My love and anger, yes, but also the essence of who I truly am.

I once read a story of a Roman emperor who was lecherous and self-indulgent, reveling in all things decadent. He held an orgy, in which he filled the entire palace with violet petals. At first it was a beautiful spectacle, the lovely perfume heightening the senses of the wanton guests. But then the petals fell harder, began accumulating like mountains of snow. The guests were buried alive under the avalanche, as all the while the emperor looked on in amusement.

I am not a lustful or powerful emperor; I am only a woman, one who has nothing left to lose. But I call upon the flowers, that they might help me now in my hour of need.

And they come. First soft and peaceful as snowflakes, drifting down into the darkness, then faster and thicker. The wet cobbles below grow slick with them. They bring color to the bleak night and perfume the tainted air of the city.

A few voices from the windows below mine exclaim in surprise, and I know that I am not the only one to see the petals falling, soft and sweet. I am cradled and caressed by them, until the mountain of petals is nearly to my window. Until I no longer feel metal under my fingers, and I am consumed with a passion so hot that it might be love, or hatred, or both. Until my heart has at last answered the call of the flowers. Until I am free.

From Le Moniteur Universel
October 16, 1815

Dearest reader,

How often do we sit and reflect on the true nature of love and not just allow ourselves to be swept away on a current of fancy and romance? Any lady might declare herself to be in love, when in truth she is simply eager to indulge in the pleasant pastime of lovesickness and yearning. And indeed, it is an unmatched exhilaration to scheme and yearn for someone of whose heart we may not even wish to capture.

And gentlemen—(yes, I know that you seek out my column, whether out of mere curiosity or even a genuine interest!)—I beg you to reflect on whether the lady to whom you pledge your heart and make all sort of pretty promises is the same person with whom you will be content to spend the rest of your natural days. For after the first exciting flush of passion and courtship, there is a lifetime of in which to nurture the steady flame of love.

Today I invite you to copy this arrangement I have designed for you. I have paired the following flowers, that you may not only communicate your desires to your sweetheart but also ensure that your love is true and lasting.

Purple lilac: the first stirrings of love
Moss rosebud: confession of love
Sweet pea: lasting pleasures
Orange blossoms: eternal love

Arrange these into a pleasing bouquet with ivy (for fidelity and marriage), and give it to your sweetheart to let them know that you esteem them beyond simply the degree of acquaintance. But beware, a garden cannot be planted and expected to thrive if it is not watered. Once declared, you must tend to your love if it is to flourish.

And I beg of you, remember you yourself are worthy of your *own* love, and if a romance cannot blossom without tending, then your own character—nay, even your *soul*—can likewise not grow without true introspection and the courage to change when circumstances demand it.

Madame Dujardin

Forty-Six

LIJSBETH

SWEET ALYSSUM: sweetness of soul.

I dream that I am an orphan again.

I belong to no one, have no one to love. Can a body truly have a soul if there is nothing tethering it to this world? And if a body is made to work and toil without hope, then what else does one have? But I must have known love once, because my soul did not break. Not in the orphanage, not during the years of servitude, not even at the hands of Isidore. I have somehow survived, and this latest turbulence is not enough to pull me under completely.

As I swim back to the surface of consciousness, there is light, and a tender touch, bringing me back out of the frigid beyond. My mother's voice, clear and sweet, rings through my mind. *You were never truly alone. You had the flowers and a promise in the shape of the locket around your neck. You had love on your side. You are more than a body and an empty heart.*

The room I find myself in is light and airy, a window open

to admit a fresh ocean breeze, and a dimity bedspread pulled up to my chest. And there, sitting so close that I can see the taut worry in his brow, William is stroking my cheek, looking as if he were about to fall headlong into my dream with me.

When he sees me open my eyes, his entire face lights up. "Lijsbeth, you're awake. Thank God." He takes my hand and imparts a long, grateful kiss onto it. His lips are soft and warm, and a shiver runs through my body. "I rode my horse half to death to find you." Seeing my concern, he quickly adds, "Merlin is fine, resting at the inn. This is the house of one of my men. It was closer. We found you near the gaol, unconscious in the street. I thought—I thought you were dead, and—"

Emotion wells up in his throat, choking out the rest of whatever he might have said. I close my eyes, let my head sink back into the soft pillow. It had all seemed like such a natural thing at the time, that my only choice was to let myself fade away. But now, seeing William's hurt and his fear, I think that I made a terrible mistake and am lucky beyond anything to have escaped what should have been my fate.

"Are you hurt? I didn't see any injuries to your body, but I didn't want to look without—"

I stop him with a shake of my head. Aside from my aching legs and tired feet, I am thankfully unharmed. There is a tray at the side of the bed with a pitcher of water, and I motion for a cup which he hurriedly fills and then offers to me. Food is next, and I take slow nibbles of pillowy-soft bread so that my stomach doesn't protest. When William is satisfied that I don't need for anything else, he begins gently stroking the hair from my forehead.

"We'll rent horses for the journey to Hampshire. You *are* coming back, Lijsbeth," he says, his voice suddenly husky as he stares at our hands joined together. "I won't let you go." His grip tightens, the muscle of his jaw clenching as if he is fighting to rein in some runaway emotion. "I should never have presumed to speak for you. You could only ever be perfect to me, but I want to know everything you see fit to share with me. I will take anything and be grateful for it. Only please, Lijsbeth, let us never be parted again, and certainly not for only a misunderstanding. If there is anything else that I have done to hurt you, tell me so that I might remedy it."

This is the moment I tell him how hurt I am that he did not want to share a bed with me. Heat rushes to my face as I try to collect my jumbled words. He doesn't prod me, though I can see that his breath hangs on whatever I am about to say.

"Y-you…slept in a d-different…" Embarrassment makes the rest of the words too hard to choke out. William sits up a little straighter, the confusion that had been clouding his brow giving away to understanding.

"You thought I didn't want to share a bed with you," he says, saving me from having to explain any further. "Damn me," he adds in a whisper, then hurriedly clears his throat in apology for cursing. Leaning back, he draws his hand over his face. He doesn't seem to be able to sit still, but finally he lets our gazes meet. "What do you know of the great battle?"

I don't need to ask what battle he's speaking about, though I don't understand why he is bringing it up now. I shake my head.

"It was…it was hell on earth," he says, his blue eyes uncharacteristically dull and flat. "The things I saw, the things I *did*… I wish that I could forget it all. But I can't, they've become part of me, however much I might hate it. I could bear it all, though, if I had a reprieve at night. But that is when it haunts me the most, and I relive every hellish moment of it in my dreams."

Even if I could speak, I would not press him. I will give him all the time he needs. I owe him nothing less.

When he finally speaks, his voice sounds as far away as his gaze. "We were holding the line, right below a small ridge. Mist was rolling in, obscuring us from view of the French. There had already been action for many of the regiments the previous two days, but this was my first time coming face-to-face with the enemy. I had discharged a weapon before, and I had killed before. I am proud to serve my country, but I am not proud of spilling the blood of another man who is only doing what he is ordered."

His throat bobs. "But I digress. The French cleared our line of sight, and we rose, sending a volley of fire into their line. It hit them hard, and many men went down. We were not without casualties, of course. I lost men who had but moments before had been eager to meet the enemy, letters and locks of hair from their sweethearts pierced by bullets on the way to their chests. But it was a young ensign who had the worst of it. We fell back, and he took a bullet in the gut. It wasn't a clean shot, and he was maimed, terribly. The screams..." William blinks away a tear before it can form. He clears his throat. "It was unbearable to hear him in that kind of pain, the kind that only death can relieve. But I couldn't leave him there, I couldn't, so I—"

My heart breaks as I watch him struggle for words. This man, who was lauded for his bravery, bears the scars of that very act as one might a yoke.

"I brought him back. That was the easy part—the running and dragging. I knew what had to be done, and I did it. I took a bayonet in the arm, but I hardly felt it." He draws a shuddering breath, watching a seagull wheel outside the window. "The hard part was all the other men along the way. The ones I couldn't help, the ones that were begging. French or English, it didn't make much difference. The look in their eyes, the outstretched hands, the screams. My God, the screams." He gives a cough, swallows hard. "Since then, I have had these...terrors, at night. I awake in a sort of dream where I think I am back in battle. The first night back in Brussels, I smashed a lamp and tore down the drapes, all while I thought I was in hand-to-hand combat for my life."

My hand tightens around his. I can't believe that what I

thought was a slight to me or a difference in our cultures was so much more, something so painful to him.

"Lijsbeth," he says presently, still focused on where our fingers are interlaced. "You are a shining light in my life. If anything were to happen to you..." He tries again. "If *I* were to hurt you, in any way, I would never be able to live with myself. I will do anything to protect you, and if it means denying myself the privilege of sharing a bed with you, then so be it."

Something wet falls upon my hand, and I look up to find that William is weeping. It cracks something deep within me to know that I did this to him, that I drove this lovely, upstanding man to despair. I know that whatever words are needed to fix this will not come easily. I wish that I could simply open my mouth and assure him that I feel just as he does. My heart knew the first moment I saw him that I could trust him, that I loved him with every part of my being. But I allowed my fears and old shades to convince me otherwise.

There is another way to tell William all that I am feeling, but to do so means having to bare myself to him completely. He will see me for what I am, but it is better than him thinking me indifferent. I am ready to share that last secret part of myself.

I close my eyes. Cornelia's heart is a garden that is abundant with flowers that bloom in love. Mine bloom in anger, when I can no longer hold it inside of me. So I reap from that deepest part of me, summoning the blooms that will help me speak.

Rue for regret. Liatris for apology. Snowdrops for hope.

One by one they fall from my fingers, fluttering to the bedspread and mingling with William's tears. Blinking, he looks with amazement at the flowers that fill my palms as I offer them up to him.

He takes them from me, cupping them gently. And because he is William, and he cares about me, wants to hear what I have to say, the flowers speak to him.

This is what I am. I ran because I was scared that you could not love someone like me. I thought it was anger, but I was scared that your love came with limits. You could not have known that Cornelia was my sister, but even still, it was not worth losing you over. If I had died before telling you what you are to me, my regret would have followed me to the grave. No matter what happens to my sister, I want to have you at my side. I do not think I can face what is to come without you.

And as for trying to protect me from yourself, from your dreams, just know that I would rather die than be separated from you. Trust me to know that I am safe with you.

I watch William, waiting for him to recoil or show some sign of fear or disgust as the flowers convey my message to him. But he only looks up with an expression of pure awe.

"Miss Shaw told me that it was you who was responsible for the roses in the courtroom, but I never thought..." He shakes his head, then graces me with the smile that I feared I would never see again. "You brilliant, brave, brave girl," he says. "You are a wonder, Lijsbeth."

I could weep for the foolishness of trying to hide what is inside me, for nearly throwing William away.

He is holding up a snowdrop with reverent fingers, gently studying the petals. "I know it will not fix everything, but I have a contact, a General Wheeler, and he is reviewing my petition even as we speak. I'll not see your sister hang, Lijsbeth."

I wish that I had William's confidence in the ability of men and that all it would take to secure Cornelia's release was a word from the right mouth. But she has three black marks against her: murder, treason, and the crime of being a woman who strove to have more than what the world saw fit to mete out to her.

After some broth and tea, William leaves me to rest. Content and drowsy, I drift off to sleep, only to awaken to the sound of voices quietly conversing just beyond the half-open door. Sitting up, I crane my head until I can just make out two figures.

William is speaking with a uniformed man, urgency in their

whispers. Despite my shaky legs, I get out of bed and pad quietly to the doorway.

"Lijsbeth." William has heard me despite my best efforts. He draws me against him with a firm hand. "This is General Wheeler."

The general hardly spares me a distracted glance. He can only be here either because he was successful in his petition to spare Cornelia, or because he was not and she is already dead.

I cannot believe she is dead, for something tells me that the locket at my neck would let me know if she were. Yet I still feel myself swaying on my feet, afraid that the worst has happened.

"The news is…it is not bad."

"Well, it is certainly not good, either," the general counters in a booming voice. He is a big man, with dark side-whiskers and a red complexion. I wonder if he was present in the courtroom for Cornelia's trial.

"Will you excuse us a moment, General?" Without waiting for an answer, William maneuvers me back to the bed. "You should be sitting for this."

I am burning with curiosity, but he seems to be at a loss for words. He scrubs at his jaw, thinking. "It would seem that your sister has escaped. Or, at the very least, is no longer in her cell. The warden came to fetch her for the final rites, only to find… Well, I'm not certain I can explain it or even understand exactly what I've been told."

I hardly hear him. My sister is free, but I need to see for myself to be certain that she is safe. I begin to rise from the bed again. William looks as if he will stop me, but I think he must see my determination, for he helps me up. I hurriedly dress in a borrowed gown, and soon we are both in a hack bound for the prison.

When we arrive, several soldiers and guards are milling about outside, seemingly in a state of confusion. Nothing looks particularly amiss until we approach the courtyard.

William pays the hack driver and helps me down. What I see steals my breath away.

A mass of thorny, winding rose vines, cascading down the side of the building, bricks and stone crumbled in their path. A hole runs straight through the wall, giving us a view into the ruined room within. The vine must have grown where the window had been, widening it and boring straight through the stone. Below, street children run through the petals, kicking them up into great clouds of pinks and purples, corals and creams. Seedlings are blooming through the cracks in the cobbles, thriving without even so much as a ray of sunlight. It is a verdant island in the middle of a sea of gray and stone.

Beside me, William is rendered speechless as he cranes his neck back to follow the path of the vines climbing the stone wall. His hand finds mine, and we stand together, awestruck.

"What has happened?" he asks a passing guard.

"She's escaped is what's happened! Used witchcraft to break down the wall. The Prince Regent himself has heard and put a reward on her head of ten thousand pounds!"

While William tries to learn more from the guard, I kneel down among the petals and flower buds, letting them sift through my fingers. I close my eyes. These are Cornelia's last words to me. They speak of hope, joy, determination. They speak of a voyage over the ocean, freedom. They speak, I think, of love.

Forty-Seven

CORNELIA

IRIS: faith in a better tomorrow.

November 1815, Paris

Paris is an easy city in which to disappear.

It is a city of freedoms hard-won, of ancient places and modern fashions. And I am the latest contradiction: a woman who has no name and no past, yet is richer and more fulfilled than most.

Though it is a late-November afternoon, the Jardin des Plantes is in full bloom. All of Paris comes to walk here, marveling at the unexpected colors that linger late into the season. When I first came to the city, I spent most of my time in the forgotten gardens of Malmaison. But soon the ghost of my afternoon with Henri there became too melancholy for me to bear, and I desired a fresh start. Here, in the beating heart of the city, I walk for hours, nurturing the gardens and groves so that all might enjoy the splendor of nature, regardless of the season.

Today it is the jasmine that has caught my fascination. Such exquisitely delicate blooms, their sweet scent rivaling any perfume that sells in one of the city's shops. Touching one of the feathery leaves, I watch as the white petals unfurl and nod to me.

"I thought I might find you here," says a masculine voice over my shoulder.

I finish nurturing the jasmine and slowly rise from the trellis to find Captain Norton standing behind me, beaver hat under his arm. He has not changed overmuch in the two months since I saw him last, except that he has exchanged his soldier's uniform for a smartly tailored cutaway tailcoat and buckskin breeches. There is an easiness about him, and he looks a great deal more content than that afternoon in my prison cell when it seemed that he would at any moment fall apart completely. "I am afraid I am nothing if not predictable, Captain. Will you walk with me?"

"There are worse things to be than predictable," he says, offering his arm. I decline, instead inviting him to walk beside me. "And it is just *Mr. Norton* now. Or *William*, if you would be so good as to humor your brother-in-law. I sold my commission and took a diplomatic position with the Foreign Office."

"Have you come for the treaty-signing, then?" All week, foreign dignitaries, generals, and other military men have converged on the city to sign a treaty that once and for all will bring peace between France and the coalition countries. There are those who feel that it is too punitive, that France is being unjustly punished for the actions of Napoleon, but I cannot be mad about anything that promises peace, not after witnessing what I did in battle.

"Yes, in part. But also to see you," William tells me.

"How fortunate I am! I so rarely am afforded the opportunity to entertain gentlemen, and in such an attractive location, no less."

"It is lovely," he agrees, stopping to admire a white rose. "I did not realize there would still be so much in bloom this late in the season."

We walk in easy silence, every so often stopping to allow

another strolling couple to pass us. After some time, I notice that William is turning his hat about in his hands. He clears his throat. "I—I heard a strange phenomenon occurred last month in the English city of Portsmouth," he says presently.

"Oh?"

"It seems that there was an avalanche of flowers at the prison and a climbing rose which grew straight up the side of the wall. The vine was so strong that it actually split the stone. It made it possible for the prisoner housed in the tower to climb out and alight on a cushion of petals below."

To hear of my fantastical escape out loud sends a little shiver down my spine. "Indeed! How curious."

"Most curious," he agrees, throwing me a sidelong look full of wry admiration.

We walk a little farther, the sounds of birds and couples chatting filling the air around us. "I heard that there was some excitement surrounding her trial as well," I tell him. "Do you know whatever became of the officer who seemingly choked on roses during his testimony?"

Captain Norton tugs at his cravat, as if the topic alone has suddenly made his throat go tight. "Ah, yes. I believe he is facing a trial of his own. A servant who was employed at Hill Cottage came forward with some rather damning testimony regarding him. It seems that he may have been responsible for Mr. Shaw's death, as well as that of his first wife."

My step falters. "Come again?"

"Yes, I believe a Betty Patterson...perhaps, Betsy? She claims that Major Reeves came to the house with the intention of demanding your hand. When you were nowhere to be found, he became violent with your uncle and shot him."

"But he couldn't have. He—" I stop myself as understanding slowly dawns on me. All the times that I cursed Betsy as a nuisance and she has protected me in the most profound way. I can hardly fathom it.

Misunderstanding my look of wonder, Captain Norton hurries to continue. "I believe that the major hoped to collect Mr. Shaw's fortune as well as frame the young Miss Shaw as the murderer. His plan was a flawed one, though, as there was never any sort of written contract found that detailed the supposed dowry he would have received, nor the title to Hill Cottage."

A seasoned military strategist could not have planned it better. It is a fitting punishment, I suppose. Any lingering guilt that I felt surrounding my uncle's death is finally lifted from my shoulders. I wonder if Betsy knows what a gift she has given me. I wonder if she knows the truth, suspected it all along.

"And the French officer who testified against Miss Shaw, do you know what became of him?" I ask.

"I am afraid I must disappoint you on that front. After his testimony he disappeared. He was not a particularly valuable asset to the English, but it may well be that the attention he gained from the trial led the French back to him and they will punish him as they see fit." Captain Norton doesn't look terribly concerned. "Men like him are opportunists, and I daresay he will resurface when the opportunity presents itself."

The apathy I find myself feeling for Armand takes me by surprise. There is evil in the world, but I cannot think that Armand ever truly meant to contribute to it. He is selfish, yes, and an opportunist, but not evil. Certainly not worth my anger.

"Regardless," Captain Norton continues, "I hope that the young lady in question will have the foresight to avoid returning to England. I should hate to see such a clever escape carried out only to have her brought back, and on additional charges."

"I am sure she is quite aware of the danger," I tell him, plucking a camellia as we walk by and twisting the stem in my fingers.

"It is a shame, though, as I imagine her sister will miss her terribly."

I wince as I envision Lijsbeth's sweet face and know that it will probably be many years until I see it again. "She must be the luckiest creature to have a sister like that, one with such a pure heart."

We have reached the gates. A peacock calls from somewhere in the menagerie, and I find myself wanting to draw out the goodbye. This is one of the few people who knows my secrets, knows who I truly am. The world can be a lonely place when you are in hiding, even if it is in plain sight.

"Please thank Mrs. Norton for sending her husband all the way to France to ensure that her sister was well. I'm sure she will be eager to see you."

"Perhaps we will take something of a bridal tour to France in the future. But until then, *au revoir*, Madame Dujardin." He gives me a short bow and replaces his hat.

The city swallows him up, a precious link to Lijsbeth gone. But my sister and I are bound now by the flowers, and I know that I only have to listen closely to them to hear her voice. Someday, perhaps, we will see each other again. I hope that when we do, we will have only good memories to share and will find in each other the friend that we were both denied when we were separated as children.

I leave behind the park and continue my stroll through the city alone, stopping in front of a shopwindow where little diamond pins and jeweled earrings are arranged on black velvet.

"Nella!"

Sophie runs across the street, hand to her bonnet to keep it from falling off. When she reaches my side, she brushes my cheek with a kiss. "I thought you might be at the park, but when I didn't see you, I figured you had continued on this way. You are rather predictable in your walking paths."

"I must be, for you are the second person to tell me as much today."

She gives me a questioning look, but I direct her attention to the gleaming jewels in the window. "Look."

"They're beautiful," she says, admiring the little diamond pin.

"Yes, and you ought to have one."

Pulling back, she gives me an incredulous look. "Don't be silly. I don't need baubles, let alone such costly ones."

"You don't need one, but you should have one all the same. You should have everything."

"And what about you? I think you would look fetching with a sapphire on each ear to match your eyes."

I laugh. "Perhaps once I would have agreed with you, but not anymore. Come." I lead her by the hand into the shop. The diamond pin costs most of what I've made from my columns in the past month, but seeing the glittering jewel sitting on her breast is worth every bit of it. Besides, now that I have my columns again, there will be more money. It seems that news of my trial, and subsequently my identity, only created more demand for my work and under strict orders of secrecy, *Le Moniteur Universel* was only too glad to be able to publish the work of the infamous Madame Dujardin. There is even now a letter in my pocket from my editor informing me that there is a large sum that I must collect at my earliest convenience.

After Sophie is done protesting that it is too much and has given up, transfixed by the sparkling stone, we leave the shop and continue on our walk.

"We need to find out about some lodgings, proper ones," I tell her. "I can't stand another night in that miserable boardinghouse."

Sophie gives me a dry look. "So you don't need sapphires, but you turn your nose up at a perfectly good room with a kindly landlady?"

"I never said I was completely reformed, did I? Besides, Madame Maistral may be kindly, but her chicken is dry and flavorless."

"Well, I wouldn't say no to a feathered bed. It's all I ever dreamed of."

"Then, you shall have it," I vow to her.

She finally takes her gaze off her new pin and gives me an adorably eager look. "I can take in laundry again, help to earn a little more."

"You will do no such thing," I tell her, taking her hand and brushing her scarred knuckles with a kiss.

"Nella! Look!"

No matter how often I tell Sophie that we must be careful using my given name here, she insists on calling me by the pet name she coined for me. In truth, I cannot fault her. What a relief it is to hear my name, my real name, from her. To know that she is now intimately familiar with not just what I am but *who* I am and loves me all the more for it. I am glad to be rid of my silly pseudonym, using it only for publishing now. *Cornelia Peusol* feels ever so much more wearable. And now I can carry a piece of Henri with me, make sure that his name is never forgotten.

We are in front of a bookshop, and Sophie has run to the big glass bow window, her face pressed against it as if she were a small child. I come beside her, and my heart gives a jump in my chest when I see what has caught her attention. "No," I murmur. "But that cannot be!"

"There is only one way to find out." Dragging me by the wrist, Sophie leads me inside.

"That book in the window," Sophie says to the shopkeeper breathlessly, "may we see it?"

He quickly takes our measure and, deciding that we are respectable enough, fetches the volume bound in green leather and embossed with a gold fleur-de-lis and places it in my hands.

I can hardly fathom what I now hold.

A Book of Thorns & Petals, Relating to the Secret Meanings and Language of Flowers, by Madame Colette Dujardin.

"I cannot put one on the shelf but a lady comes in and buys a copy," the shopkeeper laments. "Can't complain, of course, money is money. I have already had to place an order for more from the printer. Did you know," he says, leaning in conspiratorially, "it's said that she was lately an escaped prisoner from England. If that's the case, then I say good for her. Show the English a thing or two. Whoever she is, there is sure to be a pile of money waiting for her at the printer's should she ever reveal herself."

He goes on like that, but I am quite incapable of hearing him. "But how?" I ask Sophie. Inside, there are not only flowers compiled from my years of columns but also work that was never before printed. "How can this be?"

She gently takes the book from me and flips to the front. "Look."

The frontispiece contains a picture I am certain did not come from my own hand. It is an iris, each of its three petals containing a hidden initial: *C, S, H.* It is not crude, but neither is it practiced. It is the earnest work of an amateur, yet I think it is more beautiful than anything I have ever drawn.

"Henri must have gathered up all my work that I could not send in," I say in a whisper, "and sent it to the address I gave him for my publisher."

This must be the source of the large sum about which my editor informed me, and is waiting for me to collect. It is as if Henri has reached back from beyond the grave and given me one last gift, one last token of his love. He did this for me. I don't know how, but all that time, he was working toward my dream for me in secret, even when I had given up.

I try not to dwell on the injustice that he will never be able to read the words inside the book that he helped create. The world is still a cruel place, but if I let myself only see the thorns, then I will miss the sweetness of the rose. Here is something beautiful, created solely through love.

A tear rolls down my cheek and lands on the color plate of the iris.

The shopkeeper blanches at the page gently warping from my tears. "We'll buy it," Sophie says quickly.

He tells her the price, and I nearly drop the book hearing the exorbitant figure. I might have written it, but I despair of ever owning it. I spent almost everything on the diamond pin, and what little is left must be for new lodgings.

But Sophie is already removing the pin and handing it to the befuddled shopkeeper. "This should be more than enough," she tells him, hauling me out by the arm before he can change his mind.

As we walk, I cradle the book under one arm and loop my other arm around Sophie's waist. As soon as possible, we will go to the publisher, collect my earnings. And then I will take care of Sophie, make certain that she never wants for anything ever again.

"I still can't believe that we're here, that you're here," she says, leaning her head on my shoulder as we walk.

"Where else would I be, goose?"

"Nella," she says, pulling away to look at me. "You know very well where you could be if you had not decided to fight for me, for us."

I squeeze her closer. We reach a flower market, which would usually be shuttered this time of year but is now full of carts spilling over with all kinds of blossoms. Their petals shimmer, and Sophie runs ahead to look for irises. "For Henri," she explains.

I trail behind her, relishing not only the flowers but the smiles and laughter of the children skipping through the market, eager to show their parents the extraordinary blooms that they find. Even after all this time, I cannot help but look at every face that I pass, searching for a familiar pair of eyes, a warm smile. I like to imagine my mother, eternally youthful and happy, always just around another corner, laughing on her soldier's arm. Perhaps she has long moved on; perhaps she was never here at all. But *I* am here, and I am content.

My locket quivers, and I hold it against my chest. Somewhere across the water, my sister is thinking of me. I don't know that I will ever understand what it is that connects us, or how. Does the voice that whispers through the flowers belong to our mother? Or did she pass something down to us that allows us to hear the flowers themselves, all their glorious secrets that most people will never know? I suppose it doesn't matter. I am just glad that I carry such a gift within me and that it has allowed me to flourish instead of destroy me.

Sophie returns with an armload of irises, the petals spilling over and carpeting the cobbles in shimmering violets and blues. With her arm tucked in mine, we wander through the market together, until the golden evening sun turns dusky and sets on a sea of flowers.

Forty-Eight
LIJSBETH

WHITE ROSE: I am worthy of you. The truest, purest, love.

June 1817, Hampshire

Clouds are rolling across the late-afternoon sky, and I track the euphoric swoops and dives of the swallows as they pluck insects out of the air. They are free and beautiful, like jewels with wings, and there is nowhere I would rather be than in my little garden, listening to their trilling chatter.

It has taken me the better part of a year, but I finally feel at home in England. The Hampshire countryside is beautiful, the verdant hills softly folding me within their embrace. I suppose this is my homeland in a sense, but I think it is more than simply the circumstances of my birth that make me feel as if I truly belong here. I finally have someone to love, who loves me in return. So long as we are together, I am home.

William's family, it turns out, welcomed me with open arms as one might a long-lost sister. His father was just grateful that William had survived the war, and his mother was delighted to have a new daughter to dote upon. Perhaps I was not the wife they would have chosen for him, but I can't help but believe that this was the family I was always fated to have.

A figure appears at the back door, then comes down the path to the bench he built for me by the rosebushes. Civilian life suits William. I enjoy seeing him relaxed, his collar open, his sleeves rolled to the elbow as he works in the garden. Perhaps it is selfish of me, but I am glad that he has given up the army for a diplomatic position instead. I don't think I could bear having to send him into battle again. And there will be more wars, even now that Napoleon has been driven back into exile. So long as there are men who yearn for power and domination, there will be fighting. But it is how we fight for peace, how we find beauty in the moments between the cannon fire that defines us, gives our lives meaning. And I will fill mine with flowers, with children.

William brushes the top of my head with a kiss. "Will you come in now, love? It looks as if it might rain."

I smile up at him, the sunlight of my life. "Soon," I tell him, and he imparts another gentle kiss, then returns to the house.

A bird coos from the privet hedge. Another coo, but this one from the bundle in my lap. I adjust the blankets, and the little face of my daughter peeks out at me, rosebud lips pursed into a contented, milky smile. This little girl will always know who she is, will always know that she is loved. My little friend sent her to me, I am certain of it.

Some days when I look at her, I see only William, his beautiful blue eyes and noble mien. Today, I see Cornelia in her. The thought of my daughter growing up to be anything like her aunt fills me with pride. But I cannot think of my sister without feeling a thread of guilt twining through me. There was little that I could do for Cornelia besides giving her the encouragement to look within her, but at least she will not have to bear the burden of knowing that the cruel man she thought was her uncle was really our father. As far as she knows, our uncle was just that, and our mother is alive and happy somewhere.

I touch my hand to my locket, allow the silver to warm and sing. My sister is thinking of me, holding me in her heart, just as I am. Someday it will be safe to see her, and she can meet her niece. Until then, we will always have the flowers.

The first drops of rain are starting to fall, so I scoop up Violet and hurry down the path to the door where William is silhouetted against a warm kitchen, waiting for us.

The roses nod to me as I go home.

★★★★★

Acknowledgments

After publishing six books, you would think that writing the acknowledgments would become somewhat easier, but as I sit here thinking of all the amazing people who helped bring this book to fruition, I am still as overwhelmed as the first time. As a writer, I should probably be able to express my feelings at least competently, if not eloquently, yet I find that there are no words that can adequately convey the immense gratitude I have for the people who have helped me on my publishing journey.

Firstly, I feel incredibly privileged to have landed in the care of such an extremely kind and supportive editor as Sara Rodgers. I know my stories are in good hands, and I look forward to working on many more together.

I am also deeply grateful to Vanessa Wells for her meticulous copyediting and thoughtful comments on my manuscript.

Thank you to Leah Morse and the rest of the team at Graydon House, Harlequin, and HarperCollins, especially Kathleen Oudit and Mary Luna for the absolutely stunning cover.

All my thanks and awe to Ell Potter and Fiona Hardingham for bringing Cornelia and Lijsbeth to life in the audiobook.

My agent, Jane Dystel, who has been there for me since that very first phone call, and has propelled my career to places I could have only dreamed of. Thank you.

Thank you to the bloggers, Bookstagrammers, BookTokers, reviewers, booksellers, librarians, and everyone who has helped readers find my books. And of course, thank you to my wonderful readers, who allow my stories to live on beyond the confines of my imagination. I am only here today because of you.

Zaynah Qutubuddin, Becca Podos, and the rest of the Books for Palestine community for showing true humanity and light in an incredibly dark time.

The isolation of writing is eased by the incredible support and friendship of authors such as Agatha Andrews, Paulette Kennedy, Trish Knox, Rosanna Leo, Rachel McMillan, Marielle Thompson, and many others.

Special thanks to Jeanne Renee, who I am so incredibly lucky to call a friend. Someday we will hang out in a cemetery together (preferably while we are both alive).

To my friends and family, who have been cheering me on since day one, thank you. Florrie and Pippy, who maybe one day will read my books, but if not, will always know that it is all for them.

Author Note

I felt two things simultaneously when my proposal for this book was accepted. The first was: "I can't believe I get to write my Vanity Fair–inspired flower magic story!" The second was: "Oh no, I'm going to have to write about Waterloo." Military history, the logistics of moving regiments, battle timelines…all of these things fall well outside of my comfort zone. A preliminary dip into the oeuvre of work written about Waterloo left me completely overwhelmed (as well as in awe of those who have dedicated their lives studying this battle). Waterloo—or the Battle of Mont Sain-Jean as it was contemporarily known in France—was the last battle of the Napoleonic Wars which had begun in 1799 when Napoleon seized power. Over the following decade and a half, multiple European countries would become ensnared in the war, sometimes shifting alliances, changing sides, or becoming new entities altogether. The countries we know as the Netherlands and Belgium changed names, borders, and rulers, at a dizzying pace in the years between 1792 and 1839. During the very brief window of time of my story, Brussels would have been located in what was then known as the United Kingdom of the Netherlands.

I relied heavily on Bernard Cornwell's comprehensive work *Waterloo: The History of Four Days, Three Armies, and Three Battles* for information concerning the chronology of Napoleon's escape from Elba, the lead-up to the infamous battle, and his subsequent loss at Waterloo. While these historical events provided the scaffolding for my story, my book is obviously a work of fiction, and I took liberties with exact movements of specific regiments, as well as omitting a plethora of detail which I believe would have ultimately not served to further the plot.

My favorite part of researching this book was discovering the many diverse roles that women played in the Napoleonic Wars. In particular I was intrigued by the vivandières, who were women who were granted military commissions and lived and worked in the camps selling goods. On the battlefield, they would often enter the fray, not just to provide aid to the soldiers, but may times to also fight alongside of them. Additionally, many women traveled with their husbands' regiments, and it was not uncommon for entire families to live together on the march and in the camps. It is estimated that as many as 4,000 women may have been attached to Napoleon's Grand Armée at the time of Waterloo.

Another wonderful aspect of my research was getting to dive into the world of floriography (otherwise known as the language of flowers). Typically, when we think of the floriography craze that swept Europe and the United States, we think of the high Victorian era. Indeed dozens, if not hundreds, of guides were written in the mid to late 19th century which detailed the secret meanings of flowers. Some of these were based on folklore or had some basis in medicinal uses, while others were completely the whims of the author. The first generally accepted floriography guide in Europe was written by Louise Cortambert (under the pen name Madame Charlotte de la Tour). I drew Cornelia's language of flowers from a variety of these sources, the primary one being Kate Greenaway's slim 1884 volume *The Language of Flowers.* Since the meanings were often just one word, I took the artistic liberty of expanding and embellishing some of them in order to draw stronger parallels to the plot of the story.